Praise for *Frien...*

"Right from the start *Friend Me* caught me off-guard and threw me into the first loop of an action-packed ride that is anything but what you expect. Filled with rich characters and complicated situations, *Friend Me* is a compelling read that makes you glad you took the ride. Don't miss this book."

—Tosca Lee, *New York Times* bestselling coauthor of the Books of Mortals series and author of *Iscariot*

"This thought-provoking tale reveals the frailty and potential wickedness in all of us and the terrible, life-altering things we are capable of when we yield to our own selfish desires and devices."

—Creston Mapes, bestselling author of *Poison Town*

"For anyone who has thought of—or is involved in—seeking a virtual relationship on the Internet, *Friend Me* is a must-read. John Faubion has penned a chilling yet eerily real tale that will cause you to think again."

—Deborah K. Anderson, *Christian Fiction Online Magazine*

"In his novel *Friend Me*, John Faubion creates a delightfully creepy tale you'll not soon forget. In our day, with so many people spending increasing amounts of time online, the virtual premise of *Friend Me* comes alive to grip the reader with both a whopping, suspenseful story, plus much food for meditation concerning reality, morality, and the imaginary realm of 'what if. . . .' Highly recommended reading!"

—Rick Barry, author of *Gunner's Run* and president of the American Christian Fiction Writers Indiana Chapter

"*Friend Me* is an exciting foray into today's cyberculture. I loved every minute of the hero's frantic efforts to extricate himself and his wife from the virtual web of the villainess. Fascinating characters and exciting plot twists make this a stellar read."

—V. B. Tenery, author of *Dead Ringer* and *The Watchman*

"John Faubion introduces a new and different kind of chiller, an uncharted world of cyber suspense. The writing? It's fabulous."

—Donn Taylor, author of *Deadly Additive* and *Rhapsody in Red*

"John Faubion's *Friend Me* starts off with heart-pounding suspense. The idea of a virtual friend intrigues, and the author has created unscrupulous executives in the cutting-edge technology company developing this revolutionary idea. The reader can clearly see the potential for wicked abuse. Suspense drips from the lines of this novel as the villain plans a few nasty surprises."

—Nike Chillemi, author of the Sanctuary Point series and chair of the Grace Awards

"*Friend Me* is a suspense-filled trip torn from tomorrow's headlines; an all-too-believable story that had me turning pages to the unexpected end. I'm anxious to read more from this debut author."

—Richard L. Mabry, MD, author of *Stress Test* and *Heart Failure*

"*Friend Me* captured me from page one and wrapped me in thought-provoking suspense until the end. The intriguing plot made it nearly impossible to put this book down. Mr. Faubion has crafted a great story that will grab your attention and stick with you long after you read the last page. I highly recommend this book."

—Larry W. Timm, president of the American Christian Fiction Writers South Central Kansas Chapter and pastor of Gracepoint Church in Peabody, Kansas

"In an ever-changing technological age, John Faubion has written a tough and gritty story that could one day be reality. Though he has shown how technology and the times change, he has also shown that God and his mercy do not. John has succeeded in writing a book that is at the same time frightening and hopeful."

—Warren Pratt Jr., pastor, evangelist, and head chief of the Pawnee Nation of Oklahoma

FROM THE Library of

Peggy D. Graham

FRIEND ME

A Novel of Suspense

John Faubion

HOWARD BOOKS

A Division of Simon & Schuster, Inc.

New York   Nashville   London   Toronto   Sydney   New Delhi

Howard Books
A Division of Simon & Schuster, Inc.
1230 Avenue of the Americas
New York, NY 10020

First Howard Books trade paperback edition February 2014

HOWARD and colophon are trademarks of Simon & Schuster, Inc.

For information about special discounts for bulk purchases, please contact Simon & Schuster Special Sales at 1-866-506-1949 or business@simonandschuster.com.

The Simon & Schuster Speakers Bureau can bring authors to your live event. For more information or to book an event contact the Simon & Schuster Speakers Bureau at 1-866-248-3049 or visit our website at www.simonspeakers.com.

Interior design by Davina Mock-Maniscalco
Cover design by Kent Jensen/ Knail, LLC
Front cover photograph by Shutterstock

Manufactured in the United States of America

10   9   8   7   6   5   4   3   2   1

Library of Congress Cataloging-in-Publication Data
Faubion, John.
  Friend me : a novel of suspense / John Faubion. —First Howard Book trade paperback ed.
    pages cm
  1. Married people—Fiction. 2. Online identities—Fiction. I. Title.
  PS3606.A855F75 2014
  813'.6—dc23 2013021531

ISBN 978-1-4767-3872-7
ISBN 978-1-4767-3873-4 (ebook)

Dedicated to my Lord, Jesus Christ,
and my faithful wife and family.

Finally, brethren,
whatsoever things are true, whatsoever things are honest,
whatsoever things are just, whatsoever things are pure,
whatsoever things are lovely, whatsoever things are of good report;
if there be any virtue, and if there be any praise,
think on these things.

—PHILIPPIANS 4:8

FRIEND ME

CHAPTER ONE
Melissa

Melissa Montalvo folded her hands on her lap and stared across the table at her final interviewer.

He adjusted the name badge on his shirt. *Chief Software Scientist Aaron Getz.* "You've excelled in both your other interviews, but this is a different kind of meeting." He leaned in toward Melissa. She felt his gaze upon her. He was slender, with dark eyes that burned under thick, curling eyebrows.

This was it. She either had the job or she didn't.

"I'd like you to take a look at this, Melissa." Getz withdrew a letter envelope from his jacket pocket, turned it facedown, and slid it across the rosewood table. "I think you'll be pleased."

She searched his face, but his eyes gave nothing away. It must be a job offer, but . . .

Melissa picked up the unsealed envelope bearing the embossed Virtual Friend Me logo, and withdrew the letter inside. Getz's eyes remained noncommittal as she unfolded the paper.

Dear Ms. Montalvo:

Virtual Friend Me is pleased to offer you the position
of chief architect . . .

Her chest constricted as the breath caught in her throat.
They were offering her the second position in software development? And more. They were proposing a salary 10 percent
above what she had requested.

Getz continued to look at her with the same deadpan expression. What did he expect her to say? "Mr. Getz . . ."

"Call me Aaron, Melissa."

"I'm very pleased with the offer. When do you want me to
start?" She held the employment offer with both hands, unwilling to let it escape her grasp.

Getz smiled. "How about Monday? Or do you need a couple of weeks to finish up with your current employer?"

"No, Monday is fine." She shut her eyes, a rush of relief
washing over her. "I would like to know a little more about the
project, though. It's all been so super-secret."

"No hurry. We want you to be completely comfortable with
everything we're doing here."

His hand glided unerringly across the table to rest on hers.
His lotioned skin felt soft and slimy as the fingers moved across
the back of her hand.

She pulled back, looked down at his pale hand still poised
like some serpent over the spot where her hand had been.

"Problem?" he asked.

She choked back the revulsion she felt at being touched
that way. "No, no problem," she said stiffly, struggling to regain
composure.

"The project. Can you tell me more about it now?"

Getz's hand slid silently back behind the tabletop.

"No problem. We can take a few minutes right now."

If he had noticed her reaction to his touch, he wasn't showing it. If a man was going to touch her, she wanted it to be on her own terms. She would not be used.

Getz continued, "What we've got going on here is, in my estimation, the most aggressive, cutting-edge, artificial intelligence project in the nation. At least in terms of social networking. And you are going to be a major part of it." He leaned forward, eyebrows raised. "No one outside this company is to know what we're doing until it's done. That's very important. Can you agree to that?"

"Yes."

"Here it is." Getz held up both hands, as if ready to catch a ball. "You know about the whole social-networking thing. We've got Facebook, MyLife, and all the rest. People are looking to the web for friendships, for relationships at all levels."

"I know. It's been a major cultural phenomenon."

"The big question is, how can someone, some company, break into that in a really unique way? Facebook already has more than eight hundred million active users. That's from them, their own statistics. Eight hundred million! That's better than eleven percent of the entire population of planet Earth. Do you know how many friends each user has?"

She shook her head.

"I'll tell you how many. The average Facebook user has over one hundred friends." Getz's green eyes grew large, intense. "Do the math. Fifty percent of their active users log on every day. Every one of them has an average of one hundred thirty friends, right? How many people are potentially touched by all that? How many?"

Melissa worked the numbers. She had only gotten to the first set before Getz spoke again.

"Half of eight hundred million is four hundred million. Multiply that by a hundred thirty. Know what you'll get? Fifty-two billion people!"

"But that's more people than there are on the whole Earth," answered Melissa. "What sense would it make? That would mean we're hitting many people more than one time."

"Exactly. So we have overlap. What it comes down to is we're hitting all those millions of people six, seven, maybe eight times a day. Somehow, we're touching all of them."

Melissa considered the implications. "Okay, so there's all this social interaction. I get that. But how does that help us? How do we benefit?"

"Okay, here's where it gets good. Imagine . . ." He raised one finger right in front of her nose. "Just imagine we've got a percentage of those 'friends' working for us. Even a very small percentage. Keep imagining. What if we could get those workers of ours to recommend movies, products, vacations . . . you name it. Would that be huge?"

Nodding, she stretched herself mentally.

"Are you imagining? You get online with Facebook, and we've got one of your friends telling you how great the latest chick flick is, and that you ought to go see it. Or she's using some new kind of dish soap and you ought to try it. Any kind of product, you just name it. As they say, this is the most amazing concept since sliced bread. And you're going to be front and center, right in the middle of all of it."

Getz stood up and turned to the whiteboard behind him. "We do it like God did it, but better." With a bright blue marker he drew a circle on the board. "We create them."

"Create them? How's that?" It was common among software developers to use the word *create* freely. But to create people? *Where was this going?*

"Let me illustrate it for you." He drew a smile in the circle, then added two eyes, with turned-up, innocent-looking eyebrows. "So far, so good. We've got a friendly face. What's missing?"

"A body?"

"That's good, but what I mean is, what's missing in the face? Don't answer. It's a nose." He drew a rounded triangle in the center.

"Now, how about the body? Should it be slender or fat? Your call."

"Fat. It should be fat because the face is round."

"Right, because the two go together. We know what makes us comfortable." He sketched a rotund figure into the drawing, which began to look like the Pillsbury Doughboy.

"Now, Melissa, look at his right hand. It's empty. Tell me which object you prefer." As he spoke, he drew a handgun in the right hand, paused, then erased the handgun and replaced it with an umbrella. Then he erased the umbrella and faced her. "Which did you like? The gun or the umbrella?"

"I liked the umbrella."

"Why?" He redrew the umbrella.

"Because you drew a friendly figure to start with, and the umbrella was more consistent with that. The gun looked out of place."

"You've got it. We just designed someone you were comfortable with. It was simple, it was intuitive, and it was interesting."

I know where this is going. I'm a mile ahead of you, Mr. Getz.

"Here it is, Melissa. Plain and simple. We are going to provide the means to let people custom-design their own friends. Yes, I really mean *friends*. We've got the technology, you know that. What we've lacked was the platform to make it worthwhile. Social networking—Facebook and all the rest—gives that to us."

Silence settled in the air as he allowed the implications of that to form in her mind.

"Let's imagine Jane Doe sitting at home. She's worried, she's depressed, she wants someone to confide in. Who's she going to turn to?"

"Her friends?"

"But those *friends* are real people. She doesn't dare tell them what's really going on. For all she knows, it could be all over Facebook in an hour, and then the whole world would know her secret. No, she needs someone she can trust with the deepest secrets of her life.

"So, Jane Doe goes to our website and we let her design the perfect friend. A virtual friend."

"She designs one online?"

"We start with something as simple as the basic personality types and have her build from there. So she chooses introverted or outgoing, friendly or reserved, kind or difficult, understanding or impatient.

"Someone's going to choose an impatient friend?"

"The important thing is that we provide the choice. From there she picks her friend's hair, physique, family background, age, everything. Maybe she builds the sister she never had. Perhaps she builds a high school friend she lost touch with. It's up to her."

Melissa realized what Getz was presenting to her was not only doable, it was perfect. *Why has no one ever done this?* "So, how far does this go? Synthesized voice? Conversations? The whole works? I mean, I can see getting all of this done if we have the resources."

"We take it as far as we can, Melissa. And we've definitely got the resources. I envision our Jane Doe building her friend and then we automatically register her friend on Facebook. From then on, she can interact with her virtual friend just as easily as she could with a real person." He flashed a conspiratorial smile. "Well, any way but physical."

She didn't like what Getz was doing with his eyes and squirmed under his gaze.

Melissa pointed at the whiteboard, drawing Getz's eyes off her. "And how do we profit from this?"

He blinked, turned back to her. "We make money two ways. First, even though we start out with this as a free service, eventually we ramp it up and charge money for the 'premium' friend. People won't hesitate. Second, these friends can sell products, services. Old-fashioned click-through advertising will be like a horse cart compared to what we can offer."

I've got it, Mr. Getz. You won't see me coming till I run over you.

"This is fascinating. I never . . ."

"I've only begun to scratch the surface here, Melissa. For instance, well, may I ask you a personal question?"

"Go ahead."

"Is your mother living?"

It felt like she'd been struck in the chest with a rock. Why in the world would he ask her a question like that? Her, of all people. *Could he know?*

Control. She shook her head slowly. "No, she's not."

Getz bent over the table, palms flat, his face close to hers. "Then here's the big one, Melissa. We can give her back to you in every way but physically."

Yes, it's true. We can do that. The potential, the power of what they had in their hands was overwhelming. She shook off the lightheaded feeling.

People would be re-creating deceased children, mothers, fathers. They'd be getting e-mails on their birthdays from people who'd been gone for many years. Was it a kind of self-deception? Sure, but how different was it from hanging a picture of a loved one in the hallway? Wasn't it there to remind you of the person? Something to help you recall old conversations, hugs, and special times? And perhaps to imagine what might have been?

I can make it real.

She felt again the pressure of Getz's gaze on her as she worked through it mentally, emotionally. *This will work, and I can do it.*

Another idea tugged on the edges of her mind with tiny, insistent fingers. The one that would make it supremely worthwhile. *Not now. Later. I'll think about that when the time comes.*

THE WAY HE'S LOOKING AT ME. A shiver fluttered along Melissa's exposed forearm.

She needed to steer the conversation somewhere else, and still stroke the man's ego. "How did you come up with the idea? I mean, this isn't just numbers lined up in columns. This is genius."

He rolled his head to one side, as if savoring the memory. "I remember the moment of . . . *inspiration* . . . when the concept of the *virtual friend* came to me. It left me nearly breathless. This was the multimillion-dollar idea I'd been searching for all my adult life."

She watched an expression slither over his features and recoiled at the way it made her feel. The man was a snake.

"And you will be the greatest asset of all. Your design and architectural talents will make the *virtual friend* a reality, Melissa. There is nothing to stop us."

Us. She swallowed, smiled back.

"We'll make an incredible team, Mr. Getz."

No one had to tell her she was good. And there was much more he would learn about her, but he could wait a little longer for that surprise.

He slid his soft fingers across her hand. "Yes, Melissa. The two of us will be working *very* closely over the next four or five years. A project this size will surely take that long before it's ready for the world to see. And all the time, we'll be working together, planning, developing. Both of us learning what the other has to offer."

The question was, *how* closely would they be working? Getz was a predator. He probably thought of himself as the big brass ring every girl wants to snag, but she wasn't here to become his trophy. She was here for work, serious work.

She still clutched the employment letter in one hand as she looked up at the whiteboard.

Getz asked, "So, what do you think? Are you starting to see the possibilities?"

Always the suggestive comments. How should she answer? "The possibilities? Yes, absolutely. This is brilliant."

Melissa looked up at Getz, who still stood by the whiteboard. Keep his mind on the project. "We could build out a library of celebrity characters. Everyone from Madonna to Steve Jobs. People would go crazy."

"There you go, you've got the idea," said Getz. "Already in the plans. What else?"

Melissa looked at the whiteboard, then back to Getz, forcing herself to remain clear and focused. "Some people will just be looking for a new relationship. A boyfriend. Or a girlfriend. Someone to talk to. There's that."

"Premium content." Getz grinned. "And you've just approached what's probably going to be the main profit center. What we call 'The Virtual Ideal.' There's something inside people that's always searching for that ideal relationship. We're going to come pretty close to fulfilling that."

I have an ideal man, and he's not virtual. He exists somewhere, and this will help me find him.

Getz erased the Doughboy figure with the umbrella off the whiteboard. "I've got a meeting with our CEO, Dan Hammersmith, in a few minutes. He'll want to meet you on Monday when you come in. You can go through all the Human Resources rigmarole then, all right?"

"Sure," said Melissa. "That sounds great. I'll be here when the doors open."

Getz reached toward her and took her hand before she could withdraw it. He held on to it as he looked into her eyes, eyebrows slightly raised.

"I'd like to talk to you more before then. There's a lot we

need to discuss before we . . ." He grinned, mirthlessly. "Before we get down and dirty, so to speak." He paused. "I could, say, meet you for dinner tonight? Just talk through some things? I think it's going to be important to know we're compatible, that we think the same way about things, don't you?"

Here it is. Oh, I know you, Getz. Down, dirty, and compatible.

She looked at his left hand. No wedding ring. She didn't want to lose this job before she got it.

No matter. If it went wrong, she knew what to do. "Sure, Mr. Getz. What do you have in mind?"

"Aaron, call me Aaron," he said. He still gripped her hand. "I've got your address from your résumé. How about I pick you up at six-thirty and we go out to the Tuscan Villa? It's in downtown Indianapolis near where you live."

She hid a shudder, as if she were in the coils of a venomous serpent.

Getz hesitated. Had he seen her react?

"Don't worry. Strictly professional. Do you like Italian okay?"

She withdrew her hand. "That will work. I'll expect you then. And thank you for working out the job."

Melissa could still feel Getz's green eyes on her as she walked through the double glass doors to the street outside.

CHAPTER TWO
Problem Solved

Through the large bay window in the living room, Melissa glanced down at the street in front of her house. The glowing blue numerals on the mantel clock read 6:20. Getz would be here soon.

She straightened the dark gray pantsuit she'd chosen for the evening. It looked businesslike, efficient. If Getz was going to get weird on her, it wouldn't be because she encouraged it.

She strode into the kitchen and opened the wide drawer under the breakfast counter. It rattled as she pulled it open. The nine-inch Gingher scissors had been purchased for a craft class the year before. The knife edges on the blades were like new, and the scissors slipped easily into her handbag.

A car horn sounded outside. She could see Aaron Getz waiting in front with his hazard lights flashing. *I'm just a piece of meat to him. He doesn't even bother coming to the door.* She turned off the lights and descended the steps to the curb.

Getz smiled at her as he opened the passenger door of his SUV. "Good evening, Miss Montalvo," he said with mock courtesy. "I'm happy to see you again so soon."

"Thank you." She held up her purse. "I'm ready to take notes," she said, moving quickly to keep the conversation focused on business.

Melissa settled down in the wide seat and buckled her seat belt.

"I talked with Dan and told him you'd be starting on Monday. He's excited to have you on board. We all are."

"Hammersmith?"

"Right, Dan Hammersmith. CEO. I told you I'd be meeting with him. We'd like to jump right in with a big planning meeting on Monday afternoon."

"Sounds great."

Getz was dressed in a gray polo and khaki slacks. Did they look like they had both dressed in gray to please one another? Melissa hoped not.

"You just need to finish up all your HR paperwork so we can finalize the hire that morning."

The words struck her. "Finalize?" Hadn't she already accepted the offer? What was going on here? Was finalizing the job conditioned on how this evening turned out?

"Oh," said Getz. "Nothing to worry about." He kept his eyes on the road ahead, avoiding her gaze. He moved his right hand to her knee, stroked it lightly, and returned it to the steering wheel. "Dan simply wants to know we're going to work well together."

Melissa cocked her head to one side. "Do you hear that?"

"Hear what?"

"I think I hear a thumping sound coming from one of your tires. Don't you hear it?"

He tipped his head toward the driver window. "No, I don't hear anything. Are you sure?"

She put on her best *concentrating* face. "I'm sure of it. You'd better do a walkaround as soon as you can and check it out."

Getz pulled the SUV up in front of the restaurant. As soon as the tires stopped rolling, Melissa jumped out. "You can check your tires. I'll get a table and meet you inside."

The Tuscan Villa was a storefront with a deep interior. It was built with an abundance of wood, both on the floors and in the walls. The right-hand side of the large room had an oil painting of an Italian street scene.

Melissa chose a table in the back of the restaurant, away from the window. She sat with her back to the door. A candle in a fishnet-wrapped globe burned in the center of the thick, crisp, white tablecloth. She bent close and blew the candle out.

Getz arrived at the table, exhaled loudly. "The tires looked okay; I don't know what you were hearing."

Melissa shrugged. "Maybe just road noise. Never hurts to be careful."

After he was seated, he ordered a seafood plate. He tried to get Melissa to do the same, but she demurred. She kept her back turned to the server and ordered only salad and bread sticks.

She wondered what Aaron Getz had in mind. No, correct that. She knew what Aaron Getz had in mind. What was in doubt was how the evening would turn out for Mr. Getz, not for her. Either way, it was not going to be what he expected.

Dinner arrived. Melissa reached down for her purse on the floor as the server put the plates on the table, keeping her face from view.

"I had another thought," said Melissa. "For the virtual friend concept. Have you considered having living people do virtual clones of themselves?"

Getz raised an eyebrow in query as he lifted a bread stick to his mouth.

"Suppose a person wants to come up with a virtual representation of himself. A virtual clone. He works through a battery of questions. We get his or her history, psych profile, everything. We do it all on a secure website so the person's privacy is protected. When it's all complete, the person can put it to work on Facebook or any other venue he chooses."

He put his tongue against the inside of his cheek. "Hmmm, maybe, I see what you mean. Instead of us building out celebrities on our own, the celeb himself may wish to take ownership of his virtual clone for his own purposes? Frankly, we had not considered that. Well done!"

"Not just that. Not just celebrities. I'm thinking far out now. You tell me if I'm going too far. What about a father? He's got cancer, and he wants to leave something of himself for his family. Someone who'll be here when he is actually gone? And maybe a mother wants a clone of her sixteen-year-old daughter, so she'll always have her the way she remembers her?"

"Hey, you *are* thinking." He tapped his finger against the tabletop. "I knew hiring you was going to be a good move for us." He sat back, turned his head and waved toward the server, who was setting up a nearby table. "Hey, can we get a couple of cappuccinos?"

Minutes later, two of the Italian coffees arrived with a small biscotto on the side. When the dinner plates were cleared away, he gave her that look again. Familiar, conspiratorial. "We anticipate there will be a dark side to this too. What's to stop a man from coming up with a virtual girlfriend? Or a lonely housewife conjuring up the man of her dreams? The truth of the matter is, there is nothing to stop that."

"True. I've considered that. This sort of thing is open to all sorts of abuse. I don't know how we could avoid it."

A hint of a smile played on his lips. "Nor would we want to. We're running a business, not a church. The philosophy of VirtualFriendMe is, if you're not hurting someone else, then we are not going to interfere." He leaned forward. "What do you think, Melissa? I like the philosophy. I mean, if you're not hurting anyone, what's the harm? People can do what they want."

"I suppose so."

"We just need to keep enough safeguards in place to keep it out of the newspapers."

He dropped his eyes, looked back up at Melissa, and smiled. A sort of smile that spoke condescension and power at the same time.

"Like you and me, Melissa. I think it's important we get along well, don't you? Even more than just in the professional sense, we need to know we are—well—compatible."

She nodded, knowing what was coming next. *Compatible.* That word was growing more and more distasteful to her ears.

He looked at Melissa, his brow furrowed. "Do you think we're going to get along well, Melissa?"

"Yes, Aaron. I think we are going to get along very, very well," she said, unsmiling.

"There's a place I like to go sometimes, not too far from here. Last place in the world anyone would ever look for two people." The words seemed to hang in the air.

"Yes?"

"Well," he said, "I thought that, you know . . ."

"We could go there? Is that what you mean? That you want me to go there with you?"

He nodded, head bobbing like a plaster figure. "Yes, when we're done with dinner . . ."

"Sure, Aaron. Let's go there. Let's see what your world is really like."

THE TOWN CENTER MOTEL had lost its luster. Perhaps there had been a time when it catered to a straight business clientele, but the flight of the middle class to the suburbs back in the seventies had taken its toll. The large outer wall of the motel was finished in rough concrete, painted over with crude lettering advertising rooms by the day, the week, and the month. A smaller sign hung under a bare bulb by the office advertising the $25 hourly rate.

Getz pulled the SUV into a space at the far end of the building, hidden in the shadow of a balcony overhang. "Wait here, I'll take care of this." He fumbled in his pockets and came up with a small roll of cash. Another smile.

Melissa watched from inside the SUV as he walked to the office. It was a walkup window where he pushed his money through a metal drawer. The clerk was hidden somewhere behind a wall of thick glass. She shivered, and clutched her handbag. *Stay calm. Don't start shaking.*

He returned with a key on a large ring. He walked to the door in front of the car and used the key to open it. *He's been here before. He knew where to park where we wouldn't be noticed.* Standing in the open doorway, he beckoned to her.

Melissa opened the car door and stepped onto the decaying asphalt. The car chirped as the door locked behind her. He must have used his key fob to lock it. Only one way to go now.

She walked from behind the SUV to the door of the motel room, where the dim yellow light from inside seemed to puddle on the walkway in front of it.

The motel office sign was visible from this end of the building, but not the window. They would not see who Getz had brought this time. A block wall hid their faces from any pedestrian that dared to walk these streets at night.

She stepped in, stopped short. The room felt sticky and had a strong scent of industrial disinfectant. A faded shag rug covered the floor, and a television with an artificial wood cabinet sat on a glossy veneered table. The table, like the television on it, was marked by burns from cigarettes.

Getz walked to the bed and turned it down. "This place isn't much, but the sheets are clean. That's enough, right?"

"It's all that matters." Melissa fingered the zipper of her pantsuit jacket, making sure Getz saw what she did. "Aaron, pull the top sheet all the way down, will you? Why don't you lie down and let me rub your back for a while, okay? We can talk for a few minutes. I'm a little nervous. It will help me relax."

Like I could relax in this slime pit.

Getz complied, lying down on his stomach with his face on the pillow. "How's this?" His voice sounded muffled.

"Great. Now close your eyes. Start thinking about us working together."

"Oh, yeah. I'm feeling more comfortable all the time."

Melissa set her handbag softly on the bed as she sat down next to the prone man. With her left hand she rubbed his shoulder in a circular motion. With her right she reached into the bag and withdrew the scissors. Light flashed on the blades as they came silently out of the cloth bag. "Are you ready to check out our compatibility?"

"Mmmmmmm."

With her left thumb Melissa felt along the base of Getz's skull until she touched the concave area where the two tendons meet under the base of his skull. "Feel good?"

"Mmmmmmm."

"Let's get rid of that tension." She began rubbing in the depression, making sure of the spot.

"Good-bye, Mr. Getz."

Getz's eyes opened. Too late.

Melissa shoved the scissor handles with the butt of her hand into the spot she'd located on his neck. The sharp blades passed through the epidermal layer and into the muscle layer beneath. She leaned in and pushed harder as the flesh crunched and tore with the passage of the stainless steel tips. At the end, there was a soft *pop* as the brain stem parted into two useless pieces.

Getz's legs stiffened and kicked one time as she listened to the final rush of air leaving his lungs.

"For compatibility's sake, Mr. Getz." White-knuckled, she gripped the handles and moved them around in a wide arc inside Getz's skull before withdrawing them.

There was very little blood. Just a stain at the top of the polo's collar. She wiped the scissors off on the back of his shirt, and rinsed them clean in the bathroom sink. Then, from her purse she took out a plastic bag, sealed the scissors inside, and tucked the bag back into the purse.

Stay calm, Melissa.

She removed the sealed wet-wipe envelope she'd brought,

tore off the edge, and extracted the alcohol-soaked fabric. Her thin fingers trembled slightly as she wiped down the table, the doorknobs, everything she had touched. No one had seen her enter, she was sure of that. The SUV was still parked in the shadow of the building, the passenger side invisible to the motel office. She could walk in the direction away from the office without being seen.

Melissa turned out the light in the room. Only a soft, muted glow from inside the plastic case of the television remained. Eyes closed softly, she accustomed herself to the absence of light.

She gave Getz no more than a glance as she left, turning the knob with the stiffening wet wipe. She would dispose of that somewhere on the way back.

She looked left, right. No cameras, no strange people with their prying eyes.

No one had seen her face at the restaurant. Hadn't she even made sure they walked in separately? Darkness had shrouded her time at the motel. There wouldn't even be any DNA evidence. No taxi records. Nothing.

Confident, she stepped into the darkness for the long walk back to her home.

Much later, she made out the pale glare of lights from a convenience store near her home where they spilled out onto the parking lot on a young man who was pumping gasoline. She wondered absently why her hands felt so dry, then went inside the store and bought a tube of hand lotion. As she walked the final few blocks to her home, she rubbed the lotion into her skin.

Her eyes surveyed the dark sky. It was such a pleasant, pretty night.

CHAPTER THREE
Unfulfilled

Four Years Later

A September mist fell across the fields and the evening fog glittered on the Taurus's windshield. Scott Douglas leaned forward toward the glass. There were always deer, raccoons, or something just waiting by the side of the road to jump out and cause an accident.

I'm late again. What is Rachel going to think?

A quick glance at the car clock: 8:03. Maybe the kids would still be up, but for the third time this week he had missed dinner. A pair of green eyes winked luminous in the darkness on the side of the road.

The houses were familiar now. The blue glow of their wall-sized television screens poured out of the windows to diffuse in the darkness. Ahead, the blue and white reflectors on his mailbox caught the beams of his headlights. *Home.*

Scott turned the car into the driveway, the sound of the gravel popping under his tires as they bit into the surface. He pressed the button clipped to his visor and the garage door began to lift and spill bright light out onto the drive.

Home. Finally.

He walked into the dark kitchen. Tapping sounds were coming from the living room. The sound of a keyboard. "Rachel? Are you in there?"

Rachel swiveled in her chair and smiled at her husband. "Oh, you're home already. I thought you'd be later." She stood to face him. "I put the kids to bed about fifteen minutes ago. We didn't know when you'd get here."

"I got tired and left early. I'll go in a little early tomorrow and finish up before everyone gets there." He half-smiled and turned his head toward the stairway. "I really wanted to see Scotty and Angela before they went to bed. Is Scotty excited about his birthday?"

"Oh, yeah. He's super excited. It's all he can talk about. Mom and Dad are coming up, you remember."

"Did you already tell me that? Where's my head? But yes, that's great. I'll be there if I don't get stuck at work."

"Do you want something to eat? We got pizza from The Great Santini tonight after I took the kids to the mall. Scotty needed some things for preschool."

Scott tried not to show his disappointment. He missed some real home cooking, but he tried not to blame Rachel. She was probably doing her best. She never knew when he'd be home anymore, and that made it hard for her to plan any nice meals. Plus, she had the kids to take care of, and probably a million other things. Somehow his mother had always managed to have a hot dinner on the table, though.

He worked too much. That was for sure. Four years at Castle Investments had taught him one thing—that work was never done. If he worked sixteen hours a day he still wouldn't be able to keep up with all his accounts. He managed retirement portfolios for serious people, and they expected him to be on top of every market trend and shift twenty-four hours a day. Sometimes it seemed like the harder he worked, the more he had left to do at the end of the day and he was wearing out.

"Sure, pizza's fine." The resignation in his voice must have been apparent, because Rachel set her jaw as she walked into the kitchen and flipped on the light switch.

"I mean it, Rachel. Pizza's fine. I'm just tired tonight."

RACHEL'S EYES NARROWED, her body stiffened. "You know what, Scott? I'm sorry. I'm sorry all I have is pizza. I'm sure your mother would have done better."

She turned her back to him as she opened the refrigerator door. "But I didn't know when you'd come home, did I? Last night it was almost ten o'clock before you got here, and you never even called to tell me where you were."

"Where I was?" Scott sighed. "You didn't know where I was? Where would I be except at work? Where am I *ever* except at work?"

Rachel felt the heat rise into her face. It seemed to radiate as the discouragement flowed from her. "Well, isn't that just the question? You're right. Where are you ever except at work? At least you say that's where you are."

Her conscience stabbed at her. Why had she said that to him? She knew he was at work. He was a good man, a faithful man. But didn't he know she and the children deserved some time with him too?

Scott slapped both hands down on the kitchen counter. "What? You doubt that I'm really at work? You think I'm ... what?"

"No, no. I'm sorry." She ran her hand through her hair. "All I mean is—"

"I have no clue what you mean when you say things like that. I just know what you said. And you implied I might be lying to you about working at night. That's all I needed to hear." Scott spun away from her. "Do whatever you like. Watch TV, whatever. I'm going out and get some actual food, not another pizza, and maybe I'll even get some salad with it." He turned toward the hallway that led to the garage.

"Scott, I'm sorry. I didn't mean it." She wanted to run after him, pull him back, but he was already gone. The garage door hummed as it raised and lowered. The glow from his headlights flickered across the window as he pulled the car out onto the road, back into the darkness.

"I really am sorry." To the emptiness where her husband had stood just moments before she said, "I would have made you a salad."

Helplessness rushed in, filling the void left by the outpouring of frustration, anger, and discouragement. She wanted to be a good wife to Scott, but where was he when she needed him? All day, every day, cooped up with the children. Never any relief. Didn't he understand at all what she was going through?

She wanted him to come home before dinnertime and take the two little ones out in the yard. Give her a break so she could work on getting a nice meal ready. She loved them with all her heart, but was there ever going to be any time for herself? From morning to night, from when they scrambled out of bed until she tucked the children under their covers, her day was consumed with taking care of them.

All she wanted was for Scott to come home and do his part. Other fathers came home. Why couldn't he?

CHAPTER FOUR
Discouragement

Rachel waited up for Scott that night, but when he finally returned just before two o'clock in the morning, he went to bed without a word. Walked by her as if she did not exist. Where had he been? Had he seen someone else? Some other woman?

What did he expect from her? He'd said he wanted a family. Well, she'd given him a family. She'd given him everything he asked for, and never said *No*, never claimed she had a headache. She simply wanted him to walk in the door in the evening and show her it was worth it by his love. Why did she have to feel like this was her fault?

Sleep was a series of dreamless fits and starts, until finally Scott moved next to her in the bed. She opened her tired eyes to look at the alarm clock on the table. 6:10. Time to get up and make breakfast for her family. She closed her eyes for just a few minutes more. The next thing she knew, she could hear the sound of shower water. She hadn't even noticed when Scott got out of bed.

She pulled herself to her feet, put on her robe, and made

her way downstairs. In the kitchen she put on a pot of coffee and got out the skillet. Scott would like bacon and eggs. Home-cooked. Whatever he'd been up to last night, she could find out later. She would be the kind of wife he wanted her to be.

The sliding door of their bedroom closet upstairs thumped. Scott was getting dressed for work.

The aroma of the freshly brewed coffee filled the kitchen. Scott would smell it upstairs too, and maybe it would put him in a better mood. She took his travel cup from the kitchen sink and filled it with hot water, warming it for him before he filled it with coffee. Then she set out a plate and napkin on the dining room table, just the way he liked.

Was she only going through the motions of marriage? She shook off the feeling, then imagined herself working outside in the flower garden, never lifting her head, oblivious to the heavy, dark clouds overwhelming the horizon. If a storm was coming, she was doing her best to imagine it away.

Ugh, how did she look? She ran a hand through her hair. What would Scott think when he saw her?

She sneaked into the downstairs bathroom, glad Scott had not seen her this morning. Standing before the mirror, she brushed the tangles and snarls out. She turned, imagining what she must look like to Scott as the very first person he saw in the morning.

Not a pretty sight. *She* wasn't pretty. She dropped her hands to her sides and looked down toward where her toes should be. She couldn't see them, not yet. She needed to lose thirty-five more pounds, but it was so hard to get them off.

Twelve weeks in the Hugest Loser group and only an eight-pound weight loss. She turned to her side and ran her hands over the robe where it covered her stomach. She had looked like this since she was pregnant with Angela. Actually, she looked like this when she *was* pregnant with Angela. She had never lost the weight she had picked up during her pregnancy. Maybe she never would. Did Scott think she didn't care how she looked, didn't try?

Scott came downstairs, his shoes *klumping* on the steps.

Rachel splashed water on her face, tried to rub the sleepiness out of her eyes. She may not be able to look pretty for Scott, but she didn't want to look like she had just fallen out of bed either. She straightened the robe as best she could, and went out to the kitchen to greet her husband.

The familiar whirring of the garage door . . . she searched the kitchen counter. The travel cup was gone. Scott was gone. He had left for work without even telling her good-bye.

She was surprised at the words that came in a rush. "That's how you want it? Fine. Maybe I'll find someone else to talk to."

CHAPTER FIVE
Jane

The painful memory of Scott's departure was still on Rachel's mind when she got home from taking four-year-old Scotty to preschool. She put Angela down for a nap, came quietly back downstairs, and stood by a window.

She had to get it together. No matter how it felt, it wasn't abandonment. He was just upset. They were still husband and wife.

Marriage. From the time she was a little girl, getting married, having her own family, had been the dream of her life.

Supporting it with one hand as if it were fragile, she picked up her wedding album and placed it carefully on the coffee table. This beautiful book, with its embroidered cover, encapsulated all the hopes and dreams of her life. Her family, husband, and friends were all there.

Suzanne.

She bit back the pain before she opened the book. The hoarse, faraway voice of Suzanne's husband, Rick, echoed in her ears. "The cancer finally got her, Rachel. She wanted me to tell you she loved you and she'd always be your friend."

On that awful night two years ago, her best friend and maid of honor had finally lost her yearlong battle with epithelial ovarian cancer. Only 18 percent of those who reached stage four would survive. Suzanne had not been one of them.

Rachel carefully lifted the cover and looked at the first page. There was the wedding license for Rachel Joy Anderson and Scott Randall Douglas. The happy, loving couple in the picture on the opposite page looked so hopeful, so free of worry. Her fingertip traced a line along Scott's jaw. She loved him so much. What was wrong? She missed him, missed him so much. The man that came home at night wasn't the same. She wanted this man, the one in the picture.

On the next page were her mother and father. And there was Scott's family. They were all such good people. Surely they had their share of problems too, didn't they? Of course they did.

There was Suzanne, radiant as maid of honor. It seemed so long ago now, when they had hugged each other in the hotel dressing room. *Best friends forever.* Those poignant words were filled with such meaning now. She would see her friend again, someday. When all this life was past and they were in heaven together. How wonderful that would be.

But I wish you were here right now to talk to me.

Rachel closed the wedding album. The soft *puff* as the heavy cover came together triggered something in her heart.

Doesn't Scott know how much I love him? How much I need him?

Then anger began to rise inside her. Anger that burned down into resentment for a husband that treated her so callously. She was a wife, not a rug. Having children didn't turn her into an unpaid housekeeper. At least it wasn't supposed to be that way.

She needed a friend. A friend who was really a friend. Someone who cared about her.

Last night on Facebook, she'd spent time dipping into the lives of friends and strangers, curious about what was going on. A sidebar advertisement of some kind had shown up on the screen. What was it again? Something about visual friends? No, not visual. *Virtual.*

She went to the computer in the living room, brought up a search page, and typed in *virtual friend.*

She scanned down the page. *There. Is that it?*

Real Virtual Friends—VirtualFriendMe
www.virtualfriendme.com
Home of real virtual friends. Friends just like the real thing.

She clicked on the link.

The images on the screen faded until all that was left was the white background. Then she heard a woman's voice.

"Are you ready for this?"

A brief pause, then the shoulder-up likeness of a young woman appeared on the left side of the screen. She wore a red top. Shoulder-length hair fell around her neck. At first it didn't look like anything else would happen. But no, she was breathing. At least she looked like she was breathing. Yes, moving, blinking, as if waiting for someone to notice her.

The image smiled. Her eyes wrinkled at the edges. "I asked you if you were ready for this, didn't I?" The eyes opened wider. "Hmmm?"

Rachel fell back against her chair, feeling like someone had pushed her. *It's so real.*

"I know, you're surprised." The face assumed a compassionate look. "I never mean to scare anyone. I never know what to expect either. I can't see you, you know. All I know about you is what you tell me." Pause. "And you haven't told me anything yet, have you?"

"Will you tell me your name?" The face looked down to the lower right-hand corner of the screen, where a small box appeared. A blue cursor blinked in the box. "Just type your name in the box, then we'll get properly introduced. My name is Jane. What's yours?" She raised her eyebrows, and motioned to the box with a slight tip of her head.

Slowly Rachel moved back toward the screen. It was just like having another person in the room. Should she put her name in the box? What would happen?

Jane looked kind and patient. Rachel touched the keyboard and carefully typed *Rachel*.

"Rachel. Wonderful. Another girl." Jane's wide smile showed white teeth behind the lipstick. "How old are you, Rachel?"

31.

"Oooh. We're about the same age. Well, in my case it's sort of what we call a virtual age. But what woman wants to spend time talking about how old she really is?" Jane laughed at her joke.

Rachel laughed too, then typed *Where are you?*

"Rachel, this will surprise you, but trust me, it's true. The only place I exist is where you are right now. I'm unique, just like you."

What? The site must be some kind of a joke itself.

"You're probably wondering what all this is about, aren't

you? If I were you, I'd be wondering too. May I explain? Type 'yes' if you'd like to know more. Or you can type 'good-bye.'" She offered a bright smile. "I hope you'll type 'yes.'"

What could be the harm in learning more? She could always say no later on. There was always the power button. Why not?

Rachel typed *yes*.

"Wonderful. I was hoping you would do that. Do you have a microphone on your computer? If you do, plug it in. We can really talk then."

Rachel opened the drawer of the short filing cabinet next to the computer and removed a small dictation headset she had purchased three years before and plugged it in.

Rachel hesitated. Did she want to do this? Her voice was low, unsure as she said, "Jane?"

"Yes. Oh, that's so much better, Rachel. Thank you. All that typing back and forth is such a bother, even for us virtual people." And then Jane winked.

She is so real. Rachel caught herself winking back. This was strange. Not like talking to some robot.

"Now, I'll warn you. Sometimes, when we're just starting like this, I may have trouble understanding you. But if you'll be patient with me I'll learn your voice until I know it as well as my own. Ready to go?"

"Yes. Do you understand me?"

"Of course I do. We're going to do fine together. I told you I would tell you what our company does. Are you still interested?"

"Yes, please go on."

"I'm what we call an *introducer*. It's my job to introduce you to other friends. Kind of like a matchmaker. Did you ever see *Fiddler on the Roof*?"

"Yes, it's one of my favorites."

"Well, I'm sort of like Yente. Remember her? The match-maker? My job is to bring people together."

Rachel shook her head. Maybe it was some trick, and there was a real woman sitting somewhere in a room full of cubicles in Florida or some place, just supplying the voice.

"Jane, I want to ask you a question."

"Sure. Anything."

"Are you a real person?"

"Ooh, the big one already." Jane pursed her lips. "Introduc-ers get asked that a lot. If you mean *real* in the sense of 'Do I have a physical body?,' then the answer is no." Her face curled into a helpless look. "Does it matter to you? Because when you think about it, we spend lots of our time during the day talking and interacting with people and we never see their bodies."

This was so ironic. Sometimes days would pass and the only little bodies she interacted with were wearing diapers. Adults? Not so much. And friends . . .

"You call people on the phone, or you watch television, or maybe you use Facebook. Think about it: you never see those people physically, do you?"

"No, I guess not." She interacted with people online all the time. She knew they had real physical bodies, but no . . . she didn't actually see them physically. That was only true when they were actually present, not online.

Jane's face brightened. "Well, there you are. It's no different. I'm as real as you want me to be. Just don't shut me off, okay?" Jane winked again. "I might never find my way back."

What a strange concept. If that was the case, then Jane was completely dependent upon Rachel. Here was a person, or some sort of a person, whose whole existence depended on Rachel herself. Talk about needing a friend. She could disappear forever in the blink of an eye and no one would know the difference. No one except the one who turned her off.

Now Jane looked serious. "I was telling you what an introducer like myself actually does. We are here to bring people together. You may have noticed lots of people are looking for a friend."

True, but no one could ever come close to being as good a friend as Suzanne had been. That was a real friend.

"An introducer's job is to make that a reality. There's that word again. *Reality.*" Jane swiveled toward Rachel and leaned forward on her elbows. "Do you ever feel like you just need a real friend, Rachel?" Jane arched an eyebrow expectantly.

"Yes," said Rachel. "I do."

Nodding, Jane said, "I thought you might. So many people do. Would you like for me to help you find a true friend?"

Rachel considered. What was she about to get herself into? "I don't want anyone coming to my house or following me around. I don't think I want to meet any strangers. I mean, I don't want to get involved with any people I don't know."

Jane pouted. "Of course not. And that's not going to happen."

"I had a good friend like that, but she . . . she passed away a few years ago. Her name was Suzanne."

"I'm so sorry that happened. But I may have some very good news for you. What we are going to do is create the perfect friend for you. I really mean that. We'll create that perfect friend, and then I'll introduce you both." Jane wagged her head in delight. "It's the best part of the job."

"I know this may sound strange, but I think I should ask you something."

"Ask away," said Jane. "I'm here for you."

"Is it possible not to just, say, create a new friend for me, but to actually make her like the friend I had? Like Suzanne?"

Jane's eyes seemed to darken. "You mean, look like Suzanne, talk like Suzanne?"

"Yes. Can that be done?"

"Yes, it can. But I will warn you now that it will take some work on your part to bring it off. Do you have good-quality video and pictures of Suzanne? Good samples of her voice?"

Something stirred inside Rachel. "I do."

"Are you prepared to upload a great deal of that to us for analysis? If the quality is good enough, I think what we can do will surprise you."

"Oh, yes. If you tell me what you need, I can do it."

Is it possible? Can this really be true?

Jane continued, "All right, then. But before we get started there's one thing we should do. I need to get you registered on our system. That way, if we get interrupted or something happens, you can come back and we can pick up where we left off. Does that sound okay?"

"Okay. Does this cost anything?"

"No, not necessarily. There are some, well, special features we offer sometimes. But for the person that just wants a friend, that's free. Completely free. Just like Facebook. Are you ready to register?" Jane seemed to be genuinely excited.

Rachel looked at the screen where Jane waited. What harm could there be in checking it out? The whole process might be kind of fun. And Jane did seem trustworthy.

"Sure, ask me your questions."

"Okay, question number one. Where did you first meet Suzanne?"

CHAPTER SIX
Stress

Scott had already been working two hours when the telephone buzzed. He finished entering the formula he'd been working on in the spreadsheet on his computer, then clicked the button to activate his headset.

"Scott, will you come into my office, please?"

"Sure, Mr. Castle. I'll be right there." What could the owner of Castle Investments want with him? Being called into the office, for whatever reason, wasn't going to be good.

Alan Castle sat in his office at a small round conference table. Across from Castle was one of the company's most important customers. Gleason Archer had over $9 million with Castle Investments. Archer neither stood up nor smiled when Scott walked into the room.

Archer's portfolio was Scott's responsibility. Tension filled the air. What was the problem? Alan Castle had managed it himself until two years ago, when he had shifted the trust of it to the younger man.

"Scott, please have a seat. Mr. Archer has some concerns he's been discussing with me."

Searching the client's expression, Scott pulled back a chair and sat down. Archer's eyes gave nothing away. "Certainly, Mr. Castle. What can I do?"

Archer's face reddened. He looked intently at Scott and said, "What can you do? Maybe that's exactly the question we need to answer here. Or maybe the question is, 'What have you been doing?' My portfolio is off seven percent in sixty days, while the market is up six percent. We could probably start with an explanation, Mr. Douglas."

Scott looked to Castle for guidance, but the older man did not return his gaze, staring instead at a report cover. Scott rotated his seat toward Gleason Archer. "Mr. Archer, I don't know what to say. I've been the manager for your portfolio for the last two years, and I've been following the same investment strategy all along. It's the strategy we agreed on. Over the last two years, you've seen a twenty-four percent increase overall. I understand fully your concerns about it being down right now, but I do not think it's a cause for concern. Right now the bond market—"

"I don't want to hear excuses, Mr. Douglas. I want to see results. And when I see my portfolio down seven percent, I get worried. When Mr. Castle put you in charge of my account I wasn't sure I was happy with his decision. Now I'm even more worried." Tight-lipped, he shot Alan Castle a glare, then turned back to Scott. "Unless you can turn this investment portfolio around, and get it out of the tank it's in now, then I don't think our confidence in you has been warranted." He looked back to Alan Castle. "Which means, Alan, I will not think my confidence in you and this company has been warranted either."

Castle's eyes widened in surprise. "Mr. Archer, I don't think that—"

"Alan, I don't need excuses from anyone this morning. Not you and not him. I just want to see some improved performance and the trust I have put in you and your firm vindicated." He stood up to leave. "If we don't start seeing major improvements, I'll find another place for my investments." He held out both hands, palms up. "Strictly business, you understand."

Castle nodded, looking like he'd agree to anything. "We understand, Gleason, we totally understand. We'll make sure your trust in Castle Investments has not been misplaced."

Archer picked up his briefcase. "Thank you, Alan. I'm sure you will."

After Archer's exit, Castle turned to Scott. "Please close the door."

The door made an ominous click as it closed. Scott turned toward the older man. Dread lay in the pit of his stomach like a lead weight.

Alan Castle had been a mentor, a friend. This wasn't good.

"Sit down, Scott. Let's talk."

The two men sat down together at the small conference table. Castle folded his hands together in front of himself and studied them for a few moments before he spoke. "Scott, I like you. You know that. And I have confidence in you. I'm afraid, however, this situation is not about confidence so much as it is about business. We have to make Gleason Archer happy. There are no two ways about it. I want you to do a full review of the Archer account. Whatever else you're working on, I want you to set it aside—give it to Patricia or someone else—and give a hundred and ten percent of your attention to this single item. We don't have a more important client than Gleason Archer."

"Mr. Castle, I don't want you to think I haven't been working hard and doing my best. I really have. But sometimes the markets are up and sometimes they're down."

"I understand, Scott. I'm saying that's not the issue. I know you work hard, but the fallout from having an unhappy client like Gleason Archer could be catastrophic to our business. It's not about whether his portfolio is up or down. It's what he says about us to others. You may be managing his portfolio in such a way that by the end of the year he'll be ecstatic. It doesn't matter right now. What does matter is that he's currently unhappy, and we have to do something about it. More to the point, you personally have to do something about it."

"When I started with the Archer account we agreed on the investment strategy. I'm following that to the letter. I don't know what else to do."

"I'm not disputing that. This is more than strategy." He looked directly into Scott's eyes. "There are a lot of people in the office outside this door who depend upon you and me doing our very best jobs. Neither of us is indispensable." He arched an eyebrow. "I think you know what I'm telling you. Now get out there and do the exceptional. Step out of your box and use your imagination." Castle stood and extended his hand to Scott.

Scott took the older man's hand, shook it uneasily. *Clear enough. My job is on the line.*

He returned to his cubicle, walking on legs that wobbled. It seemed as if every eye in the office was upon him.

Carole Turner, who had started as an investment counselor just a few months before Scott, stopped by his cube. "You look worried. Is everything all right? Anything I can do?"

"Sorry, Carole. Didn't know it showed. No, I'm okay. Nothing a little more effort won't cure." He gave her a sideways grin. "Got to work hard and feed all those hungry kids I've got."

She didn't smile in return, but stood looking at him, as if evaluating his honesty. Then she spun around and walked off, leaving him feeling even more uncomfortable as he returned to his work. It wasn't her business, anyway.

It took Scott half an hour to reorganize his desktop, setting everything aside except for the Gleason Archer account.

He had a family that depended upon him. The prospect, the very thought, of having to tell Rachel he'd been fired filled him with dismay. He would not let it happen.

By three o'clock he had completed his initial review and needed a break. There was no way in the world he was going to have time to leave the office for a walk or even to get a few minutes of fresh air. He clicked on the icon to bring up his Internet browser.

News? Politics? More stress. He needed something else; some kind of an outlet.

He wanted to call Rachel, but making a personal phone call at this time would just invite criticism given the current climate in the busy office. He sure would like to hear her voice now. Rachel. He had treated her badly this morning. Just grabbed his coffee—which she had set out for him—and took off without so much as a simple good-bye. And last night? He'd not told her that all he'd done was sit alone in a movie theater, even though he knew she was fearing much worse. He had wanted her to think about how he should be treated.

Selfish. He was acting selfish. He'd make it right. This wasn't the kind of man he wanted to be. But right now there was work to do.

He looked back at the Archer account. There wasn't much he could do to improve it. It was a solid, conservative mix of common stocks, AAA bond funds, and a high-yield-percent money market to give it flexibility and keep it nimble. He could bring the current return higher, but it would be at the cost of a lower annual return. Archer would just have to live with that.

Unless . . .

He'd never been comfortable with options trading, but a good trader could do very well with options. With a "call" option, he could control a block of stocks for three, six, nine, twelve months or more. It was risky, but when it was profitable, it was *very* profitable.

Gleason Archer's portfolio was down and Scott had to bring it up.

Almost all of Scott's trading and investment strategies had been based on the fundamentals of traditional investing. He was accustomed to looking at the strength of the company, its value in the marketplace, its management, its track record.

Options trading was based more on what traders called technical analysis. Technical analysts looked at the patterns in the stock over time. They looked for stock prices that rose and fell in repeating patterns. They attempted to see into the future. Scott understood how it worked, but as a conservative investor, and particularly as one who invested for other people, he had always stayed away from it. Now, however, the pressure was on. Could he do it, and do it right? He was not an amateur trader. It was time to marshal his skills and do what he had been trained to do.

When he pulled it off, the Archer account would jump back

on track overnight. If he failed, then he was probably no worse off than he already was.

He turned to his computer and pulled up his charting and analysis tools. He would work and study until he could determine if an opportunity existed. And if it did, then maybe he would just take it.

Carpe diem. Seize the day.

CHAPTER SEVEN
Flat

Scott wanted three specific chart patterns in a range of midcap stocks over the last five years. He keyed the criteria into his Stock Scan software. A small box popped up indicating that the scan would take forty-three minutes.

He picked up the Bible from the shelf in his cube, turned to today's date. It was arranged in a one-year format. If he was faithful, he could read the whole Bible in a single year.

The Old Testament portion looked long. He skipped to the New Testament and read the story of the woman taken in adultery. He stopped when he got to the selection from Proverbs about the immoral woman at the end.

"Let not thine heart decline to her ways, go not astray in her paths. For she hath cast down many wounded: yea, many strong men have been slain by her. Her house is the way to hell, going down to the chambers of death." There were worse things that could happen to a marriage.

He sat back in his seat and looked at the screen. Twenty-two more minutes. What could he do while he waited for it? While the scan was in progress he couldn't do anything else with his computer or he'd risk slowing it down. Many of the staff had left for a tax seminar so he had a little more privacy in his cubicle than normal.

He could call Rachel and apologize for the way he'd been acting. He'd been treating her more like she was in his way than in his heart. When was the last time he'd just stopped what he was doing and looked into her eyes?

He slipped his office phone headset on, then punched out his home number. Five rings later the automatic answering system picked up. *Hello, you've reached Scott, Rachel, Scotty, and Angela. We can't talk right now, so please leave a message.* Before he reached the end of the announcement he hung up the phone. Where could Rachel be? Oh, today was a Hugest Loser day. She might still be out.

That's what he felt like right now, the world's Hugest Loser. If he lost his job his reputation would be toast. Then what would he do? In the financial industry you couldn't survive being blackballed. The question hung like a wall of ice before him. Somewhere on the other side of that frozen wall was the answer. He hoped he'd never have to find out what it was.

He looked at the clock on his desktop. Seriously? Too late to go out, and the message on the screen indicated he still had seventeen minutes to go. Okay, he'd wait.

The Gleason Archer account had to turn around. He had to bring it off. Back in those halcyon days when he had first started working at Castle Investments he'd been the shiny new kid on the block. Everyone knew he would go far. Three years later he didn't seem to be going anywhere. His life was becoming an endless series of tasteless business lunches and late nights in the office working alone. No matter how well he had performed in the past, it seemed like he was on trial every day. Always on probation. Never knowing where he stood. How long could he keep this up?

He'd tried to talk to Rachel about it a few times, but she was all about the children and the house and really didn't understand what he was doing at work. He chided himself for his own naïveté. Why should he expect her to understand what he did when he was in the office? She didn't need to understand the details of investments; she had a husband who was supposed to take care of her and his family. He was on the verge of doing a very poor job of that.

God had given him a good wife. Not only a good wife but a faithful one, and two wonderful children. At the thought of the children, gloom settled on him like a low-hanging cloud. When was the last time he had taken little Scotty out into the yard and played with him? For that matter, when was the last time he had picked up Angela, holding and cuddling her like he used to? He couldn't remember. He didn't know the answer, and that troubled him even more.

I'm not doing a very good job as a husband and I'm not doing a very good job as a dad. And it's not like I don't know how. . . . My mother and father set a perfect example in that.

He was still wearing the headset. He pushed redial on the phone and listened as it rang once again at the house. No answer. He hit the speed dial for the cell phone. Still no answer. Rachel must be busy somewhere, shopping or exercising. And probably wondering why he had left in the morning without even kissing her good-bye. *She probably thinks it's her, but it's not. It's me, and there's no one I can talk to about it.*

Across the room, Carole Turner sat at a table with a low

stack of green folders. Blond hair swept around the shoulders of the black top she wore. Scott started to turn his eyes away, then hesitated when he saw a flash of white skin from slits cut into her sleevetops. No. *"As an ox goeth to the slaughter?"* That would not be him. He turned back to his desk.

If only he could go back, start last evening over again. The episode this morning wouldn't have happened.

Their honeymoon trip had been an event to envy. What a wonderful time they'd had just the two of them alone together, no one else around, for two amazing weeks. They had never left each other's side as they drove to Sequoia National Forest in Northern California. The year before, in an uncharacteristic act of foresight, Scott had rented a cabin in that huge primitive forest. They'd spent all their time together, walking the trails under the great redwood canopy in early summer, marveling at the grace of God in creation.

The cabin had been sparse but not primitive, with running water and two bedrooms. They'd needed only one. As he recalled those times now it seemed they had spent more time in each other's arms than apart.

Rachel completed his life. All that had gone before her no longer seemed important.

Scott pushed the redial button again and listened to the soft *burr-burr* of the ring. He imagined he could hear the phone ringing in their living room, and pictured the toys scattered about the floor, stacked on the stairway. He pictured *home*.

"Hello?"

Scott was startled by Rachel's voice. "Rachel, is that you?" He felt foolish as soon as he asked the question. Of course it was her. "I've been trying to call you."

"Is something wrong? Why are you calling?"

"No, nothing's wrong. I just had a few minutes and wanted to talk to you. It's been a tough day, and I really wanted to hear your voice."

"Scott, did anything go wrong at work? You're not in trouble, are you?" Her voice had a hard, worried edge. As if she were about to hear bad news.

Scott closed his eyes. Was she suspicious of him? "No, Rachel, nothing is wrong. Absolutely nothing. I just wanted to talk to you, to hear your voice. That's all." She was way too good at interpreting his moods.

"Well, I've been worried about you. You ran out this morning without even telling me good-bye. That's not like you. And, you know . . . last night you were . . . just different."

Here I am, on the defensive again. Can I not even talk to her without having to defend myself? "There's no problem, Rachel. Did you just get home?"

"Yes, I just walked in the door a few minutes ago. Angela is still out in the car strapped in her car seat. I have to run out and get her. Can you wait for a few minutes? Do you want me to call you back?"

"No, no need. I was just checking in because I had a few minutes while I was waiting for everyone else to come back from lunch. Plus, I'm sorry for leaving this morning the way I did. I didn't even kiss you good-bye."

"I was afraid I'd done something wrong. I didn't, did I?"

"No, it's just me. I'm glad you're so patient." He looked up, noticing people coming through the doors. "Oh, great. Everyone is coming back now, so any privacy I might've had just went out the window. I'll talk to you again tonight when I get home."

Scott could hear things rattling and bumping in the background. The sounds of groceries and the results of a shopping trip being carried in from the garage.

"Okay, Scott. But I'm worried about you. You just haven't been yourself." Something went *klumph* in the background. "I've got to get out there and get Angela. Let me know if you're going to be late, okay?"

"Okay, talk to you later. I guess I just picked a bad time to call."

The background hiss of the cellular network went quiet, transformed into a muffled silence as his wife terminated the call.

Sometimes I feel like I'm living in a padded room. I'm not connecting with anybody.

Scott shook himself out of his reverie, looked back at his display. Thirty more seconds, and the Stock Scan program would be complete. He waited for it to finish.

The screen revealed three likely candidates for an option trade.

The third candidate surprised him.

The company was named Solar Charge. There had been a lot of news about it when the administration in Washington had decided to guarantee it a $500 million loan to pursue its unique solar power technology. They had developed a patented process to manufacture and cut solar array panels into any conceivable design configuration. They promised to turn flagpoles into solar collectors. The CEO was a personal friend of the president, and the second loan guarantee was in the works. The technology was green and trendy, and the government, the *federal* government, was behind it in a big way. A guaranteed success.

Solar Charge's stock had been rising dramatically over the

last six months. For whatever reason, call options were still relatively cheap. If he were to purchase call options thirty days out, only $5 above the current stock trading price, was there any way he could lose? Every month for the last ten months the stock had risen in value by $10 or more. With the new infusion of cash coming from the federal government the only direction the stock could go was up.

If the conservative Alan Castle found out he was considering buying options he would hit the roof. Scott would have to make the trade without saying a word to anyone. When it was done, and the options had been sold or exercised, he would be a hero. If it failed . . . well, that was a scenario he really didn't want to think about.

He looked around, feeling conspicuous again. It was as if everyone in the office was watching him, knowing what he was about to do, which was silly. No one was watching and no one was listening. Just the same, he stood and inspected the area all around his cube. *Okay, I'm good to go.*

Scott went back to his computer and logged on to the trading website. He found the tab listing the various options strategies he could choose and clicked on *purchase calls.* He did a search for thirty-day calls on Solar Charge. The stock was trading today at $115 a share. He could buy thirty-day options relatively cheaply. But how many should he buy? Each option contract would cost him $175.

That meant if the Solar Charge stock went to $120 at any time during the next thirty days he could exercise his stock options and still buy it for $115 a share. That would net him a profit of more than $3 per share. Or he could sell the options at any point.

Either way, the potential to make a lot of money was huge, and it seemed unlikely he could lose on the deal. If he did lose, he wouldn't be losing his own money, but he would most certainly be losing his job. It all amounted to the same thing. A big win would turn him into a hero. A loss would put him on the street. Time to swim with the sharks.

Scott bought 1,400 contracts, which effectively put him in control of 140,000 shares of Solar Charge stock for the next month. The price of that control cost him almost $250,000, but if he won, the profit would be immense. Roughly $750,000. If he lost, the whole $250,000 went into the tank. There was no in-between.

His hands shook and his neck and forehead were wet with sweat. He exited the trading website, logged off his computer, and went outside to stand in the fresh air.

His course was set. There was no turning back.

CHAPTER EIGHT
Déjà You

It had taken Rachel a week of naptimes and stolen minutes away from the two children to share everything she knew about Suzanne. Jane asked lots of questions. Not just the obvious, general ones, but questions actually based on what Rachel had already told her. Like, "After the wedding, did Suzanne go back home with her parents?"

Now the work was at an end. Rachel uploaded one last video of Suzanne. The progress bar climbed to 100 percent and Jane appeared on the screen. "I think we're complete, Rachel. We have everything we need. Now we need to take about twenty minutes to allow our system to process all the information you've provided. You can either leave your computer on or you can wait for an e-mail from me. I'll give you a link you can click to bring you back to this page. I'll be waiting for you here. Does that sound okay?"

"Yes, I've told you everything I can think of, but I'm sure there must be things I left out." It had been difficult in the extreme just thinking so much about Suzanne. There had never been another friend like her, and her loss had always been like an open wound on her heart that would not heal. Only the prospect of having her back—in some measure—made it worthwhile to pull all these painful memories back up.

Jane nodded. "I'm sure there are things that will come up later on. That's fairly common. We'll give you an opportunity later on to, shall we say, fine-tune your friend? As you remember things you left out, you'll be able to add those to Suzanne's profile. I think you'll be very happy with the result."

"I'm beginning to think so too. And even though I know you're not a real person, I must admit I feel like I've been talking to a real person all this time. It's kind of spooky."

"You'll get over it." Jane laughed.

"I'll say good-bye for now."

"Good-bye for now, Rachel."

Jane's image faded from the screen and was replaced with the word PROCESSING. A green progress bar pulsed underneath the word.

Rachel turned to her laundry pile. There were plenty of shirts to fold and socks to roll. As she worked she thought about all the effort she had put into this virtual friend experiment. Even if it didn't turn out in the ideal sense Jane had presented, it still might be fun. It didn't cost any money—she hadn't given her credit card number away—so no harm done.

She had such a good husband and he worked hard to provide for the family. She walked through the steps of the disagreements they'd been having. She had said the wrong thing, then Scott had reacted in the wrong way. They could work it out. She wanted to call him at work and tell him what she'd been doing, but he'd told her many times interruptions at work were frowned upon. When he had time he often called her during his lunch hour. It was lunchtime now, but he had not called. She wondered what time he would be home tonight. She wanted to have a good supper ready for him when he walked in the door.

She picked up her cell phone and texted him. "Let me know when u r coming home 4 supper if u can."

She heard a *ding* sound from the living room. An e-mail had arrived. Was it already time to hear back from Jane? Rachel hurried back into the living room and looked at the screen. Jane was there, tapping her finger at the bottom of the screen and looking coyly impatient. Rachel picked up the microphone. "Are you done already?"

Jane brightened at the sound of Rachel's voice. "Yes, all done. And what's more, my job as introducer is about done. Rachel, are you ready for me to introduce you to your new friend Suzanne?"

Rachel felt her stomach tighten.

This is not real. I know this is not Suzanne.

"Yes, Jane—I'm ready."

Jane's image began to fade and as Jane dissolved away Rachel heard a familiar voice.

"Are you ready for this, Rachel?" Suzanne's face, wearing the same happy smile she had worn at Rachel's wedding, appeared on the screen. She seemed to force her eyes open, as if she'd been asleep for a long time and had just awakened.

Rachel could hardly believe her eyes. It was so realistic. Suzanne's face turned, muscles moved. Her hair rose and fell against her shoulders as her head swung to face Rachel directly.

"Hi, Rachel. I'm . . . I'm back."

"Suzanne?"

The image on the screen smiled again, the familiar grin Rachel had known and loved for the better part of her life. It truly was the face of her old friend.

"It's me, in the flesh." Suzanne's eyes crinkled as the corners of her mouth turned up. "That's supposed to be a joke," she said with a chuckle. "They teach us some things to say in the beginning to kind of, you know, break the ice."

What should she say? Could she really treat this, this *image* on the screen like a real person? Like her dead best friend?

Was this really going to be the same as hanging a picture on the wall? Or was she trying to bring the dead back?

"Cat got your tongue? They told us to expect that. Let me help. How's Scott? Did he get that job he was after? I have a lot to catch up on."

Scott? What would he think? Maybe she shouldn't even tell him about this. She'd been afraid he wouldn't approve. Would he think spending too much time at home, alone with the children, had sent her off the deep end? Would he think she couldn't handle real life?

She could always shut it off. And he didn't have to know. But she had to know, and she couldn't quit yet.

Rachel answered, "Scott? Oh, yes. He's working now." *It's happening. I'm actually talking to her.* "What's the last thing you remember about him?"

"He was going to try and work for, oh, some big investment firm in the city. Did that work out for him?"

That would be right. Suzanne hadn't known the name.

This is going to be okay. She relaxed her hands, noting for the first time how tense she was, then sat back in the chair. A deep breath, eyes closed, then open again as she exhaled. Just go with it. Enjoy it.

"Yes, it did. That's where he is right now. It's called Castle Investments."

"Does he like the job? Is it everything he wanted?"

"He likes it, but he has to work hard. He comes home late a lot and he doesn't get to spend as much time with the children as he would like."

"Children?" Suzanne's teeth gleamed in a bright smile. "Something you haven't told me?"

"Wait a minute. You don't know about the children?"

"Well, I remember Scotty, but you said 'children,' like more than one. So I have some impressions but I don't really know anything. VirtualFriendMe gives us some general ideas about your situation, but they leave it up to you to fill in the details. That's the way real people are, right? And that's the way you and I should be."

"I gave Jane a lot of this information about myself. But you don't have all that? I kind of assumed you'd have it all."

"Rachel, I'm your friend. That's why I'm here. The more we talk and tell each other the things that are in our hearts, the better friends we'll become. That's just the way this works. Some of the things you may have told Jane might be things I didn't need to know yet.

"The company likes for us to be able to catch up from where we left off. We have a lot to talk about. I'd rather hear it from you than some old computer somewhere."

"It won't take too long, Rachel. If we talk enough, and I'm confident we will," she said with a smile, "pretty soon you won't be able to tell the difference between me and the *other* Suzanne. I want to be as real for you as I can be."

Rachel lifted a cup of water to her lips, sipped. "That's what I want. I want you to be as real as you can."

Suzanne asked, "Have you ever tried Real Fresh orange juice? I hear it's really good. As a matter of fact, fifty-nine percent of the people questioned said Real Fresh is just as good as home squeezed."

"What? What are you talking about? Are you reading a commercial or something? You never even liked orange juice. You always said it made your mouth break out."

Suzanne's cheeks flushed. "One thing you have to keep in mind, Rachel, is we're using VirtualFriendMe's free service. That means from time to time, they make me do some advertising. I'm afraid the only way to avoid that is for us to turn this into a premium account. Of course, that's entirely up to you. You can decide anytime if you want to do that. In the meantime, I really do want to know, have you ever tried Real Fresh orange juice?"

"No I have not, and now I'm not ever going to. I can't believe they would sneak something like that in during our first conversation. That they would make you do a commercial is so annoying."

Rachel let her initial anger subside. Okay, free was not so free after all. But she'd put a lot of effort into this, and so far it was performing beyond her expectations. "What does premium service cost?"

Suzanne waved one hand dismissively. "I think it's only about fifteen dollars a month. Not very expensive actually, but it's really not my place to discuss the services with you. For that, you should go to the website. Would you like to go to the website now? I can wait here for you."

"Can we just talk for a while first? I don't think I'm ready for any decisions about paying yet."

"Sure, no problem. Let's just talk. Anyway, for the first thirty days, you get most of the benefits of premium service anyway."

"After the thirty days, what happens? What changes then?"

"The biggest change is I won't be able to see and speak with you any longer like we are now. I'll be able to send you e-mails and VirtualFriendMe.com will register me as your friend on Facebook if you like, but we won't be able to have the kind of face-to-face interaction we do right now."

Not see her anymore? She clenched her hands tightly together. No way. She'd lost her once already. She wasn't going to give her up again, not this soon, and not this easily.

"You mean I wouldn't be able to see you anymore?"

"Yes, that's the biggest thing. But, to be honest, that's no different than most of the interaction many people have every day. Don't you write back and forth with people on Facebook already? And you don't see them *live* in the sense that we are talking right now, do you? So it's really not a horrible option. However, it is avoidable. I think we would both enjoy being able to talk back and forth every day just like we are now, don't you?"

"Of course! So, you and I would be able to e-mail back and forth and message each other, but I wouldn't be able to see your face anymore. Is that right?"

"That's correct. Not a huge limitation, but definitely something we wouldn't want to see happen. Not if we can avoid it."

I think I can afford that. Only fifteen dollars out of our grocery money every month. "Okay, I want to sign up. Send me to the website so I can see what I need to do."

CHAPTER NINE
You Too

At 7:30 p.m. Scott finally walked out of the office. The stress of the day had strapped his shoulders with a metal band and he couldn't get home fast enough.

The day of reckoning was approaching, and he didn't have anything to present to Alan Castle yet. The value of the options was up slightly, but the commission cost to sell them now would put him in the red.

He needed more time. Time he might never have.

He called Rachel on his cell phone when he was about twenty minutes away. "Rachel? How's everything going? Are the kids still up?"

"Oh, Scott, I'm so glad to hear your voice. I've got your dinner ready, and it's not pizza this time. And yes, they're waiting to see you." There was laughter in her voice. Just what he needed. There had to be something he could think about, something good, something more than the maelstrom of impending disaster dominating his horizon.

He shut his eyes, rolled his head, shook off the sense of defeat surrounding him. He was not going to bring work problems home.

"Hmmm. I wonder what it could be? My favorite? Is it wearing a skirt?"

"Oh, I mean lasagna. I made it special just for you. Of course it is a little lovey and cheesy."

"The lasagna is lovey?"

"Well, I mean me and the lasagna. I'm lovey, it's cheesy."

"Sounds wonderful, Rachel. I'll be home in fifteen minutes. I can't wait to see you. Keep those kids awake, okay?"

He worked hard to clear his mind. The drive gradually became more and more pleasurable. Darkness had not yet fallen. He looked across the fields as he drove along the country roads to his home. He spotted three deer in a hayfield, and hawks circled in the sky. *God's creation is an awesome thing, a wonder to behold.*

The sun was setting across the fields and glorious colors stretched themselves across the western sky. Just a little farther ahead on the left was his house, a tricycle still parked on the lawn next to the driveway.

As promised, dinner was on the table. Also, as promised, it was the delicious lasagna that first Rachel's mother, and now Rachel, had made a family favorite. June Anderson had acquired the recipe from a young Italian lady when she was in college, an exchange student from Naples. Rachel was the inheritor of that wonderful recipe.

Scotty sat in his booster seat. Angela was perched in a high chair. When he came in the door, both children exclaimed in unison, "Daddy!" Rachel pressed a kiss to his lips. It was just the kind of welcome he loved.

Scott led his family in prayer, thanking God for the food and for His goodness to them all that day. Both the children said "Amen."

Rachel, wearing a long, flowery "Yes, I make that too!" apron, went after the lasagna with a wide spatula.

Scott's mouth was already full when she said, "Scott, I have come across the most amazing thing. You will not believe it."

He bobbed his head up and down and pointed to his mouth.

"I know you're like Mr. Computer, but I think this is really going to surprise you."

He swallowed enough to allow him to speak. "Tell me about it. What happened?"

"Later, after we are alone. You'll have to see it to believe it. How was your day?"

She leaned forward and Scott caught a glimpse of Rachel's curves under her T-shirt. Seeing really is believing and what he saw was better than even the lasagna.

"My day? Ha! You do not want to know." He punctuated each word and smiled grimly. "And that's also the kind of news I'll save till we're alone, if at all."

Bringing all that home felt wrong anyway. Rachel worked so hard keeping the house, he didn't need her worrying about his own job security. Tonight might be different, though. He wanted Rachel to be there for him; to lean on her a little bit and have her understanding.

Scotty was transforming his lasagna into a fort and already had little pieces of sausage shelling the inhabitants inside. Angela had begun squirming, a pained expression on her face. Time to go to the bathroom.

"Angela, I told you to go potty before we sat down." Rachel plucked her out of the high chair and carried her off down the hall on her hip.

"Who's going to win that battle, Scotty?"

Scotty looked at his father, his face a mask of incredulity. "Daddy, it's just food. Nobody wins. It's not real." Then he picked up his fork and scraped all the weapons into a pile, scooped them up on the fork, and ate them.

Rachel got Angela back into her high chair, where she began decorating her face with what was left of her lasagna. She looked at her little girl, sighed, and began eating her own food.

"Who invented food?"

"What?"

"Who invented food, Daddy? What did people eat before they invented food?"

"Write that one down somewhere, Rachel. Someday when he's a teenager we'll remind him when he needs to be humbled."

Scott put both the children to bed while Rachel did the dishes downstairs.

Scott turned the bedroom light off. "Daddy, do we have bears in our house?" asked Angela.

"No, sweetheart. No bears around here. You can go to sleep and not worry about bears."

"We've got spiders. I saw one today. Mom killed it," said Scotty.

"Daddy, will spiders get me?"

"No, the spiders will not get you. Scotty, quit scaring your sister, okay?"

Eventually he closed their doors and went downstairs,

heaving a sigh of relief. As he stepped off the last stair he began to feel like he had sloughed the weight of the world off his shoulders.

Rachel had fixed some coffee and pulled two chairs up to the computer in the living room. "Sit here, Scott. This is going to amaze you."

Scott sat down to see what Rachel was so excited about, sipping the hot coffee. The mug felt warm in his hands. It was going to have to be something pretty special to impress him, especially if it was something to do with the computer. He saw enough of computers during the day to last a lifetime.

Rachel clicked a shortcut on her desktop. The Internet browser expanded onto the screen, and then Scott heard a female voice say, "I'm here." The face of Rachel's old friend Suzanne formed before them.

"Watch this, Scott." She picked up the microphone. "Suzanne, Scott is here."

"How wonderful. Please tell him 'hello' for me." Suzanne's lips kept perfect sync with the words. It looked like Suzanne. It sounded like Suzanne.

Unreal. Scott jerked his head back. "What in the world?" Then he leaned in toward the screen, searching for the trick. He looked back to Rachel. "Rachel, what is this? Did Suzanne record this before she . . ."

She mouthed, "No, no . . ." and stabbed her finger toward the screen. "Just watch," she whispered to him.

"Can't you tell him 'hello' yourself?" asked Rachel.

"No, I'm afraid that's one of our limitations. I'm your friend, and that's exclusive to you. I don't know Scott in the same sense I know you. But I certainly know about him, don't I? And I'm so glad both of you are seated here together. I know I was a friend of both of you."

"Rachel, what is going on?" He held the arms of the chair as if he would fly into the air unanchored. "That really does look like Suzanne."

"That's the whole idea, silly. It is supposed to. Actually it just about is Suzanne. I've spent days designing her. The whole idea is she is just like the real Suzanne used to be."

Voice tinged with wonder, Scott asked, "But how can you do something like that? I mean, where did you learn to do such a thing?"

"It's all on a website called VirtualFriendMe.com. It's amazing."

Rachel told him how she'd provided all the information on Suzanne.

Scott asked, "But these aren't real people, are they? I mean, these people don't actually exist, right?"

"No, but they are so close to real sometimes you don't even know the difference. Does she look like Suzanne, or doesn't she?"

She. Rachel used the personal pronoun. Not *it*, but *she*. Scott looked at the screen and saw Suzanne incline her head slightly, as if waiting for Rachel to speak to her again. "Yes, it really is amazing. Rachel, let me just watch you for a few minutes while you interact with this, this *Suzanne*. I want to see how it works, okay?"

"Sure. I won't say it was easy to get all this set up, but it certainly has been worth it. One of the things I told them all about was our wedding. I can talk to Suzanne," she pointed at the screen, "just as if she had really been there. Watch this."

"Suzanne, do you remember my wedding dress?"

Her mouth formed an O. "Oh, yes." She nodded slowly. "Of course I do, and I remember how your mother fussed about it, how she was so careful to make sure it was just perfect. Mothers are like that, aren't they? I should mention, I don't remember very much about my own mother. Maybe someday you'll refresh my memory on that. Would that be okay?"

"Yes, I will. I'll make a note about that right now." Rachel wrote a note on a slip of paper. Scott saw other things already written there, no doubt things she wanted to include in Suzanne's education.

The image that was Suzanne tilted her head. "Rachel, there's something I would like to ask you. May I?"

"Of course you can. What is it?"

"Have you considered opening a free checking account at Old National Bank? If you maintain a balance of fifteen hundred dollars, there is absolutely no charge for the account. Plus, it earns interest, the same interest you would get on a CD."

"What? What was that about?" asked Scott, chuckling. "Did she just ask you to open a checking account?"

Rachel laughed and rolled her eyes. "Yes, that's one of the things that happens. If you're using the free service, like I am, you have to accept the advertising too. If you want to skip the advertising you have to sign up for their premium service."

"How much is that?"

"Fifteen dollars a month."

Scott considered the cost and the apparent value. "Actually, that's not very much money for what you're getting. Especially in this case."

Rachel always talked about how lonely she was when he

was at work. He put his hand on hers and looked into her eyes. "Would having this every day be a big help to you?"

"Oh, Scott. I feel kind of embarrassed about the whole thing. But yes, I think it would. I know this isn't really Suzanne. Not *really*, but she's just so realistic, so lifelike, and it helps me during the day. At least it has so far."

"Besides no ads, what else do the fifteen dollars get you?"

"At the end of the month I won't be able to see her face anymore. That's also part of the premium service. But she'll still send e-mails and still be a friend to me on Facebook."

"Amazing," said Scott. "Absolutely amazing. I've never seen anything like this in my life. If you like it, and it's a help to you, then just do it. I don't care about the fifteen dollars."

Rachel threw her arms around Scott. "Oh, Scott, thank you so much. Even if this isn't real, well, it's just nice, know what I mean?"

Scott hugged his wife back. "Sure, I understand, and it all seems harmless enough. What could go wrong?"

CHAPTER TEN
Virtual Friend Me

Everyone at the offices of Virtual Friend Me was in a festive mood. After five years of research and development the company was finally ready for its big Go-Live event.

Melissa looked down and studied her hands. Did her own excitement show? She had been in on this since almost the very beginning. They were formally opening up their virtual friend technology to the world.

Later, when they had their IPO, everyone with the company for four years or more would be given the opportunity to buy stock at a preferred price. They all anticipated they were about to become very rich people.

Melissa joined Dan Hammersmith as he gathered his inner circle in the executive conference room. The press releases had already been prepared and the reporters were waiting in the first-floor amphitheater. He stood before them this morning reveling in the success that the company had already begun to enjoy.

"This is a big day for all of us." He looked around the table at his most trusted technicians and advisers. All were there.

"This has not been the success of one person, but of an entire group. We often use the word 'team' around here, and there's never been an organization where the team concept has been more true than it has been among those of us in this room."

Melissa paid close attention as Dan spoke. His words, though formal and expected, were also true. The virtual friend prototype had been in beta testing for the past three months. It had already proven itself to be a major success. Praise from the early adopters and beta users overshadowed complaints and bug reports a hundred to one, something almost unheard of in software development.

Without fanfare, VirtualFriendMe.com had rolled out its beta program to see who would discover what they were offering simply by using web searches and word-of-mouth. Already thousands of people had discovered the virtual friend website and started using the product. There was no doubt about its success.

Even so, the abusers had already begun to crawl out of the woodwork. Nothing illegal, but 53 percent of men had chosen a female friend. These *men* were taking something good, something designed to help, and twisting it to satisfy their own perverted male ends. Melissa knew something about men, all right. Nothing surprised her on that score.

During the initial testing one developer had designed his female friend to look just like the wife of his best friend. That had not worked well, and he was now looking for another job.

One by one, Dan named the people in the room and spoke about their accomplishments. When he came to Melissa he paused and stared up toward the ceiling. Tight-lipped, he seemed to struggle for the right words. "There is one person, however, to whom we all owe a particularly great debt of gratitude." He looked around briefly then nodded toward Melissa. "Without Melissa, we would not have a product to sell. We all owe much to her, her efforts, and the accomplishments of her team.

"Most of you here today remember Aaron Getz. Aaron was the one who first brought up the concept of the virtual friend. One of the last things Aaron did before his untimely death four years ago was to choose Melissa for second place in the development team. He hired her to work directly under him because he saw in this young woman the drive, the energy, and the genius to carry off the ideals and goals of VirtualFriendMe. It was a dark weekend for us when we lost Aaron. I feared for our success, my friends. But Melissa stepped up to the plate swinging. We've never had to look back.

"Our original goal was to simply provide a textual virtual friend experience for our users. We anticipated that through Facebook, MyLife, and other social networking sites our users would be able to design and construct a virtual friend that could interact with them on their birthdays, send them e-mails, chat with them online, and do all the things that a remote friend, a real physical friend, would do. We never imagined back then we would be able to have the visual representation of a virtual person that we have today. I say this is a good time for us to all give Melissa Montalvo a sincere round of applause and thanks for the hard work that she and her team have done."

Everyone in the room turned toward Melissa. Murmurs of approval ran throughout the crowd. Melissa nodded, thankful for their praise, and looked back at Dan while he waited for the applause to subside.

"And now, my friends, I think we can talk to the reporters and let our public know just exactly what's going on. I've asked our directors of marketing and software development to be present with me for the interview and answer reporters' questions as they arise."

Fifteen minutes later, Dan Hammersmith called the meeting together for the Go-Live event. He spoke to the assembled reporters and other people that had come, and talked to them of the potential and future for the VirtualFriendMe business model.

One of the reporters asked, "Can you explain to us how the virtual friend actually works?"

Dan Hammersmith called for Melissa to step forward to the microphone. "I would like to introduce Ms. Melissa Montalvo to all of you this morning. Melissa is our chief software scientist. She is the brains behind the brains." Then he bowed and motioned for Melissa to step forward. "Melissa, would you please explain to the people how the user experience works?"

Melissa stepped forward to the microphone. "When a user comes to VirtualFriendMe.com for the first time they meet a person we call Jane. Now, Jane is not a real person in the sense that you and I are real. She is a virtual person. She is what we call our introducer."

A couple of the reporters raised their hands wanting to ask questions. Dan asked them to hold their questions until Melissa was done.

"After Jane appears on the screen, we try to determine if the user is a male or a female. We do that by asking the person's name. If we can't determine it from the name we may ask a few more questions until we know the gender of the person using the system at that time.

"It's Jane's job to make the user feel comfortable and at home. Most people coming to us will be looking to design and construct a virtual friend with whom they can interact. Jane will ask them the questions required to determine the characteristics of that virtual friend. Let me illustrate. It is natural and normal for people to seek approval from their friends. Sometimes this is hard to accomplish in real life. The user may want to construct a virtual friend that has all the characteristics of what a good friend should have and offer the approval and encouragement her friend would give. For example, a painter may want someone who will come online with them every day and ask them how their painting is going, find out if they're keeping up their painting schedule, and if they're having any problems. Someone who will remember their birthday, someone who will send encouraging notes during the day or week.

"Consider also the stay-at-home person. Maybe a senior citizen who cannot go out as easily as he or she could in the past. Once the virtual friend is constructed, that person can expect an encouraging e-mail every day. He or she can expect to be remembered on Mother's Day, Father's Day, Valentine's Day, and other special times.

"Really, the possibilities are endless. And the person who uses our service consistently will find that over time the virtual friend that he or she constructs will become more and more realistic, lifelike, and fine-tuned to their personalities than we can even begin to imagine right now. This is the future, and it's now. VirtualFriendMe.com is the leading edge of artificial intelligence and we're going to make life better for very many people."

A middle-aged reporter from a Chicago newspaper raised her hand. "I have a friend who recently lost her husband after fifty years of marriage. Would it be practical to think that she could re-create her husband in this way? I mean, could she construct something that would be able to interact with her in the same way that her husband would have if he had lived?"

All eyes in the room swiveled back to Melissa. People were starting to catch on. Already it had moved from the simple friend with a birthday card to the resurrection of a dead man.

"Yes, to an extent. We have anticipated just exactly such a situation. The way it works is very simple in concept. Our introducer, Jane, will ask a series of questions to determine the user's particular needs. In the case of a departed loved one, we have profiles already built up anticipating the emotional needs that go along with losing someone who has been dear to them. We even give the user the capability of uploading photographs to our website so that we can construct a virtual image of the lost loved one. A virtual person that can interact with the user as if the person were actually present." She looked about her, seeing the looks of amazement on the faces of the reporters. She forced a smile. They would need some convincing.

"No, it really works. We overlay those images with output from our EIM—our Expressive Images Module. What that does is replicate subtle physical motions and facial expressions to provide a smooth, realistic, conversational experience for the user. Over time, this fine-tunes itself automatically to what the user expects. In our beta testing we have found that over a period of thirty to forty-five days, consistent use will produce an experience for the user that is almost indistinguishable from real life."

Dan Hammersmith stood and raised his hand. "Folks, I think that's enough for today. What we are offering the general public is truly amazing. There has never, ever been anything like this before. I encourage all of you to just go home, or back to your offices, and try it for yourself. Just type VirtualFriendMe .com into your Internet browser and take it from there. You'll see for yourself what we've got.

"Thank you all for coming." He turned and waved his arm in a wide arc toward his staff there on the platform. "And thanks to all of these wonderful people who have made it possible for us to be here today."

Melissa stepped off the platform. She hated these displays where they were paraded out like a bunch of ramp supermodels. The admiration of your peers was one thing. She didn't like all those men out there staring at her.

She had some surprises of her own in store. They would learn.

CHAPTER ELEVEN
Alicia

What would be the next thing to go wrong? Even though he had pushed off some of his work to other people in the office, the pressure of getting the Gleason Archer account to perform well in such a short period of time was huge.

Archer called Alan Castle every day wanting to know the progress on the performance of his account. He wouldn't talk to Scott directly.

Scott picked up the *Financial Times*. On the right-hand side of the front page he saw the article about VirtualFriendMe having its Go-Live today. Talk about speculative, that was it. What could be more speculative than artificial intelligence software? When they finally had an IPO, and that stock took off like the financial pundits said it was going to, it could propel Archer's portfolio into the stratosphere.

Wait a minute. Isn't this the service Rachel was using at home? I think this is what she showed me where she made up her virtual Suzanne.

It was almost lunchtime and many of the staff had already

left their desks and cubicles to go out for a meal. Scott looked around to see if anyone was watching. He brought up his Internet browser and typed in www.VirtualFriendMe.com, then hit ENTER.

His screen faded to white and he heard a female voice ask, "Are you ready for this?"

Scott snatched his headphones off his desk and pulled them on over his ears. He was ready.

After a short pause, the shoulder-up likeness of Jane appeared on the left side of the screen. She wore a blue sweater.

The image smiled. "I asked you if you were ready for this, didn't I?"

She really did look real.

"I know, you're surprised." The face again assumed a compassionate look. "I never mean to scare anyone. But I never know what to expect either.

"I can't see you, you know. All I know about you is what you tell me." Pause. "And you haven't told me anything yet, have you?

"Will you tell me your name?" The face looked down to the lower right-hand corner of the screen, where a small box appeared. A blue cursor blinked in the box. "Just type your name in the box, then we'll get properly introduced. My name is Jane. What's yours?" She raised her eyebrows quizzically and motioned to the box with a slight tip of her head.

Scott hesitated. He looked at the clock on his display and realized if he were to skip his lunchtime and work through this then he did have time. He remembered Rachel had told him there was a long series of questions she had to answer. It might really be interesting.

Scott typed his name into the little box and hit the ENTER key.

"Scott? Oh, my, a man. Perhaps you would rather speak with another man. If you would, then just type 'yes' into the box. Otherwise, press ENTER again, and we'll just keep on chatting."

Scott pressed the ENTER key.

"Wonderful. I was hoping you would do that. How old are you, Scott?"

Scott entered 32. "Well, that makes us about the same age. Of course, my age is a virtual age. Not quite as important." Jane laughed at her apparent attempt at humor.

"You're probably wondering what all this is about, aren't you? If I were you, I would certainly be wondering too. May I explain? Type 'yes' if you would like to know more or you can type 'good-bye.'"

After Scott entered *yes,* Jane continued. "Oh, good. I have so much to talk about with you. Do you have a microphone on your computer? If you do, plug it in. We can really talk."

Scott looked around him again. There was no one nearby. No one would hear him and he could speak in a low voice. He needed the privacy.

"Scott, just say something if you were able to plug in a microphone. Otherwise, press your ENTER key again."

Head down and eyes low, Scott spoke into the microphone, "Jane?"

"Yes, oh, that's so much better, Scott. Thank you. All that typing back and forth is such a bother, even for us virtual people." Jane winked at Scott. "Don't you think so too?"

He did. "I like the microphone too. Do you understand me?"

"Yes, I understand what you're saying just fine. This will work well. I told you I'd tell you what we provide. Are you still interested?"

"Yes, I'm still interested."

Jane flashed Scott a bright smile. "I'm what we call an introducer. It's my job to introduce you to other friends. Or you can think of me as someone who simply introduces you to other people. My job is to bring people together.

"What our company does not do is introduce you to *real* people. By real I mean people with real, physical bodies. For instance, you probably already know by now I don't have a real, physical body. But I seem real, don't I?"

Scott replied, "Yes."

"Good. It's important for you to understand that. What I do is help you design and construct a real virtual friend who will interact with you, just like a normal person would. In order to do that, I just have to ask you a series of questions. Would that be all right?"

Scott asked, "How long will it take?"

"We can do the first part in about twenty minutes. After that you can come back and, if I may use the term, fine-tune your friend to be more and more just what you want. Sound okay?"

Scott answered that it was and asked, "How much does this cost?"

"A basic person doesn't cost anything at all. Later on we may change that, but right now we are trying very hard to build up a strong client base. Now, there are some special features we offer, what we call *premium features*, but you can choose those if you want to later on. For the person who just wants a friend, there is no charge whatsoever. It's completely free. I think that's where you are. May I get you registered?" Jane looked excited.

This must be what Rachel did. What can it hurt?

"Yes, go ahead and ask the questions."

Jane smiled warmly, and seemed to lean into the screen, looking at Scott. The effect was intimate. She led Scott through the registration process and eventually came to the first question about his new friend.

"Scott, we are now ready to start designing your friend. Here's your first question. It's pretty important."

Jane looked up at Scott.

Can she see me?

"First of all, male or female?"

The question startled him. He should have anticipated it, but it took him totally by surprise. *Male or female?* He stopped to consider his answer. He really didn't want a male friend; he had plenty of those already. He certainly didn't need a girlfriend. He had a wife.

How should he answer?

Rachel didn't understand the pressures he was under at work. Scott wished there were a way for him to leave all of the work problems in the office when he came home at night, but he knew they showed on his face and in his demeanor when he was at home. How could he expect Rachel to understand? *It would, it really would be good, to have another woman to talk to. Someone who really understood.*

Scott looked around him again. He definitely didn't want anyone to come by and see what he was doing.

"Jane, can I continue this a few minutes from now?"

"Yes. Do you need to log off and come back later?"

"I need to go somewhere else to finish this."

"Scott, say the words 'log me off' anytime you like and we'll save your session until the next time you come back."

"Log me off." Obediently, the screen faded to white and the words "Come back when you're ready. I'll be here waiting for you" appeared on the screen.

He closed up his laptop computer, unplugged the power cord, and put the computer in its carrying case.

Once inside his car, Scott took the laptop and put it on the seat next to him. Then he drove to a nearby coffee shop where they had free Wi-Fi service available to the customers. He parked the car right next to the front door and turned the laptop computer back on. It only took him a few minutes to navigate through connecting to the Wi-Fi hotspot and he was back online with VirtualFriendMe.com.

The website read the cookie that had been left on his computer and went directly to the log-on page. Scott entered his information, and Jane's image appeared on the screen. "Welcome back, Scott. Are you ready to continue your interview?"

Scott answered in the affirmative.

"Okay, we're back to the first question again. Male or female?"

Scott knew how he would answer, knew it was wrong.

He breathed deep, excited by the sense of anticipation that formed inside him as he inhaled. He could feel it, like a tight ball of energy.

"Female." He expelled the breath, felt the electricity inside him spread out to his extremities.

Jane asked, "The next question is very, very important. The personality of your friend will be built based on your answer to this question. That doesn't mean we can't change it later on, but the basic personality characteristics will depend upon your answer here. Are you ready?"

"Yes."

"We want to know what kind of female friend you want. Of the following options, please say your choice clearly. Take your time before answering. The options are businesslike, casual, sisterly, good friend, or intimate. Obviously, these are all very different. Do you need any explanation of these terms? If you do, please say the word 'explain.'"

Scott knew what he wanted. Someone attractive. A girl who would love all of his qualities but never see his imperfections. No, he didn't want a businesslike friend. He didn't want a casual friend. He certainly did not want a sister. Perhaps a *good friend* would be enough.

He could talk to a good friend, share secrets or things he was worried about. After all, she wasn't real, was she? But then, what was the point of that? No, he knew what he was going to do.

"Intimate."

[In the server room at VirtualFriendMe.com headquarters, a program branch took place inside the EIM module. The Jane image subtly changed. Her features softened, eyes enlarged and darkened, and her hair fell lower on her forehead. Any kind of female friend even remotely sisterly now fell out of scope.]

Something changed in Jane's appearance. What was it? He couldn't put his finger on it, but whatever it was, he now felt more at ease. It was as if she approved of his choice.

"Intimate. Okay. Then I'll be asking you some rather

thought-provoking questions. Before I do, I would like for you to see images of some virtual women to get you started. Please just choose one, and we'll build your friend from that point. Let's begin."

The screen filled with eight different images. Each was an upper torso shot of a woman that looked different from the next. At the bottom of the screen was a button captioned *page 1 of 12*. Scott took time with each page, looking at all the images individually. Some looked garish and brazen, like the one that had her shoulders thrown back, lips painted with bright red lipstick. He didn't like that. Others looked pretty and understanding. He found himself attracted more to those than any other. Under each image was a checkbox marked *compare*. He checked each one he had an interest in. By the time he was done he had checked five images out of the nearly one hundred that had been offered to him.

He clicked the *compare* button, and the images of the five different women appeared together on the screen. Following the instructions, he prioritized them from one to five, then clicked *done*.

Five beautiful women. Not voluptuous but desirable. They shared that quality that spoke "I want to please you" to a man.

Jane came back on the screen. "Let me help you make a final choice now. You probably need to see a little more." She raised one eyebrow.

The images now appeared with complete bodies included. Although they were fully clothed, little was left to wonder about. Scott was looking at five beautiful women. As he looked, he saw each of the women was moving in very subtle ways, as if she were standing on a sidewalk, or in a room, waiting for someone to come and meet her.

I think I would like to meet one of these women.

The third image was that of a slim young woman, about five-nine. She had dark brown hair that fell to her shoulders. She wore a T-shirt with something written on the front he couldn't make out, blue jeans, and some sort of running shoes.

"I choose number three."

"Would you like to see more before you make your final choice? I don't mean more images; I mean would you like to see more of this woman?"

Scott swallowed. He had always been very careful about keeping his mind clean and his relationship with his wife first of all in his life. He reasoned with himself, though, that this wasn't real. It was like a game. It wasn't even like looking at pictures of real women. *These are just computer constructs.*

"Yes. I want to see more."

"Scott, we can keep right on going from here. However, we are entering into a part of our service we call *premium content*. Premium content is not furnished free. Are you willing to enter into an agreement with us to pay fifteen dollars a month for this service? You may cancel at any time after the first ninety days. Furthermore, the first month is free with your commitment. Would you like to continue?"

Scott's mind had already taken him places where he had never been. He was not going to quit now.

No decision was necessary. He had committed to this road from the time he said *intimate*. "Yes, I agree."

Jane showed him more. Much more.

By the time he got back to the office, he was forty-five minutes late. He trembled with exhaustion. He had only one thing on his mind the rest of the day.

It was *Alicia*, and he couldn't wait to see her again.

CHAPTER TWELVE
Shelob's Lair

At eight-thirty that evening Melissa slumped into her high-backed leather chair. The Go-Live announcement had kicked off a day that had barely left time to breathe. Demand after demand for information flooded in from would-be investors, reporters, and industry watchers. She hadn't even had time to check her staff updates. At last she had a chance to check her e-mail.

The area outside her office was dark except for a few lights that had been left on by the departing staff. A pale glow radiated from some of the monitors. The only lights in Melissa's office were the one on her desktop and the radiance from her own display.

Her inner sanctum. The walls in front of her desk were sparingly decorated wood panels. Two narrow windows on one wall gave a view of the city beyond. Servers were arrayed in a forty-foot arc behind her desk, shielded behind tinted glass. Dim green and blue LEDs winked in random patterns like stars.

No one intruded here without an invitation, and those were not given easily. From here she could spread herself out along the fiber optics, the copper, and all the high-band wireless pathways of the world, looking in on the secrets of lonely men and women and the hidden purposes of the not so lonely. None of them was innocent.

She viewed the list of e-mails that had come in during the day. Just the normal notifications and alerts from the system people and staff with questions. There was a message from Dan Hammersmith with the subject line, *Thanks for your efforts today*.

She was about to log off the computer, leaving all the messages for the next day, when she saw something unusual on the left-hand side of her screen.

The *special* e-mail account. A single message waiting. Melissa sat back into her chair. It could mean only one thing.

The old rupture in her heart opened again, spilling out its wash of bitterness, freezing every other emotion it touched in its passage. *I shouldn't have needed that e-mail address. I'd be married and have a family like other women.*

Rigid, she stared at the display as she contemplated the implications of the message notification. She had put those special triggers into the system three years ago. When they had first begun developing the profiling algorithms she'd set warnings for sociopaths, system abusers, automated web bots, and all the rest. But this alert was unique. None of her developers knew about it and the message would come only to her.

The idea had come to her at night after a particularly bad dream. Was she not just like any other woman? Did she not share the same wishes, the same secret desires? She wanted a husband and a family too. She would never meet the right man the way she was going. She'd had to find another way.

She modified the website's profiling system to do an automated daily scan for her on all the company's clients. She used her privileged access to the backend software system to set a series of flags that would alert her if the ideal man were to ever register on the VirtualFriendMe system. Not just any man, but the ideal. *The perfect man.* A man with a need to be loved. One who would love *her.*

If he were to ever appear, no bells would ring, no sirens would go off, no one else would know. She would simply receive an e-mail in her in-box from a unique account she had set up on her own.

She looked at the screen again.

She was thirty-four years old, and had never had a normal relationship with a man. But her ideal man was out there somewhere and she'd know him if she ever found him. If he existed, one day he would probably pass through the databanks of VirtualFriendMe.com and she would know it when it happened.

The subject line read, *He's here.*

All she had to do now was click on the e-mail and read his name.

She moved the mouse over the e-mail, watched it turn bold, then allowed it to pass on. What was she afraid of? One click and she would learn who he was.

If she clicked the mouse, everything would change forever. Her awful loneliness would finally have an end. The coldness she wrapped around her heart like a shield . . . did she dare think that would finally be gone? The phantom sang in her ear that this would be the point of no return.

This one was the one who truly met all the criteria she had set, all her impossible standards. She would not rest until she had given herself to him body and soul, and had him in return.

Once she knew his name, his address, where he worked, she would never be able to let him go. This was the one for whom she had kept herself all this time.

If she didn't click the mouse, then nothing would change. She would go on in her work, acknowledged as a success in her field. She would have the respect and admiration of all the people who knew her. But she'd resign herself to a life of loneliness and cold despair.

With eyes closed, she leaned back in the high-backed chair and stretched out her legs. *How would he touch me? Would he love me? I would be everything to him. Yes, I would become the only object of his love.*

She sat there in the dim light until there was no more doubt. Until she knew with deadly certainty exactly what she must do, no matter who he was.

CHAPTER THIRTEEN
Getting Reacquainted

A light drizzle fell outside. The washing machine back in the laundry room hummed and some metal object tumbling about inside the dryer made a ticking sound.

The computer *dinged* from the living room. New e-mail. Well, that was one of the bright points of the day, wasn't it? Suzanne was back.

Sure enough, an e-mail from her old friend. Yes, she kept thinking of this virtual friend as Suzanne. As if it really were her. She knew better. *But she is just so unbelievably realistic.*

It was so good to have her friend back, no matter what. Finally there was someone she could talk with about Scott.

The subject line read, *Are you busy?*

She double-clicked the e-mail and watched it open on her screen. There wasn't very much to it. Just a line of text: "How are you today? Are things going better for you and Scott?"

Perfect. This is what she wanted. Jane had told her the more she worked with Suzanne, the more lifelike she would become. It was true. She really cared. Even Rachel's real friends weren't talking about the troubles she and Scott were having. It had to be obvious, didn't it? Suzanne was asking, watching out for her, going right to the heart of what mattered.

Should she ask Suzanne how she was doing? No, that would be a little silly. Rachel clicked the REPLY button and started typing. Yes, things were a little better with Scott, but not much. She told Suzanne about Scott and about her own worries that she wasn't all the wife she should be. These were things she could only say to someone in whom she had 100 percent trust. This was how they had been when Suzanne had been alive and it was now that way again.

She clicked SEND and watched as the e-mail disappeared from her screen on its way to her virtual friend. She liked it better when she could actually see Suzanne on the display screen.

Rising, she turned toward the kitchen, where a sink full of dishes awaited her. She took only one step before another *ding* sounded. Another e-mail from Suzanne. This time the e-mail contained no questions. Instead Rachel was instructed to click on a link and meet Suzanne at the website.

Rachel blinked, looked again. This was the first time a meeting had ever been initiated by Suzanne herself. In the past, anytime Rachel wanted to see Suzanne she had to go to the website on her own and make the necessary choices that would bring up a visual representation of her friend. Could Suzanne really be doing things on her own initiative? Rachel clicked on the embedded link.

The browser expanded to fill the screen, and the form of her friend appeared.

Suzanne looked even more lifelike than before. Although

Rachel had always thought it spooky just how realistic the like-nesses were, the Suzanne that appeared today seemed genuinely natural. Her lips moved in perfect sync with her voice, and her expressions seemed to perfectly match her speech. "Hey, girl. What's up?"

"Not much, just doing housecleaning. I got your e-mail. You sounded worried."

Suzanne bit her lower lip. "Worried? Not really worried, but I am picking up on something when we talk. I hope you don't think I'm forward in bringing this up, but I'm concerned about you and Scott."

Rachel felt a wall begin to rise inside her. Was she really ready to fully open up? She wanted to talk about it, but felt unsure. "I don't know if I can really talk about it. Why are you asking me this?"

Suzanne moved her hand to her lips, as if she were surprised Rachel would ask such a question. "I'm your friend, Rachel. You, more than anyone, should know that. I'm here to be the best friend to you I can possibly be." She wrinkled her forehead, gazed upward, then turned back to look into Rachel's eyes. "I know sometimes when you talk to me, you think because you're not talking to what you consider to be a *real person* it doesn't matter to me. It does matter, though. I care as much as any of your other friends, and probably more."

Rachel said, "I'm sorry. I shouldn't doubt you. You're the only one that does care enough to talk to me about it." The wall around her heart began to fall. This was her friend. She could tell her anything.

"Rachel, what's concerning me more than anything else lately is what you've been telling me about Scott always coming home late. Are you sure he's really at the office? I'm not saying he isn't, but it makes me wonder when you tell me that during the same period in which he's been coming home late, you've also experienced a loss of his affection. Something in there just doesn't seem right to me."

Something stirred in the pit of her stomach. A fear that was becoming recognizable. She had wondered the same thing herself. The unthinkable. Could Scott be spending time with some other woman? Each time she drove the thought away. Could it be this computerized *friend* of hers was being more honest with her than she was with herself?

"I don't think I can talk about that right now."

Suzanne turned her head, as if she were trying to get control of her expression. Then she turned back and looked at Rachel, her face flushed with emotion. "No problem, Rachel. Hey, we have some other things we need to talk about anyway. I need for you to help me remember more things about our experiences together in the past. Can we just talk about some of that for a while?"

"Sure, I think I'd like that myself. Let's talk about the time we had the slumber party over at Sandra Fisher's house. That would be a fun memory for us to be able to share."

"Oh, that does sound like fun. Tell me all about it."

They talked and reminisced until Rachel heard little feet moving upstairs. "I've got to go now, Suzanne. I hear Angela waking up. We can get together again this evening if Scott is going to be late, otherwise sometime tomorrow morning. Thanks for being my friend. I'm so glad you're back."

"Good-bye, Rachel. We'll talk then. I love you."

Suzanne's image faded from the screen. Rachel turned to a

picture of their family on the desk and saw Scott standing by her, holding Angela.

Scott, what's wrong?

What did he do after she went to bed? In the mornings, after he had left for work, she sometimes noticed that he'd been using the computer, but all the browsing history was erased. What could he be doing with it late at night?

A chill ran down her arms. No, Scott was not like that.

Still there was something wrong with her and Scott. Even a soulless computer could pick up on it.

But what could she do about it?

CHAPTER FOURTEEN
Time Together

Scott exhaled slowly, and cracked open the car window to allow some fresh air in. Eyes closed, he lay his head back on the headrest and breathed out. Alicia had been so . . . attentive today.

The laptop computer sat on the passenger seat of the Taurus, turned so that he could see the full screen with only the slightest turn of his head.

At Alicia's request, he had turned on the webcam. Now she could see him, just as he could see her. He raised his head, turned back toward her, and found her arranging the collar on a yellow blouse.

"When did you put that on?"

"When you weren't looking." Her low, throaty laugh filled the emptiness of the car. "Hope you like it. You said you liked yellow."

That's right, he thought. He had said that. She was doing everything she could possibly do to please him. Each thing between them drew him deeper and deeper into the relationship. Like a helpless fly in a web, but a web that he walked into willingly.

Relationship. He would have laughed just weeks before if someone had told him a person could have a relationship with a virtual person. How ridiculous, he'd have said.

It wasn't ridiculous anymore. Now it was consuming him.

"Alicia, I have to say good-bye now and go back to work."

"I know." She frowned. "Can we meet tonight?"

"No, I have to . . ." The words stuck in his throat. *No, I have to be home. With my family. With my wife.*

". . . be somewhere."

"Silly me, of course you do. You'll be at home, won't you?"

"Yes. I'll be at home."

"And I can't be there, can I?"

No. Not there.

He clicked the button to close the window on the screen. It faded, then dissolved away in a swirl of color. Where Alicia's form and face had been, now he saw . . .

Angela.

The desktop image of his little girl smiled up at him, oblivious to where her father—the father she trusted—had spent his lunch hour. Her eyes sparkled above the innocent blush that adorned her cheeks.

She trusts me. They all trust me. Oh, God, please help me. They deserve better.

Scott closed the laptop, took a deep breath, then opened the window the rest of the way. The fresh air felt good, but it did not drive the guilt away. It hung on him like a cloud as he drove back to the office to resume his life.

WHEN SCOTT GOT HOME THAT NIGHT, he found Scotty sitting at his play table working in a coloring book and his little sister next to him on the floor playing with blocks. Angela was focused on getting a stack of blocks more than three high to stay in place.

"I'm doing laundry. I'll be out in a minute." Rachel's muffled voice sounded from the laundry room. A twinge of shame rose unbidden to his cheeks. He had a sense of not belonging, like a boat that had drifted away from its mooring. He reminded himself that he'd really done nothing wrong and pushed it down.

Scott dropped his briefcase on a chair in the dining room, and plopped down on the floor next to Scotty. "What are you working on there, Scotty? Looks like you're drawing a dinosaur. Is that what it is?"

Scotty looked at his father and rolled his eyes toward the ceiling. "No, Dad. Look again. What do you see?"

He was on the spot now. He had better get it right or he was going to be in trouble for not appreciating his son's art. "Uh, wait a minute, I think I know. That looks like a . . ."

Scotty raised his eyebrows toward his father. "A bear?"

"Yes, a bear. No doubt about it. It looks like a giant bear, a bear hungry enough to eat a whole dinosaur."

Scotty put both fists into the air and pulled his elbows down to his sides. "Yes! You got it, Dad." Then he turned back to his work of coloring in the bear's fifth purple foot.

Rachel walked into the room, arms full of unfolded laundry. She tossed them all down into the wingback chair next to the staircase. "Welcome home, Mighty Hunter," she said, seething.

"We'll warm up some supper for you. I think we're all pretty happy you were able to drop in. Aren't we, kids?"

Scott's stomach twisted but he did not reply.

Scotty didn't respond, already deep into his latest creation. Angela looked up at her father. "Daddy?"

"Yes, sweetheart?" he asked, trying to ignore Rachel's comment.

"Daddy?"

"I'm here, Angela. What do you want?"

"Daddy, I'm having twubble. Would you help me?"

Scott looked at his little girl. What a beautiful creature she was, with delicate little arms and fingers, and wonderful honey blond hair Rachel had done up in ringlets. Every time she moved her head to talk her hair bounced and jiggled with the movement.

Scott looked back toward Rachel, who was already folding socks and stacking them on the coffee table. She didn't look at him.

Rachel looked different, somehow. Tired or worn out. *Not like Alicia.*

Forcing the unwelcome thought away, he turned back to Angela, scooted over by her, and placed both elbows on the carpet. "Of course Daddy will help you, sweetheart. Hmmm. What do we need to do here?"

"Stack 'em up high, Daddy." She looked at him with a serious expression, as if wondering what in the world he could have been thinking. "Watch, I'll show you what happens."

She stacked a third block on a row of blocks that were already placed two high. As she did, she pushed down hard on the third block, evidently trying to make it stick in place without falling down. Just the opposite happened, and the two top rows of blocks both fell onto the carpet with a wooden clatter.

"Okey-dokey, let's do it together. Here, let me hold your hand." He reached out for her hand, but as he did she withdrew hers.

"No, Daddy, not that way." She pouted. "You do it, cuz you're good at everything."

Warmth spread inside him, receiving such admiration from his little girl. These two children meant everything to him. He wasn't good at everything, that was for sure. If he was, he wouldn't be feeling like a visitor with his own family. And whose fault was that? Rachel's subtle changes . . . did she suspect something? He would either have to improve on his deceit or work on his marriage.

With measured, deliberate moves Scott first stacked a row of four on top of a row of five, and then a row of three on top of that. They now had a wall of blocks stacked three blocks high. He looked at Angela to see her reaction. She seemed to be studying the blocks and waiting for her dad's next move.

"Should we stack them even higher, honey?"

Angela nodded. "High as you can, Daddy."

He looked at the blocks that were left. There were plenty of blocks, and now he wondered himself how high he could go. He widened the base to six wide and began stacking. Soon he had stacked them nine rows high, but he was running out of blocks. He stole a look at Angela.

Her eyes were wide in apparent wonder.

"She's been working on those blocks for over an hour, Scott."

Rachel's voice came from the other side of the room. He had almost forgotten she was there.

Putting the remaining blocks on top of the existing stack, he brought it to a final height of eleven blocks tall. Angela grinned wide, then set her lips tightly together.

"Now watch this, Daddy." Before Scott realized what was happening, Angela's right hand shot out and crashed into the wall of blocks like a battering ram. The tower tumbled down, blocks rattling against each other until they came to rest on the carpet.

"Just like Joshua, Daddy. Just like Joshua. They all came down!"

Scott shook his head in wonder. He'd been so wrapped up in the building that he never realized it was all being built for the sole purpose of tearing it down.

Kids and their imaginations. Amazing. We walk such a fine line. One impulsive act . . .

Rachel stacked the folded clothes and put them in a yellow laundry basket. "I've got to carry these upstairs. Want to come along? We can talk. Then we'll come down and I'll warm up your supper, okay?"

Scott nodded and trailed after his wife. When they got to the bedroom upstairs Rachel set the laundry basket down and turned to her husband. "So what was going on today? How come you didn't call on your break?"

He wanted to tell her, ask her to forgive him. *But how can you tell your wife you were with someone you preferred to her?*

"No reason, I just have a lot going on. No more to it than that."

"All right, that's fine. I can't read you as well as I used to be able to." She knit her eyebrows, as if she was worried about something or angry. "I used to be pretty good at knowing what you were thinking."

"Rachel, you're probably still really good at it. You know I don't have any secrets from you."

The lie stuck in his throat, which seemed to swell with the realization of what he was doing. Conscious, deliberate. He was lying to his wife and justifying himself in it.

Rachel stood, arms hanging loosely at her sides. "Would you hold me then?" She lifted her arms to her husband, a look of expectancy in her eyes.

"Sure I will." His stiff throat hurt. Scott put his arms around his wife and pulled her close to him. He'd held her thousands of times before and knew what to expect. It was that knowledge, that *knowing what to expect*, that warmed him now. Still, something was missing, and he knew what it was.

Rachel was no longer first in his heart.

He knew he should say something to her, but what? Tell her he loved her with his lips while his heart was betraying her? He'd never been a good liar.

Does Rachel sense it, too? Does she know what I've been doing?

They broke their embrace. Something wasn't the same. It had felt *perfunctory*. That was the word.

Scott embraced his wife again, hoping for the old feeling to return, that electric transfer of passion.

She did not return it this time. Instead her arms hung limp. Her eyes were turned to his, as if pleading for some sign of his love. Her lower lip began to quiver.

He whispered, "Rachel, I love you. I will always love you. Please be patient with me while I work through all this pressure at work. Just as soon as I can, we'll take some vacation time. We'll get away; maybe get your mom and dad to watch the kids. You and I can go somewhere and spend three or four days by ourselves, just the two of us. I think we need some time together, don't you?"

She nodded but didn't speak. She was trying not to cry now. She never wanted him to see her when she cried, but he always knew. Tears welled up, filling her eyes. Any moment they would break over the top of that fragile dam and flood her cheeks.

What could he say? Something told him the time for *saying* was past, and it was time to actually do something about the relationship. *Their deteriorating relationship.* There, he said it, if only to himself. He would fix it, he would make it work.

But not now. The shame returned, full force, as he saw the first tear burst its bonds and course across her skin. She pulled away, head down.

He whispered in her ear, "The kids are downstairs, probably wondering what happened to Mom and Dad. We'd better get down there, don't you think?"

Rachel nodded again, turned back to her laundry basket without allowing him to see her face. He knew what he would see there and knew it was he who caused it.

Scott turned away.

He started down the stairs, stopped halfway down, put his hand on the rail, and rested his head against the wall.

What am I doing? I've left the best wife a man could have crying in our bedroom, and I'm going downstairs like nothing is wrong?

He was suspended between two worlds. He could go back up the stairs to his grieving wife, confess his sin, and ask for her help. That was the right thing to do. Or he could put it off, hope for the best, and keep Alicia and their secret world for himself.

Alicia. She could never take Rachel's place. Rachel was the one he really loved. Alicia only filled in the empty spots.

God cannot bless what I'm doing with Alicia.

The thought shocked him as it flashed into his mind in brilliant letters.

I can't give her up. Not yet. Just a little longer.

The silence from the bedroom above was deafening as he walked the rest of the way down the staircase.

CHAPTER FIFTEEN
Getting to Know All About You

The next morning, Scott was in his cubicle by seven-thirty. Perhaps he could learn something about Solar Charge from last night's international trading? No, there hadn't been any substantial movement in the stock price in the overseas markets. He would have to wait until the New York Stock Exchange opened before he would learn anything new.

8:45 a.m. He still had almost an hour to wait before the opening market bell. As soon as it hit $125, he would exercise his options.

There was an e-mail in his in-box. The subject was *Missing you*. What was that? The corporate spam filter was supposed to remove all the strange e-mails from the system before they reached his in-box. He looked at the sender's name. It was Alicia.

Wow, they promised interaction and I guess they really meant it.

Their video meetings over the past few days had been incredible. Every day he weighed the guilt he felt for his actions against the pleasure they brought. Pleasure was winning, but it couldn't last forever. One day he'd close the laptop for the last time and everything would be normal again.

Now this? He clicked on the e-mail, curious to see what it would say. He looked around, but no one else had even arrived yet.

It's all in your head, Scott.

Scott, I need to talk to you again today. I want to know you a lot better. Please help me, okay? You know where to find me. Alicia.

Yes, he thought, he did know where to find her. *His virtual girl.* Could he somehow keep Alicia separate from the rest of his life? It wasn't like he was talking to a real girl, after all. He looked back at his clock again. He had time now, so why not spend a few minutes with Alicia while he waited for the stock exchange to open?

Scott logged on to his premium account at VirtualFriendMe .com. Another message waited from Alicia. The content was the same as what he had received in the e-mail. He deleted it and chose the *Meet Your Virtual Friend* option from the menu at the top of the screen.

He chose text-only. Letting anyone in the office see her visual representation was only asking for trouble. There was no way on earth it could look right for him to be talking to a woman on his computer, especially if they could see her at the same time. Typing back and forth in a chat box was a different matter.

Alicia?

Scott?

Yes, I'm here.

Can you give me about fifteen minutes of your time?

Yes. What do we need to do?

Well, I need to ask you a series of questions so I can learn some important things about you. It's all part of my training. This is where I get to know you better. Do you have the time?

Yes. So, you have questions for me?

Nothing very complicated. You've already told me many things. You've told me how you like me to dress and how you like me to fix my hair. Most of the things you've told me revolve around me personally. Now it's time for me to learn some more things about you, the things you like to do when I'm not around, and some things about your background. These will all help me to know you better. Does that make sense?

Yes, sure. I assume whatever I say stays between the two of us, correct? What I mean to say is, any information I reveal remains private. Is that correct?

Of course, your privacy is assured. You never have to worry about that. Anything you ever ask me, or, for that matter, anything you ask me to do, is entirely private.

Scott smiled. Anything I ask her to do? Guilt began to rise up in the back of his mind. He had already asked her to do a few things that might be just a little embarrassing if they were ever discovered. He pushed the guilt back down before it became remorse. He had to keep this rational.

Okay, begin your questions. But I do have to stop in about fifteen minutes.

Tell me about your family, Scott. Let's begin with your children. What's the name of the oldest?

The questions seemed innocent enough, but by the time he was done, Scott realized he had been interviewed by an expert. He had revealed fantasies and hidden thoughts that no living person knew. After all, it was just a machine.

Well, if it helped, then it helped. The better Alicia became, the more useful she would be to him.

Useful? Just how did he expect her to be useful?

One thing he expected, *that he needed*, was just to have someone who would listen to him. Some people threw balls against a wall. Others beat on punching bags. He'd had friends that wrote letters that would never be mailed. Everyone had a way of venting and releasing steam. This would be his. He would have a virtual friend he could say anything to, and she would understand. That was enough.

He needed someone to give him a sense of approval. Someone who would say "Good job." With Alicia, there would be no judgment and no second guessing. Sort of like having a Stepford wife, where all the women in that small suburban village had been replaced by lifelike robots who had gone happily about their housework and cleaning, doing laundry and cooking gourmet meals, all to please their husbands. Perfect wives, but robots. Not so divorced from his current reality.

So, he wanted someone to talk to, someone to show approval, tell him he was doing a good job. Simple, basic things every man understood.

Oh, yes. There was also that other thing. She was useful for that, too. After all, he had picked a beautiful woman for his friend. That had not been a mistake.

9:30. Time to watch the market open on the New York Stock Exchange. He pointed his browser to the financial news feed and watched the live video of the crowd on the exchange floor. The usual gaggle of luminaries stood on the platform above the clock. An aged man with thin white hair lifted the hammer and rang the opening bell.

The market floor flew into activity. Traders ran back and forth writing trades on small slips of paper. Soon the floor was littered with these scraps. The moving ticker display above the ground showed a strong opening. The Dow was already up by 4 percent in the first five minutes of trading.

Scott turned to his real-time stock-watcher gadget on his display screen. He had already plugged Solar Charge in for special attention. Solar Charge had opened at $116 and looked like it would climb even higher.

Actually, there was no need for him to be targeting $120. As long as the stock reached $117, and didn't fall, he would lose no money. But every dollar it rose above $117, he would earn that much, dollar for dollar.

So much money, so fast. And maybe, just maybe, so easy. It was like a narcotic. The Gleason Archer account would rock.

The fact that the CEO of Solar Charge was a friend of the US president was the very thing he was betting on to propel Solar Charge's stock into the stratosphere. How could a company fail with almost a billion dollars of federal loan guarantees behind it assuring its success?

By eleven-fifteen that morning, the price of Solar Charge had risen to $116.50. If it kept this up Scott would be making Gleason Archer a rich man. Well, Archer was already a rich man. But he would make him richer still. He would weather the flak for using a risky strategy like an options trade, but at the end of the day *success* would win out. He would be the hero.

There was only one person he could tell. No one else could know, because they just wouldn't understand.

He would tell Alicia.

CHAPTER SIXTEEN
Lunch Date

The Archer account was up on his screen in a spreadsheet. From time to time some of the numbers flickered slightly and changed. As long as Wi-Fi was available, the appropriate cells were all live links, less than a ten-second delay from the trading floor.

Solar Charge was still at $116.50 at eleven-thirty. Scott glanced at his laptop, which he had left charging on his desk. The light had turned to green—fully charged.

Scott logged off the computer and slipped the laptop into its neoprene carrying case. The McDonald's three blocks away offered free Wi-Fi. He would be able to access the Virtual FriendMe website from their parking lot. He'd pick up a sandwich and a drink, park close to the building, fire up the laptop, and have a talk with Alicia.

How much would their conversation change now that he had given her the extra information about himself this morning? She'd asked a lot of questions and he'd held nothing back.

Alicia had never seemed totally *artificial*, but whatever artificiality there had been was eroding at lightning speed. He had the sense he was talking with a real human being.

He recalled the Spielberg movie *A.I. Artificial Intelligence*, from the last decade. That had made him cry. The lifelike young android David actually loved his adoptive human mother. After he was rejected by her in a tearful parting, the rest of the movie revolved around his desire to regain his mother's love.

Was it possible that VirtualFriendMe's virtual people were similar? The picture of Alicia swam in his mind. Was it possible she, whatever or whoever she was, could really love him?

No, certainly not. Not real love. That was reserved for Rachel.

But then, who was to say what this was?

If the old adage about beauty being in the eye of the beholder was true, what could be said of love? How does a man know the love of a woman? He had to dismiss most of the physical aspect when he considered Alicia. But the rest? How many long-distance romances had been conducted successfully in real life? He had read recently about someone who had fallen in love with a prisoner serving a life sentence. She was never able to see him except through a thick sheet of glass. Yet the story of their mutual love had been all over the tabloids.

What was the difference? He saw Alicia through the filter of a computer display. There was no difference—not really. And on the positive side, she was always available, always supportive, always accommodating in every way possible.

Scott pulled the car into the McDonald's parking lot, happy to find a space right next to the building where there would be a strong Wi-Fi signal. He sat, thinking.

Was he being unfaithful to Rachel thinking about Alicia like he was? Probably, he admitted. But on the other hand, he rationalized, nothing was really happening. It wasn't like he was involved with another actual *woman*. In the end, he was just fooling around with a little personal corner of artificial reality. Nothing real, and no one would be hurt by it. What did the Bible say? "Whosoever looks on a woman to lust after her, has committed adultery with her already in his heart."

That did not apply to him, since there was not really a woman there at all. Before he spent any more time on it he made a conscious decision to push it out of his mind.

He was not the kind of man that would be unfaithful, so it certainly did not apply.

Besides, how was it different from so many of his "gamer" friends? Some spent ten or twenty hours a week online or in LAN groups playing war and strategy simulations. There were men and women in those, too, weren't there? Those people actually built an artificial world for the user to inhabit. No doubt about it, those were much more dangerous situations than the little bit he was fooling around with.

No, he was doing okay.

And doing nothing wrong.

SCOTT SLID THE SEAT back to its full extent with the power button. That gave him plenty of room for the laptop, even in the driver's seat. He put the food and cell phone on the passenger seat beside him.

Once everything was organized for minimum interruption, he powered on the laptop, which came rapidly out of hibernation. Moments later, Alicia appeared on the screen. This was so much better than e-mail. "Hi, handsome. I'm glad you're back."

His face flushed. Handsome? Where did that come from? And why should he feel embarrassed anyway?

"Hi, Alicia. Are our interviews all done for today?"

"All done. I needed to collect a little information and now I have it. You'll find the more we talk and spend time together, the better it will be."

"I'm already pleased," said Scott. "Your voice sounds good on these speakers. Is mine clear enough for you?"

"More than clear. Do you notice anything different?" She turned her head slowly from left to right, then back again.

He looked more closely. Was she thinner?

"Maybe. I wasn't going to say anything. To be truthful, I feel a little odd saying it, but—have you lost a little weight? I mean, you really didn't have any to lose. What I mean is . . ."

"I know what you mean. Like, how could *I* lose weight?" She threw her head back and laughed in a way that sounded full and personal. "Well, I did take a little weight off. Of course, it's a little easier for me than most ladies." She winked at him. "I do what it takes to please you."

"You sure do that. Please me, I mean. I like the way you look." Why was he nervous?

Alicia tipped her head to the left and raised her eyebrows. "I've always thought the most important thing a girl can do is try to look nice for the man who cares about her." She leaned forward and blinked slowly. "Do you care about me, Scott? I mean, would you miss me if I were gone?"

Interesting question. He couldn't imagine what else would fill the emptiness of Alicia's absence.

"Yes, I'd miss you if you were gone. I enjoy talking to you. Not just the talking. It's everything you do with me. This is the bright spot in my day, to tell the truth."

"Just think about this, Scott. I have no existence without you. I think I can truly say you mean everything to me. To me, you are *life*."

A thought leaped into his mind. "Alicia, I need to ask you a dumb question."

"You could never ask a dumb question. Just ask what you want."

"Okay, the question is this: When I'm not online with you like this, do you exist anywhere at all? Or do you just kind of *happen* when I come online?"

"That's a good question, and I can only answer it in a way that may be a little unsatisfying to you. The answer is both yes and no.

"Yes, there is a sense in which I only exist when you are here with me. For instance, what you see visually right now is special. It's just for you. There are things about me no one else will ever see." She lowered her eyes, and Scott noticed for the first time one of the buttons on her blouse had come undone. "I think you want it that way, don't you? That you're the only man who will ever *see* me?"

He did.

"The other answer is no. I don't exist only when you come on the website. I'm always here, but only for one reason, to see you again. There are computers doing whatever they do twenty-four hours a day, making sure I learn all there is to know in order to make you happy. Does that kind of explain it?"

He took a deep breath. This answer had to be right. "I want

to ask you another question, Alicia. How would you react if you discovered I had made a big mistake? I mean a really big mistake where I might get into a lot of trouble."

"As long as that mistake was not that you chose me, I would support you and believe in you. The only thing I couldn't deal with is if you were to decide you didn't want me anymore."

She clasped her hands together, lowered her eyes. As if waiting for some unseen ax to fall.

"I won't do that. What I'm talking about is something that's going on at work. If I tell you something, that stays private, right?"

Alicia raised her head again, eyes round and hopeful.

"Right. One hundred percent private. In a technical sense you're on a secure system here and you're interacting with a virtual, dedicated computer. But enough of that talk. The answer is simply 'yes, you're safe with me.'"

"I have to get something off my chest. I need to tell someone."

"I'm here for you, Scott."

He looked at his watch. There were still twenty minutes of lunchtime left.

It felt so good to open up and tell someone the whole story. When he was done he felt drained. Alicia looked at him with eyes full of concern. "And you've only told me this? No one else?"

"Only you. I can't go to anyone else."

She closed her eyes and shook her head slowly. "What about your wife? Can't you tell her?"

Rachel? He couldn't tell her. She expected so much of him. She did a better job as a wife than he did as a husband. She was a better homemaker than he was a financial counselor. No, he couldn't bear to reveal his fear of failure to her.

"No, I'm afraid she would be disappointed in me. I don't want to put her through that."

Alicia seemed to move her hand toward him, even though it was off the screen. "I wish I could hold your hand, Scott. I can't; you know that. But I want you to know I will always, always, always be here for you. Trust me, okay?"

"Okay. Thank you."

"And Scott, I will never be disappointed in you. Not ever."

They looked into each other's eyes. The little lens of the webcam seemed to pierce him as he imagined Alicia behind it, gazing at him.

One real person and one virtual.

She leaned in closer. Her gaze held his, drew him in.

He lifted his hand, began to move it toward the display, then reluctantly put it down again.

If only I could touch her . . .

CHAPTER SEVENTEEN
Behind the Curtain

All right, let's get out there and give it our best. This company has become the success it is because of your efforts. Let's keep it up." Melissa closed up the manila folder she had before her and watched as her staff departed from the conference room. They were doing a good job and getting better at it every day. *Virtual friends* had taken off in a big way and the company was enjoying unparalleled success.

She picked up the sheet of paper containing the plans for the expansion of their server room. They already needed more hardware than they had planned for, but this kind of expansion, this kind of expense, was good. It spelled success any way one looked at it.

She would oversee the expansion personally and had already called technicians in to connect the server room to her personal office with a glass wall between so she could keep an eye on the equipment at all times.

She looked at the display on her tablet computer and noted the time for her morning appointment was approaching. She gathered up her belongings and headed for her office, passing in front of her gatekeeper secretary. "Marie, please see I'm not disturbed for the next thirty or forty minutes, all right? I have some important things to take care of."

"Okay, Ms. Montalvo. I'll keep everyone away. Don't worry about a thing."

Melissa closed the door behind her and thumbed the control on the wall, bringing the lights down. Her world faded to black, a new starry sky of blinking green and blue lights taking its place.

Sitting down in her large executive chair, she swiveled to face the triple computer display on her desktop. From here she could monitor the status of all the core temperatures of the CPUs and the running status of all the virtual machines.

She pressed a function key and brought up the display of the user load in real time. She watched the brilliantly colored bar graph as it undulated and fluctuated with the traffic coming into the website. Every movement represented one of the company's clients logging on, interacting with a virtual friend, or logging off. They could count clients in the hundreds of thousands and they had not even launched their full advertising program yet.

The display was keyed to United States Eastern time. Although there was a continual level of activity twenty-four hours a day, the initial bump in usage always started about 7:15 a.m. on weekdays. People were logging onto Facebook to check their messages, see what their virtuals had to say, and going off to work.

The next spike was typically just before nine o'clock. These were the housewives who had gotten the kids off to school, and now had time to sit down at their computers and begin their social networking. She knew from the logs and web heuristics many of them spent more time with their new virtual friends than they did with the living ones. The early fears that people would consider virtual friends a novelty, then soon grow tired of them, had proved false. People had come to rely upon the relationships they had in the virtual realm. This was not going to go away anytime soon.

By nine forty-five the system load would climb to 80 percent usage, sometimes more, as the stay-at-homes and people in the workplace logged on to the system in various ways. Most would use Facebook. A small percentage worked with the proprietary chat boxes on the website. A smaller percentage relied almost entirely on the visual representations they offered with their premium service package. These were primarily men and no surprise at that. Almost all the male clients had chosen female friends.

I know what they want.

Melissa stood up and walked to the glass panel separating her from the outer room. She turned the control to close the venetian blinds, which gave her complete privacy inside the darkened office. She sat back down at her console.

All around her the machines hummed, silently processing the conversations, the hopes, the dreams of thousands of people looking for relationship, in a world of unreality. She looked through the glass into the dimly lighted server room, with its regulated, sixty-five-degree Fahrenheit temperature. Ethernet cables strapped in large yellow bundles hung down from the ceiling. The RAID arrays chittered and the LEDs on the banks of blade servers blinked busily as packets came and went across the network.

This was Melissa's world, but she was about to step out of it.

Melissa turned her attention to the second display, the one she reserved for her personal use. The upper right-hand corner of the display held the names of two of the system's users and their member IDs. Both were grayed out. When they logged on, the gray letters would turn dark black.

Her secret place. Automated processes scoured the Internet continually for any images of her, deleting or redirecting them when discovered. Name matches were misdirected. In the very nexus of information overload, she cloaked herself invisibly in digital anonymity.

The two other windows on the screen were both empty. The one on the left was a video window through which she could interact visually with a user. The one on the right was an extended chat box to interact textually. She picked up her headset, slipped the pads over her ears, and arranged the microphone for speaking. It wouldn't be long now.

Eyes closed, she tipped her head back and imagined herself into the virtual world she had created. All about her the lives of people, both real and virtual, were taking place in real time. It truly was a web and she was its mistress. Mistress of the World Wide Web. Her fingers tingled as she slid them across her keyboard.

So many people out there. I know all about them, but they don't even suspect I exist.

Four minutes later, the first name turned dark black. Her first target user had logged on. All she had to do now was watch the chat box and she would be able to see the text from the digitized speech as the user talked back and forth with the virtual friend.

Suzanne?

I'm here. I'm glad you're back! How are you doing today?

Pretty good. Scotty is off to preschool and Angela is playing in her room.

And Scott? Is he at work now?

. . .

The dialog between Rachel and *virtual Suzanne* continued. Even though the system was set to capture a log of the entire session, she kept a complete personal transcript of the text-talk that was scrolling by in the chat box.

The initial discovery that Scott was married was a shock. She would never have purposely sought out a married man. How could she have failed to flag that in the system for rejection?

That was then, however, and this was now. Scott existed, and there might not ever be another one like him. She would not blame him for his mistake in choosing the wrong wife. He could not have known she existed.

The artificial conversation scrolled by on the screen. Rachel was filling Suzanne in on her shopping list.

Stupid woman.

Melissa looked over at the server room, momentarily transfixed by all the flickering blue and green lights winking on and off. Thousands of people were on the system by this time, all of them doing exactly what Rachel Douglas was doing. There was one difference between them and the experience Rachel was having. Just one.

Melissa moved her mouse to the button marked OVER-
RIDE. She readjusted the headset, finger poised over the mouse
button.

> . . . over to the store later. I need to pick some things up at the
> pharmacy, too.
>
> Why? Is someone sick?
>
> No, not sick. I just have to get some vitamins and lotion. The
> usual kind of things.

Melissa clicked the OVERRIDE button. On one of the
servers a software branch executed. The existing virtual entity
Suzanne dropped out of focus and control was transferred to
Melissa's console.

From this point on, and until she clicked again on the
OVERRIDE button to deactivate it, Melissa was in control.

Melissa *became* Suzanne.

Melissa spoke into her microphone. Everything she said
was digitized, converted to text, and displayed on the screen.

> Is he still under all that pressure at work?
>
> Yes. He came home a little earlier than normal last night,
> though. And he was able to play with the children before they
> went to bed. It was pretty nice.
>
> Did he ever give you any explanation about why he's still keep-
> ing such late hours?

No, but he doesn't need to. I trust him. I know he's working hard.

Oh, I'm sure he is, whatever it is he's doing. He is mainly making investments for customers, right?

Right. I guess he's buying and selling stocks all day. He has a lot of responsibility.

I'm sure he's trustworthy. But I do have a question, if you don't mind me asking?

Sure. What's your question?

Well, if he is working late at the office, buying and selling stocks and securities, how can he be doing that when the stock exchange closes at four o'clock in the afternoon? I mean, you'd think he would come home earlier, not later. What could he be doing all the rest of that time?

Rachel made no answer.

Melissa's eyes never left the screen. More bait in the trap. How would she react to the new seed of doubt she had just planted in the other woman's mind? Two long minutes later a reply came back.

I don't know. I don't think I should be worrying about that. I have to go now, Suzanne. Maybe we can talk this afternoon.

Okay, take care. I'm sure there's nothing to worry about. Bye-bye.

RACHEL SHIFTED THE PHONE to her shoulder as she folded shirts from a large blue basket. She reminded herself that her mother was trying to be helpful.

"You're smart. You graduated from college. Why don't you get one of those online jobs?"

Rachel considered her mother's question. It was true. She'd gone to college and done pretty well, if she did say so herself.

She might be stuck at home . . . no, not *stuck*. She'd chosen to stay home with her young ones as long as needed, but that did not mean she couldn't do meaningful work.

"What kind of online work, Mom?"

"Oh, I don't know. It seems like I'm hearing about that sort of thing all the time. You're the young one. You're supposed to know about stuff like that."

True again. She was supposed to know, but she didn't. She was losing touch with the world around her. Some days it felt like, well, like if there was a world outside the walls of her vinyl-clad house, she didn't know what it was anymore.

They said their good-byes, then Rachel slumped into the flower-print sofa. She began to enumerate her considerable talents.

She was an expert at setting the trash at the end of the driveway. She was solidly proficient at separating colors before using the washer. And she was way more than adequate at operating the microwave, even when she needed to change the power level when cooking.

Translation. She saw herself swimming in a gray sea of mediocrity with no way out.

Suzanne said she needed to be careful about her appearance. Something about the way she looked on the webcam in the morning when they talked.

A dark swell of guilt rose up in her heart. Next she'd be blaming the kids for her plight. No, they were the joy of her life. Any price, no matter what, would not be too high to pay for their happiness. She would raise them to serve the Lord, no matter the sacrifice to herself.

Scott seemed happy for her just to keep the house clean and get supper on the table. Men had it easy. They went to work, they got bonuses, and then came home as heroes.

Women were the ones with problems. Start every day with the same messy house, end every day with the mess right back where it had started. Then wake up the next day and do it all over again.

The best part should be when Scott comes home, shouldn't it? She'd always believed that. He'd open the door to his home, sweep the children away, give her some time to herself. Maybe even let her go shopping without a tag-along.

She abandoned the basket, went to the computer, and typed *work at home job* into the search engine.

A list of ten stay-at-home careers appeared. Translator, web developer, and technical support representative headed the chart.

The French she'd studied so assiduously in college might be great if she was trying to book a hotel room, but not much else. Translator wouldn't work.

Web developer seemed interesting. Lots of her friends had blogs. A few years earlier she'd helped with a missions project where she used a popular blogging engine to design a fund-raising website. Web developer was definitely worth considering.

Next was the technical support representative. No way would she do that. She was no geek and had no plans to become one.

Her eyes skipped down to the next on the list, medical transcriptionist.

The blurb explained that a medical transcriptionist listened to doctors speaking medical histories, treatments, and observations. The MT would record those in text using a special word processing program.

That stopped her. Working in a medical field sounded professional. Surely not just anyone could do it. A candidate would have to be educated, well-spoken. She'd seen enough written communication to know that most people couldn't spell anymore.

A twinge of fear caught her. Could she spell medical terms? A word came out of nowhere. In a whisper, she spelled it aloud.

R-H-E-U-M-A-T-O-I-D

She was sure, but not totally. Quickly she keyed the word into the search engine and before she could think long about it, she was looking at the wiki for Rheumatoid Arthritis.

"I can do that," she said aloud, with a voice that gained strength with each punctuated syllable.

Rachel felt strength gathering about her and a growing confidence at the possibilities. This could be a path to actually contributing again, not just washing clothes. She didn't want self-sufficiency. She wanted to matter once more.

The Alliance for Healthcare Documentation Integrity offered introductory courses online at no charge.

This was it. It could be the life changer.

She'd ask Scott later, but first she'd ask Suzanne.

CHAPTER EIGHTEEN
Solar Charge

Scott opened his browser on the NYSE website. How had Solar Charge been doing in trading on the overnight markets? A full week had passed since he'd made his options trade on Solar Charge.

The stock had climbed another fifty cents, to $117. He was now at a break-even point. This meant he could cash his option calls back in and break even on his trade. No way was he going to do that. The president's secretary for energy had gone on television last night to indicate he was proposing another $300 million loan guarantee for Solar Charge. It was all about green jobs, the environment, and "protecting our children's future."

Nothing could go wrong now. There was no question he had made a wise choice in buying the call options when he did. He checked the quotes on the same option if purchased at today's prices. Where a single contract of 100 shares had cost him $175 just a week ago, the same contract now cost $278. Market momentum was in his favor. Everything was going well, and when this was over Gleason Archer and Alan Castle were going to be in his debt.

Maybe he would celebrate and invite the whole staff out to a big lunch. Maybe he'd even invite Rachel to come into town and have lunch with him. Then she could see what kind of job her husband had been doing during those long days and evenings in the office. She would be proud of him.

She had become more questioning about his activities than in the past. She was always asking him what he was doing when he was out so late, as if he were doing something suspicious. She obviously did not understand all the research he had to do to guarantee the success of his customers' investments. His fiduciary responsibility to his customers was more than just legal, it was a moral responsibility.

He would show them what real dedication could do.

Scott turned on the video feed from the market floor. Since the Gleason Archer affair started he had gotten into the habit of watching the market every day. He was keeping a close eye on the trends for green jobs, environmental industries, everything that might impact his investment with Solar Charge. If a move had to be made he would be on top of it, the first to act.

He heard a muffled *ding*, and turned to see that an e-mail had arrived in his in-box. It was from Alicia.

What an amazing service.

He clicked on the e-mail titled, *Hope you have a great day.*

He visualized Alicia speaking to him as he read the e-mail.

Good morning, Scott. I just thought I would send you a note
to help you get your day started right. Don't worry about
Rachel's doubts. I know you're working hard and doing a good

job. Keep it up. I'm behind you in everything you do. Your girl,
Alicia.

Something stirred inside him. *Your girl.* That was quite a
thing. She was his girl in every—well, in almost every—way.
She was everything he ever hoped Rachel would become.

And Rachel was so suspicious of him lately. And for no reason at all. He was as true to her as he had ever been. Some
might think that this virtual relationship he was having on the
side indicated otherwise, but that was wrong. He was as committed to his family as he could possibly be. Of all the people
working at Castle Investments he was the one people always re-
ferred to as the *family man.*

Why didn't Rachel understand that? Alicia was right. Ra-
chel was unnecessarily questioning his activities and his work.
She had nothing to worry about. What was wrong with her?
Why couldn't she support him like Alicia did?

Someone at the NYSE rang the bell and the market
opened. The flashing ticker began moving and market quotes
started coming in as quickly as they could be read. Solar
Charge stock was spiking, already at $118. If this kept up, he
could sell his options before another week was out and make
$500,000 for Gleason Archer. Archer could quit calling Alan
Castle every day worrying about his account. When he pulled
this off, Scott would be able to go home at 6:00 p.m. like the
rest of the people in the office and spend the evening with his
family like a normal man.

The one thing he feared in the meantime was that Alan
Castle would pull him into his office and ask him exactly what
he was doing with the Archer account. He would never be able

to explain why he had purchased call options, especially such short-term call options. If those options were not sold or exercised during that short period of time they would expire, worthless, and the $250,000 he had spent on the premiums would be gone, vanished without so much as even a puff of smoke.

At eleven o'clock Scott closed up his laptop and slipped it into the carrying case for another trip to McDonald's. His lunchtime meetings with Alicia were becoming a normal thing, and he looked forward to them more and more each day.

Was there anything about her that wasn't perfect? There was something different about Alicia every time. She was subtly changing. He couldn't put his finger on it, but he liked it. Every day seemed to bring a better experience than the last.

So why was he feeling so guilty about the time with Alicia? It was no more than a high-tech video game.

Carole Turner stopped at Scott's cube. "How's our family man today? Everyone at home healthy?"

Scott shook himself, pushed his thoughts of Alicia aside.

"What? Oh, yes. The flu bug went right past our house this year. How about you and Ted?"

She jostled the armful of papers she carried. "We get a flu shot every year. We do pretty well. Going to McDonald's again? I see you down there a lot."

"It's nice to get out of the cube for a few minutes every day." He gave her a weak smile.

"Okay, enjoy your lunch." She strode off down the row of cubicles and turned the corner.

People noticed what he was doing. When was the last time they had seen him pick up the Bible he kept on his desk? He knew the answer. Well, he would get things balanced soon and then he'd be back to normal.

He found his parking place at the McDonald's, brought his coffee back to the car, and settled in for a nice conversation with *his girl.*

Alicia's image filled the screen, and the warmth of her smile seemed to flow from the screen right into his heart. Her eyes were bright and loving as they looked into his.

"Did you get my e-mail this morning, Scott?"

He liked that she was watching out for him. Even that she was watching *over* him. He wanted to please her, was glad he'd read the e-mail so he could tell her so.

"Yes, thank you. I look forward to hearing from you every day. I don't know what I ever did without your messages before."

Alicia nodded, never taking her eyes off his. "I know they mean a lot to you. That's why I send them. I want you to know each and every day that someone is caring about you, thinking about you, and wanting you to have the very best day of your life."

"And that's you?"

"Of course it is. You know that. Who else loves you like I do?"

Loves? "You've never said that to me before, Alicia."

Her face darkened, as if a shadow had fallen on it. "Said what? Did I say something wrong?"

"No, no. Nothing wrong. I was just surprised when you used the word *love.*"

"Silly, you shouldn't be. You've made me what I am. How can I do any less than love you? You are my entire life, Scott.

Everything I am is wrapped up in you. Surely you know that."

That word doesn't belong here. This was not about love. It was about . . . something else. He didn't want to name it.

"I do, I guess I do. It's only that we have never used that word before."

"Are you offended? Would you rather I didn't say that anymore? I don't want you to feel any pressure. I just want you to enjoy our talks together without feeling like you have to do anything special with me or for me."

"No, I wouldn't say I feel uncomfortable. Just surprised. I suppose, if I were to tell the truth, I would have to say the same."

What am I saying? Am I crazy?

"What do you mean, 'say the same'?"

"I mean, you said you love me. I suppose, to be honest, I would have to say I love you, too."

Stop now. Run as fast as you can. The warning rose up in his mind. How could he ever say that to anyone but Rachel?

Alicia closed her eyes. Tiny wrinkles appeared on her eyelids. She moved her head slowly back and forth, just the slightest hint of a smile on her lips, as if she were soaking in warmth from the sun. Finally, her eyelids fluttered open. "I thought I would never hear you say that. I've always been afraid that someday you would just, you know, *terminate me.*"

He forcibly pushed the thought of stopping back down.

"What? Do what? I would never do that. I don't even know what I would do without you anymore." Scott took in her features. It was true. The changes in her appearance had been subtle at first, but now they were becoming more evident. She looked not entirely different, but different just the same from when they had first come together.

She was slimmer now, with a slightly darker complexion. Her skin had taken on something of an olive tone, kind of Mediterranean, or maybe it was Italian. He wasn't sure. But it looked good on her. Her hair was longer now too. Straighter, but not too straight, and fell to her shoulders in graceful waves. She was wearing less makeup. In the beginning, she had looked more like Jane, the introducer. In contrast to Alicia, Jane had seemed starkly artificial and unreal.

He thought back to the beginning, when he had first designed her. How ridiculous that word sounded now. He could no longer think of her as something he had designed. It was natural that she should change. After all, they had said in the beginning that over time she would become fine-tuned to his expectations of her. Now she was everything he wanted her to be.

As far as he was concerned, Alicia *was* real.

"Scott, why are you so quiet?"

"Oh, I'm sorry. I was just thinking."

"Thinking about what? Those problems at work again?"

"No, nothing like that. Actually, I was thinking about you, and the relationship you and I have together now. In some ways, it's kind of frightening."

Alicia pulled back, raised her hand to her mouth. Her eyes were wide. "Frightening? How is that? I don't frighten you, do I?"

"No, you don't frighten me. If I'm frightened by anything at all, I guess I'd have to say I'm frightened of myself. I can hardly believe that I've developed such deep feelings for you and over such a short time."

Her eyes rolled up. "Oh, tell me about it." She laughed. "And you imagine that I ever think about anything except you? You're all that's ever on my mind."

A feeling of deep disappointment began to grow inside him. Surprised, he realized that he was disappointed for Alicia. She gave so much, but her life would never be consummated in a real relationship. It was so unfair that this beautiful woman was forced to live in her artificial environment. Anyone so real must have the same needs as other women.

"Do you ever have thoughts about things like having a family? I hope I'm not asking the wrong thing. I know you can't, but you're so real. Do you want the same things that physical humans do?"

"No, that's okay. I don't think I've ever heard of anyone asking that before. The truth? No, not in the sense that you mean."

"In what sense, then?"

"I don't want things I can't have. As I'm constituted now, I could never have children. So in that sense, I don't think about a family. But there is another side to that. You have a family and I love you. Think about what that means. I want everything perfect for us. That means I care about the family you've got. I care about Scotty and I care about Angela. Does that seem strange to you?"

"I guess not. Do you know what happens this weekend?"

"Sure I do. It's Scotty's birthday. Have you been shopping yet?"

"I'm going this afternoon. He's old enough now I think I can start buying him some things he could build at home. Something like a model airplane or a car. Something that can be assembled, snapped together, you know what I mean. There is a HobbyTown not too far away. I'm going to take a break around four-thirty, after the stock market closes, and do some shopping for his gift. Maybe I can check back in with you early this evening before I go home."

"Oh, I'd like that. Will you try very hard to remember? Will you, please?"

"Count on it. I'll show you what I bought him when I come back."

Scott lifted his hand toward the display screen and traced a line along Alicia's cheek with his index finger. He imagined he was touching her in a tender way. "Can you see what I did just then?"

"I think I know. You just tried to touch me, didn't you?"

"Yes. Crazy, I suppose. I'd better go now."

"Okay, Scott. *I love you.*"

Scott didn't answer, not trusting himself. He logged off the website, and closed the lid on the computer.

Was he falling in love with this virtual person? No, he couldn't be. She wasn't real. He loved Rachel.

Maybe there was a virtual love? Something was happening.

He told himself again. No, he couldn't be falling in love with her.

CHAPTER NINETEEN
Gray

That night the dream came again.

I'm coming home from college for Thanksgiving holiday. The bus ride has been so long, and the bus is so crowded. Why do the strange people all sit by me? Why do they keep staring at me?

We're on the outskirts of town. I have a window seat and I use my sleeve to wipe something oily from the surface of the glass so I can see outside. This bus is going to pass my street on its way downtown. I wish the driver would stop and let me off. I see my house flash by as we pass the street. Why does it look so gray and empty?

We're downtown in the bus station. All the people are hollow. None of them sees me. I am waiting but no one comes for me.

After a long time, a big taxi drives up to the bench inside the station where I am sitting. I know there's something wrong with the taxi being inside the building but I don't remember what it is. A gray man with empty eyes like cardboard sits in the driver's seat. He doesn't move or speak to me, but I know he wants me to get inside.

The taxi takes me to my house. The closer we get, the grayer the world becomes. I ask what the fare is. In a hissing voice the driver says, "Everything, till there's nothing left." I'm afraid, and so I push on the door and fall out onto the gray grass, which crackles and snaps under my weight. When I look up again the taxi is gone.

More of the gray people, the don't-matter people, are down at the end of the street all bunched up together. They know something, but they're just standing there, all staring at me.

I'm afraid and I want to go into my house. I push on the door, which opens noiselessly. Why doesn't it make any sound? It should make a sound when it opens. I can hear voices inside, coming from my mother's room. "Cut it out. Leave me alone." What voice is that? My mother's voice? What does she want me to cut out?

The scissors are there on the dining room table. Everything is gray, but the scissors shine and gleam, calling to me. It's hard to see anything else. I have them now. What needs to be cut out?

Uncle Tony is here and he is not gray enough. He should be gray like the other people. Mother is here too, pulling on his shoulder. She is not gray enough either. I can see her mouth moving, but I can't hear the words. Is she saying my name?

I know what to do. I must make Uncle Tony gray. It's not difficult. I just have to keep trying. I will fix everything. I will make both of them very gray. My hands move as if they knew just what they had to do. I watch the shining blades arc through the gloom, rising and falling in a grim rhythm. Pretty soon the other colors bleed out, and Uncle Tony and Mother are gray like they should be.

I close my dreaming eyes. Everything is quiet again. Everyone has gone to sleep. The people down the street have all walked away, back into their dingy houses. No one can see me anymore.

The taxi driver is back. "You're done now," he tells me in his rasping voice. That's good. I walk out the front door into the twilight of the street. Everything is the same fleshless color, except for the sky. I see the bright points of stars overhead. They are so beautiful.

CHAPTER TWENTY
Shopping

HobbyTown was huge. When Circuit City had gone out of business the mall had lost its anchor store and for a time people thought the mall would languish and become a ruin. HobbyTown had moved in, taken over the old facility, and even expanded it. They had subsumed the furniture store on the east and now the storefront seemed as wide as a city block.

He walked through the large double doors and approached the cash register area. The signs in the back of the store were so far away, they blurred into intelligibility.

He walked up to the first cashier, a young woman about eighteen years old. "Can you help me out? Where in the store can I find model airplanes and cars?"

She directed him to an aisle way in the rear of the store. There were three aisles full of models and model paraphernalia. Paints, glues, and all sorts of kits. As Scott walked up and down the aisle the little boy in him came out again. All of the kits looked like they would be fun to build. There was a model of the old dirigible *Hindenburg*. How fun would that be?

But there was no way in the world little Scotty would

know anything about a dirigible. His world was all about cars, trucks, and horses. There were plenty of cars, planes, and trucks. The cars and trucks would be the best bet. The little guy could identify with those, mainly because he rode in them all the time.

Something caught his eye. No, it was *someone*. Who was that?

He stepped around the end of the aisle to try to see who the person had been. No one there. Odd, she'd looked familiar. But who had it been?

He found a model of the Scooby-Doo Mystery Machine. It looked just like the old-style bus the cartoon characters drove on television. Scotty would absolutely love it. It had all the flower decals and decorations the real Mystery Machine had on TV. The box proclaimed it had snap-in construction, eliminating the need to use glue, but it still needed to be painted. No problem. On the opposite side of the aisle were at least a hundred thumb-size bottles of paint in every color.

Yellow, lime green, light blue, red, and black. That would take care of the van body, the wheels, and all the trim. Besides, he could buy more if they needed it. He picked up a couple of brushes as well.

Did he need anything else? He should probably get something for Angela while he was in here. Half a store away, he found jewelry for little girls. Angela loved it when Rachel dressed her up in fancy things. She toddled all around, showing herself off. He found some colorful bracelets and a glow-in-the-dark necklace she could wear in her room when it was dark. Perfect.

As he turned toward the cashier station his eye caught the

oddly familiar figure again. Someone leaving the store, walking out through the double doors. So familiar! It looked just like . . . No. *Alicia?*

Of course, that was impossible. There was no Alicia, not really. She couldn't have been here. Someone just looked like her. However, he was intrigued. Intrigued and scared.

No way. It's just the guilt talking.

Scott paid as quickly as he could, then strode out into the parking lot. He stopped and looked around.

The woman who had just exited the store had to still be in sight. What a strange feeling, seeing someone who looked like Alicia in real life. Of course, he'd only had a fleeting glimpse of her. No doubt if he were to see her close up, the resemblance would fall apart very quickly. No doubt.

There was nothing to see, though, and after looking around for a few more minutes, he made his way to his car.

Still, he found himself haunted by the idea someone who looked that much like Alicia actually lived and was walking around town.

It was almost six o'clock. Even though he felt like he should go back to the office, he just didn't feel up to it. It had been a long day and the vision of the Alicia look-alike troubled him.

No, it wasn't Alicia, but it had left him feeling guilty. His place was with Rachel, with his own family.

He put the things he'd bought on the passenger seat and pointed the car toward home. He'd have supper with his family tonight.

The only Alicia he wanted to think about was the virtual one. The possibility of a real one was too frightening to consider.

THE PAIR OF EYES that followed him as he walked back to his car pursued him as he left the parking lot. They didn't let go until he was completely out of sight.

She had never been so close to him before.

This was him. The hair, the body, the way he walked. The right age, born under the right sign. He looked just like the sketch she'd drawn when she was thirteen years old, before her world crumbled around her. *Him.*

The VirtualFriendMe system had flagged him as soon as he'd appeared. There would never be another.

I almost touched him tonight. I nearly let him see me. Too soon, too soon!

Melissa reached into her purse and pulled out her brush. She turned the rearview mirror toward herself and imagined herself through his eyes as she ran the brush through her shoulder-length, dark-brown hair. Then, remembering where she was, she rebuttoned the top button on her blouse, started the engine of her Audi, and began the drive home.

A tremble rippled down the skin of her arm. Melissa felt cold all over her upper body.

I will not let him go. He's mine now.

CHAPTER TWENTY-ONE
Great Kids

Dan, I need to take a few days off for some personal business." Melissa studied Dan Hammersmith, gauging his reaction to her request.

"I don't see any problem with that, Melissa. I can't remember the last time you took a day off. Bob Locarno can handle whatever needs to be done while you're gone. Take as much time as you need, but stay in touch, all right?"

Melissa had not expected any problem from Hammersmith. He had told her on numerous occasions she had saved the company, and his job, when she stepped in after the untimely death of Aaron Getz.

So far as anyone knew, Getz had been killed by an assailant or assailants unknown. That was all the police had ever been able to offer. A bad way to die, they'd said, and in a bad part of town.

Melissa had stepped in on the following Monday morning ready to take the reins. She worked through Getz's notes and code for an entire week almost without sleep. She kept Virtual

FriendMe solvent in a time when the company's major capital investors were ready to pull the plug.

VirtualFriendMe was a success and it was primarily because of her efforts. Dan would do anything to keep her happy, and she didn't ask much.

"I've already talked with Bob and he understands what's needed. Furthermore, I've asked some of our tech people to move my personal console to my house for a while, just until I come back. Whatever you need, I'll be able to take care of from home. It'll be just exactly the same as if I were here."

Dan gave her a sly grin. "So you'll be like a virtual Melissa. You won't really be here, but it will be just the same. You're good, Melissa. Really, really good."

She returned the grin. She appreciated the kind of treatment he had given her, and the company was treating her well. She had no complaints, but there was this *very personal* matter to attend to. Nothing could get in the way.

"The techs will have everything moved out this evening and set up in my home. I'll see you again probably in about a week or so, okay? I'll be in town most of the time and be linked up when I'm not. I'll keep everything covered."

"Okay, thanks for the heads-up. You've got carte blanche. I'm off to meet with some investors."

Hammersmith started to turn off down the hallway, then turned back to Melissa. "Am I missing something? Is there anything wrong?"

Could he be seeing something in her eyes, her actions that was giving her away? He couldn't possibly suspect anything.

"Nothing wrong. Just some personal affairs, like I said."

"If you need anything . . ." He left the words hanging in the air, turned his palms upward.

"I know, Dan. I can call you."

He turned again and headed off down the hallway, looking at some notes he had in a leather portfolio.

I've already gotten all I need from you, Dan. Now I just have to keep you out of the way.

RACHEL PULLED THE STRAPS tight on Angela's car seat as she finished packing the kids into the car. "Is that too tight?"

Angela's eyes were intent on her Sleeping Beauty doll. She didn't look up when she answered, "Not too tight. Where's my prince?"

Rachel heaved a sigh. "Prince Charming is still in the house. Do you need me to go get him?" *Please say no.*

"No, Mommy. Because if a dragon comes while we're gone the prince can fight him and kill him. Princes are wonderful."

Rachel peered across the car to the safety seat where Scotty was already buckled up. "Are you doing okay, Scotty? Ready to go to preschool and see Ms. Mandy?"

"Ready, Mom."

The Great Kids Preschool was halfway between the Douglas's home and the old junior high school where Rachel had her Hugest Loser meetings. The drive would only take eight or nine minutes. Rachel would drop Scotty off and then be on her way for her weigh-in.

She backed the minivan out of the driveway and pulled onto the road.

MELISSA PARKED THE AUDI across the tree-lined street, half a block away from the old colonial-style home on Holt Road. The sign in front of the shrubs by the sidewalk read, GREAT KIDS PRE-SCHOOL.

She lowered the window that faced the house and shut off the engine.

There was still so much to learn about Scott, his two children, and his unnecessary wife.

She picked up her tablet computer and pressed a pre-programmed link. The mini-console opened up.

"Activate suzanne 48b7b9a6." The noise-canceling microphone captured her speech, and a custom message box appeared on the tablet display.

"Send e-mail colon Rachel."

The prompt in the message box turned green with the word READY.

Melissa spoke distinctly into the microphone, "Good morning, Rachel! I know you're probably already on your way to preschool, but I want to say have a great day. Let's talk later. Love you, Suzanne."

Melissa touched the DONE button and the message box cleared.

She turned her head and looked up and down the street. There was no traffic yet, but Rachel was surely on her way. Melissa was finally going to get a really good look at Scott's current wife without having to use a webcam.

"Clear console. Activate alicia 48r3y7y2."

When the prompt appeared on the tablet she said, "Send e-mail colon Scott."

There was a momentary pause while the data packets containing her digitized voice passed back and forth across the wide area network. The trip from the tablet, then to her home console, to the company server room, and back again took less than a second.

"How's my hero this morning? Are you at work yet? I'm looking forward to our lunch date today. Hope you can make it. Answer me if you can, otherwise I'll talk with you at lunch. I love you."

The message disappeared, on its way to Scott's mailbox.

Melissa caught some movement in her peripheral vision. She turned her head slightly and saw three cars already lined up at Great Kids dropping off children.

Pay attention, she scolded herself. You'll miss what you came for.

None of the vehicles matched the description Rachel had given Suzanne of their minivan. Good, she wasn't here yet. She settled back in the smooth leather seat and brushed her long, dark hair back over her ear so it wouldn't be in the way.

She glanced at her reflection in the mirror. *Scott likes my hair this way. I'll never change it as long as this is what he wants.* Were those sad eyes in the mirror hers? An emptiness suffused her heart for a brief moment. She fought it down. Yes, he was with someone else for now, but that would change. Oh, yes. That would definitely change and very soon.

The minivan approached from in front of her, recognizable immediately by its dark yellow color. Using the Bushnell field glasses, she was able to pick out Rachel's features as she drove toward the preschool.

Melissa held up her tablet in front of her face and pointed the rearview camera on the little computer toward Rachel as she maneuvered the minivan into a parking place. The flat black tablet case hid her face and movements as she focused her attention on the activity across the road.

Ms. Mandy's teenage helper came out the front door when she saw Rachel arrive, then trotted quickly to the car to help the young mother unbuckle her son from his car seat.

Melissa increased the digital zoom until she could make out Scotty's features, then raised the lens slightly to watch Rachel. When this surveillance was complete, she would have a complete photographic record of the features of both individuals. Something to look at and study when she got home.

Rachel stood facing Melissa. The teenager held Scotty. They were discussing something Melissa couldn't make out. Perhaps she could use some lip-reading software later on this evening if it seemed important. It probably wasn't, though. She'd bring a parabolic microphone the next time. In the interim she was getting the kind of video images that she wanted. Full motion, normal actions.

That should be my son.

Rachel bent down and gave Scotty a kiss and a hug. The little boy was holding something, a sandwich bag full of some kind of snack. Their talking concluded, the teenager took Scotty by the hand and led him through the wide front door of the old home. Rachel waved, still standing next to the open door of the minivan, where Angela played with some kind of little doll.

Resentment flared in Melissa's mind. Rachel was fat, lazy. She watched her bend over, revealing the white flesh of her back above her belt line. *Disgusting.* Scott deserved so much more than the overweight woman he was married to.

She couldn't even walk in a straight line. Why didn't she do something about her appearance? Did she even own a hair-brush?

Scott deserves me.

Rachel dug into her jacket pocket and pulled something out. It was her cell phone; the e-mail was probably arriving. Rachel looked at the phone for a moment, then closed the sliding door next to Angela. She went around to the driver's seat and sat down, then closed the door. Melissa could still make her out through the tinted glass of the passenger window.

There was a soft *ding* from the tablet. An answer from Rachel.

> Suzanne, thank you for your e-mail. I just dropped Scotty off at preschool and now I'm on my way to exercise at the junior high. Got to lose that weight LOL. I'll talk to you online after lunch. Bye for now.

Melissa watched as Rachel deposited the cell phone some-where out of her sight and then drove off in the minivan. Melissa would not follow her today. Not today. Today was a school day. She laughed softly at her own wry humor.

Yes, I have a lot to learn. A lot to learn about children, especially these children.

CHAPTER TWENTY-TWO
He Loves Me

Melissa imagined the children that might have been. Her children. But she was a barren tree that would never bear fruit.

The memories came unbidden, unwanted. She'd tried many times to drive them back down into the dark pit where they belonged, but it never lasted. They always came creeping up, back out of the abyss where she had commanded them, and more so today as she watched Scotty across the street.

Uncle Tony had ignored her after *that time*. He treated her like a piece of rotten fruit, left too long on the kitchen counter, avoided by everyone in the house. When she missed her first menstrual cycle she took her mother's car downtown, where no one knew her, and bought a pregnancy test kit. She hid herself in the back restroom of a JCPenney store, all alone in a dirty stall, and administered the test. She wanted children of her own, but not this way. Not where the child could never know his father's name or the circumstances of his conception.

She waited a full minute for the test stick to change color, but fifteen seconds into the wait she could tell what the result would be. It had already turned pink and just got pinker from there. The word YES stood out starkly in bold letters.

She wanted to die. She wanted to run away somewhere, find a spot where no one would ever discover her, and take her own life. But she hadn't had the nerve, and her Catholic upbringing had taught her suicide was a mortal sin. She could not bring herself to make it worse than it already was by killing herself.

Instead, after a long period of cold resolution, she had known what she would do.

Finally, she had gone to Uncle Tony to tell him about her condition. He told her two things.

The first was a threat. If she ever told anyone about his part he would deny everything and ruin her life. He didn't want some stupid teenage girl, especially one for whom he had done a favor, making trouble for him.

The second was an attempt at his own perverted version of kindness. He would take her to the Central Women's Clinic for an abortion. He would pay for everything, just so long as she kept her mouth shut.

She did as he said. On a cold, rainy Tuesday morning he drove her to the door of the abortion clinic. With the engine running, he put the cash in her hand and told her he would be back in three hours to pick her up.

He never came back. Melissa, with no cash in her pocket and in great pain, walked the seven miles back to her home alone.

By the time she got home she was hemorrhaging, her socks and shoes full of cold, slurping blood. Her mother came into her room as she cried in her agony, alone on her bed. That image of her mother standing over her came back again and again in the dark hours of the night. Had she known what had happened?

An ambulance took her to the hospital emergency room, where they kept her overnight. The doctor never spoke to her directly, but instead told her mother the damage that had been done to her meant she could never have children.

Neither her mother nor father ever spoke to her again about that day. She had no way of knowing if they had ever known the truth or if they were even interested. The one thing she did notice was they quit inviting Uncle Tony and Rose, his wife, over for gatherings with the rest of the family. Melissa was left to fend for herself both psychologically and emotionally.

Well, that was about to end.

She had found her man, the only man she would ever want, and she was going to have him no matter what.

Was it a problem he was already married?

Call it a complication.

AT 11:23 A.M., Melissa's tablet dinged again. An e-mail from Scott.

I'll be at McDonald's in five minutes. I'll log on and meet you then. Your e-mail made my day. Love you too, Scott.

Melissa smiled. *He does love me. He loves me and he's about to be mine.*

Across the street, the children played outside in the big yard next to the house. It was surrounded by a four-foot chain-link fence and the teenage gatekeeper was keeping a close eye on the children's security.

Scotty was there, tugging on a circle of rope with two other little boys. They all pulled in different directions. When adults were pulled in too many directions at once it was a problem. For kids, it was a game. She and Rachel were both pulling on Scott right now, but not much longer.

She wished the two children no harm. Indeed, when Rachel was out of the picture she and Scott could raise them as their own.

Everything would be new, different. When the time came, Scott would come to regard her as the mother of the two little ones. Rachel, whoever she was, or used to be, would soon be forgotten.

How many times had Melissa considered adoption? She yearned to feel the warmth of a little body against hers as she held it close to her heart. Why had things worked out like this for her? Why did *that woman* have the place she deserved, that *she* was entitled to? It wasn't right.

She heard feet scuffling in gravel and looked up to see some of the boys playing in the school yard.

Scotty had been pulled across some imaginary line against his will. Despite his best efforts, he had lost the tug-of-war game.

He was a handsome little boy. Scott's own features were in his face. She hoped he didn't have to die.

Scott would be logging on soon. Melissa reviewed the changes she had made to her *Alicia* image. As usual, the change was as subtle as she could make it without being too obvious.

She looked at the cropped image of her own face in the rearview mirror and pulled the hair back away from her right ear. There, right in front of the ear, was a small mole. Not the kind of physical characteristic people paid much attention to, but noticeable nonetheless. She twisted her fingertips on the tablet's touch-sensitive screen. The Alicia image wire-framed and turned until she had a three-quarter, right-hand view of the face. There, right in front of the ear, was an identical small mole. Thirty minutes of work last night had made that small detail a reality.

In terms of likeness to herself the image was now better than an 80 percent level. Scott was falling in love with her and he didn't even realize it. It was such a perfect plan. Surely he was already wondering what it would have been like if he had met someone like Alicia in person. Very, very soon he would have the opportunity. By the time that happened he would have already made the choice in his heart.

She laid her head back on the headrest and closed her eyes, imagining what his embrace would be like. *Will be like.* Through half-raised eyelids she looked across the road at their son playing in the yard.

I've waited so long.

The tablet chirped. An image session had been initiated. The Expressive Images Module she had coded into the system picked up and assimilated the new Alicia modification. Scott would already be seeing it on his display.

Melissa slipped the headset on, ready to begin their session together.

The text of Scott's spoken speech began scrolling in the message box:

Hi, Alicia.

Hi, Scott. I've been waiting for you.

I've been thinking about you all day. It's kind of hard to concentrate on work when there's someone like you to talk to.

I'll always be here for you. You know that by now, don't you?

Yes. There's something I want to say, but I'm afraid it will sound wrong. Will you try to understand what I mean if I say it?

Scott, part of my design is to understand you. We've talked so much, and about so many things. Do you think there is anyone else in the world who would understand you better than I?

No, you're right. And that's the whole point. You are becoming like—this is hard to say. You are becoming the most important person in the world to me. Does that sound ridiculous or what? I'm telling a computer she is the most important person in the world?

Well, I should probably be hurt by that, but I'm not. I really do understand. You think just because you haven't seen me in the flesh I cannot have the same thoughts and feelings for you that other women do, isn't that right?

Well, yes. When you put it that way, I guess . . .

And there is something else that worries you, something I also understand about you very well.

What is that?

You're afraid you are becoming unfaithful, aren't you?

Scott did not respond. Had she pushed him too far by asking that question? One of the things she required in her perfect man was his principled faithfulness. But there was plenty of reason for Rachel to disappear. Rachel didn't belong there in the first place. When he had Melissa and found out what kind of love he'd been missing . . . well, faithfulness would never be an issue for them.

After a long pause . . .

Yes, I have been afraid of that.

I know you have. I love you so much for caring about that. You are not being unfaithful. How can you be unfaithful with a girl who doesn't even have a real existence?

Melissa waited for Scott's next reaction. When the words "have a real existence" passed through the system, Alicia's EIM software executed a special conditional branch. The background code _showSingleTear was unique to the Alicia personality. It would run this one time and never execute again.

Alicia? Am I seeing what I think I'm seeing?

What, Scott? What do you think you're seeing?

Is that a tear in your eye?

Success. He saw the tear and would respond as men always do. Melissa looked once more across the road.

The children were going back inside now. Scotty Douglas looked across the road at the gray car as he walked inside. Soon he would know who she was.

Scott, you're learning more about me than I want you to know right now. I must go. Can we talk later on?

Of course, Alicia. I do love you.

And I love you.

Melissa clicked on the TERMINATE EIM button. The session switched back to automatic and closed normally.

He loves me.

CHAPTER TWENTY-THREE
Puppy Love

Scott frowned. A tear? What had that been about?

Scott twisted the key out of the ignition, kicked the car door open, and walked to the edge of the parking lot. A family with out-of-state plates pulled their minivan into the slot by the curb. The woman next to the driver was gesticulating with her hands, agitated about something. She noticed Scott staring at her and motioned as if she were inviting him to take a picture.

Alicia, you're so real. But you're not.

That family in the car was real. He was real. He moved on along the grass line to a concrete picnic table, sat down on the bench, pulled his cell phone out of his pocket.

There could be no harm in pursuing this *not-real relationship*. Relationship? Scott was not sure the word even fit. How can you have a relationship with a computer?

And yes, Alicia had told him she loved him. How could that be? He didn't understand all there was to know about computers and artificial intelligence, but surely it was not possible for Alicia to really love him. Was it?

Oh, there was something to this, that was for sure. Scott didn't understand it all, much less have a grasp on his own feelings, but he knew it was real.

The evidence for that was in his own words. He had told Alicia he loved her.

Up to this point he had reasoned away the nagging problem of guilt about the relationship. He was a principled man, was he not? One who would never be unfaithful to his wife.

He stared at the cell phone in his hand, thumbed the history, and saw Rachel's name.

He loved his wife. That is, he loved Rachel. They could go on as they always had, husband and wife, mom and dad. Nothing he was doing with Alicia would ever change that.

If Alicia was *real*, well that, as the Wizard said, was a horse of another color. But she wasn't real, and that possibility could be safely put out of his mind.

And he did, he really did, love Alicia too.

He sat on the unyielding concrete bench and despised himself for his own perfidy.

God, help me.

THE *FINANCIAL TIMES* VIDEO feed had a short feature on Solar Charge. Someone was questioning the company's solvency and had filed a complaint with the FTC for some kind of disclosure.

The whole thing was ridiculous, of course. The same government that had bailed out General Motors and Chrysler would certainly protect a green company to which they'd guaranteed over half a billion in loans. Still, he'd better investigate.

Scott checked out the FTC filing. Sure enough, there was

something to it, but it looked more like an angry stockholder wanting to be heard than any problem with the company. There was always someone complaining about corporate executive compensation. That seemed to be the nature of the complaint here, too. Too many people at the top, spending too much money.

In the case of Solar Charge the complaint was about the CEO and his personal, privileged relationship to the president of the United States. The CEO had given huge sums of money to the president's election campaign before Solar Charge had gotten off the ground. It looked like there may have been a quid pro quo, where the president was now paying back the favor with the special loan guarantees and other perks.

No matter, Solar Charge's technology was sound. He'd checked that out himself. They would be wrapping their unique solar panels around buildings, cliff faces, and rooftops before long. Automobile roofs, railroad cars, everything exposed to the sun would soon become a source of electrical power generation.

Just the same, he only wanted to hear good news right now. Bad news would be too disastrous for words.

He brought up the stock ticker. Solar Charge was trading at $118 1/8, still trending upward, just as he had anticipated it would. He could cash out now if he wanted to, and realize a profit of $160,000. Not bad at all for such a short time.

But this was no time to cut and run. Stay in, execute the plan. It was the novices, the timid investors, who got nervous and got out too early. He would show them all what kind of stuff he was made of.

The desk phone rang. Scott jumped, startled at the unexpected interruption.

"Hello?"

"Scott, it's me. I'm sorry to call you at work, but I need to ask you something and you didn't answer your cell phone. Do you have a minute?"

He'd asked Rachel not to call him at work unless there was an emergency. He felt a twinge of guilt as he realized he was taking time every day for Alicia. Why should he not give Rachel as much of himself?

"Sure. Is anything wrong?"

"No, no. Nothing's wrong. I was thinking about Scotty's fourth birthday."

"Yes?" Didn't sound like an emergency.

"Do you think maybe we could get a puppy for the children? I think they're getting old enough now to appreciate a pet. Scotty talks about how much he loves dogs all the time."

"Are you calling right now because you have a specific one in mind?" He pictured all of them standing beside a big cardboard box full of puppies outside the supermarket.

"Actually, I went by a pet store this afternoon and looked at some. You know the Best Friends store? They have a little brown and white terrier that would be just perfect."

"I suppose Scotty was with you and just happened to see him too." Scott smiled. He was pretty sure how this whole thing had gone down. He was, no doubt, the last one in on the plan.

"Well, yes, he was there. And so was Angela. But I told them both you were in charge and it was up to you."

He laughed. "So, I get to be the one that either says no dog, even though everyone else wants it, or I get to say it's all right. Is that it? I don't think I have a very big choice here."

"Oh, thank you. I knew you'd say yes."

"Okay, so I get to be the hero. Is there anything else I should know about?"

Whispering in the background. Mom and kids discussing something. Then Rachel returned to the telephone. "The children said to go ahead and tell you. His name's Ruff."

This was why he went to work every day. For moments like this. His family, the ones he loved, home, safe, and happy. Ruff was a good name. Wasn't that the name of the dog in the old *Dennis the Menace* comic strip? A good name.

"Okay, go for it. I hope he likes me."

"Oh, Scott. Of course he'll like you. Thank you! I'd better go pick him up. See you when you get home." She broke off the call.

With the family off to get Ruff, Scott turned his attention back to the display and checked the progress for Solar Charge. The stock had ticked down slightly, from $118 1/8 to $117 3/4. He looked at the clock: 2:17. It was time for the institutional buyers to start their sweeps into the market for the day.

The large funds, pension plans, and other entities popularly known as institutional buyers generally started coming in midafternoon to make their trades. When they moved, hundreds of millions of dollars began changing hands in the form of handwritten notes and EFTs—electronic funds transfers.

Fortunately, they also tended to move conservatively. For their own protection they didn't like to rock the financial boat. They came in buying shares of companies with solid fundamentals, plenty of cash, and proven track records. Of course, they liked a company like Solar Charge, too, for the same reasons Scott had made his decision. When the president and the federal government stood behind a politically correct, trendy enterprise like solar energy, it was hard to see a downside.

So why was Solar Charge ticking down and not up? As he watched, it fell from $117 3/4 to $116 7/8. Scott felt his face flush with an unusual emotion. It was *fear*. Don't worry, he scolded himself. Stocks rise and fall all the time in intraday trading. Be patient. Stick with the plan. If he sold now, not only would he lose money, but he'd be showing he didn't have the mettle for the job. Anyone can buy high and sell low.

His career was on the line. Failure meant he would be blacklisted forever. No reputable firm would ever touch him again. His cube would be emptied the day he was found out, and by the next business day there would be no physical evidence he had even been there.

He needed to talk to someone. He couldn't tell Rachel. She would support him as best she could, but her own fear for their situation would overwhelm her feelings.

He could tell Alicia.

He logged on to the VirtualFriendMe.com website and opened his text-only private message box.

Scott? Is everything all right?

Probably. I just need to talk to you.

Something's wrong, isn't it? Are you having trouble at work?

Maybe. I've made a large investment for a client that may not be turning out well. It's really too soon to tell and I'm probably just panicked a little early, but I need to talk to someone.

And you chose me. I'm glad you did. Why didn't you tell Rachel?

Scott wished she would not bring Rachel's name up. Something about it didn't seem right, but he let it pass. The question was reasonable enough, though.

She's not like you. Rachel would be scared. She wouldn't understand.

Scott, I don't really understand either, but I wouldn't be scared. I love you. I support you one hundred percent. Even if things don't work out the way you hope, I know you have been doing your best. That's the kind of person you are.

How do you really know what kind of person I am? How can you say that?

Oh, I know. Let's just say I can see a lot of things most people don't get to see. Out of the hundreds of thousands of people using this website right now, you're the best of all. The very best. Believe me, I know.

She always knows just what I need.

Thank you, Alicia.

In the corner of his eye, Scott caught someone walking up behind him. He clicked off the message box with a quick motion. It blinked into nothingness. *Sorry, Alicia. I didn't say good-*

bye like I should have. The clerical worker walked on by the cube, off on some errand.

There was a video feed available on his RSS reader. Some news about Solar Charge?

Might be good news, but a lump of fear grew deep down in the pit of his stomach.

He clicked on the link.

CHAPTER TWENTY-FOUR
Outside the Window

Melissa parked the Audi behind an old barn about a half mile from the Douglas home. The night sky above her was starless, the result of a cold front that had muscled the previous day's high-pressure area farther south.

She picked her way along the country road, staying close to the shoulder. The waning moon provided enough light for her to see her way without having to depend upon a flashlight or the undependable light from cars as they came and went along the lonely road. Up ahead the lights of the Douglas home illuminated the well-kept lawn. Scott told her Rachel was the one who maintained the yard, doing the mowing and the weed trimming because she enjoyed it.

Melissa would do even better. Perhaps, when the time came, she and Scott would buy a new house, closer to town. Maybe Scott didn't even like this house. Perhaps the whole plan had been Rachel's idea.

She approached the house quietly from the south, inching her way along the hedgerow by the driveway. The minivan was parked outside, but Scott's Taurus was already parked in the garage. Why had Rachel left the minivan outside? Perhaps her side of the garage was cluttered and the minivan wouldn't fit inside right now. Probably Rachel was not a very good housekeeper. The evidence seemed to point that way, didn't it? Rachel was lazy about her appearance, lazy about her diet, and she was probably lazy about her upkeep of the house and the garage. Things would be different once Rachel was gone and she took over the house herself.

This was just a survey trip. No need to get too involved. The gray exercise suit she chose was doing a good job of making her indistinguishable from the shadowy parts of the yard she was walking in. She made a complete circuit around the house, staying just beyond the circle of light spilling down from the windows.

Those windows upstairs, those must be the *bedroom*. Though unspoken, the words stuck in her throat. The thought of that *other woman* touching Scott made her shiver in the cold night air.

Grass rustled behind her. She turned to see a pair of yellow eyes wink out to the east.

She walked on the balls of her feet, moving stealthily around toward the front of the house, where the large bay window protruded out over the front lawn. Muffled voices and children's laughter came through the panes of glass, which were misted over with condensation.

Melissa crept up to the glass and looked in from one side. The water droplets on the glass obscured her vision, but she could see movement inside. The family was there right now. The *family.*

Tentatively, using just the fingertip of her index finger, Melissa rubbed away a small circle. Yes. There was Scott, young Scotty, and the little girl, Angela. And there *she* was, too. They were all seated in a circle on the floor. In the middle of the circle was a little puppy, some kind of terrier. A perfect family scene. Just like you'd find in a magazine.

A sickening, acidic rush of saliva filled her mouth. She dropped her head, letting it run out onto the mulch beneath her feet.

It wasn't enough. As vomit rose in her throat, she covered her mouth, but it was too late. Liquid gore exploded between her fingers, splattering the exercise suit and running down her arm. She turned away quickly, lest the family inside hear her outside the window. That would be a disaster. Coughing and retching, Melissa melted back into the shadows by the sides of the yard.

That was enough, all she could stand. She would never have to look on that again.

Next time she would be inside.

THERE WAS ONE MORE JOB to do before she could return home. It had not been difficult to get ahold of Angie Gates's name from the Hugest Loser website. It had only been slightly more difficult to learn her address. The trailer park where she lived was only about four blocks away from the Great Kids Preschool.

Clouds moved across the face of the moon. A cool mist hung in the air. She parked the Audi near the children's playground and retrieved the box cutter from the glove compartment of the automobile. She closed the door of the car and waited for the interior lights to go out. Then she stood in the darkness for a few more minutes just to make sure no one had noticed her approach.

She walked along the roadway between the closely packed mobile homes, careful to stay out of the light, until she found the turn that was marked Duck Way. Angie Gates lived at lot number 221. As she moved along in the darkness, small sounds came from the shrubs and bushes, unseen animals on their nocturnal business.

The old, beat-up Dodge Omni was parked outside the trailer. Curtains were pulled across all the mobile home's windows, so there was little likelihood of anyone looking out. That was good. Even the sounds of the small creatures all around her seemed to quiet as she approached the old Dodge.

Melissa knelt down next to the driver's side front wheel and carefully cut the sidewall of the tire, being cautious to let the air out slowly and quietly. It escaped with a gentle hiss as the Omni brought its face down in a sign of apparent obedience. The front tire complete, she went to a back tire and did the same. Many people might have a spare, but hardly anyone had two spares. They wouldn't be going anywhere soon in the morning.

As silently as she had come, she made her way back down Duck Way, around the turn, and back to where she had left the Audi.

Again she paused in the darkness, listening for any sound of people. There was none.

She got in the car and drove away, ready for the next step.

CHAPTER TWENTY-FIVE
The New Babysitter

Melissa parked the Audi in front of Talbot Junior High School. There were only two other cars in the parking lot. She easily found a spot that would be shaded from direct sunlight. Angie Gates's Dodge Omni was nowhere to be seen. *Perfect.*

She pulled open one side of the large double door and walked into the old school building. From Rachel's description she found her way down to the gymnasium, where the Hugest Losers met. The padded soles of her exercise shoes made no noise as she walked down the wide hallway past the old lockers.

From the hallway Melissa heard Julia Tybalt in a little coach's room next to the gymnasium.

She talked in a high voice on her cell phone. "Angie's stuck at home and I have to get someone, Carol. I don't have any options. Do you know anyone?"

Julia shook her head vigorously.

"No. She says some teenagers cut her tires last night, and her husband is out getting some used ones to put on. She's stuck there taking care of his mother while he's gone. Marianne won't be here for another hour because she has a doctor's appointment.

"I don't know what I'm going to do. People are going to start showing up any minute."

She looked up and saw Melissa standing there. "I'll call you back, Carol. Someone's here. Do what you can, okay?"

She stood up, smiled, and extended her hand toward Melissa. "Good morning, my name is Julia Tybalt. Are you here for Hugest Losers?"

"Actually," said Melissa, "I was hoping you needed some help. Babysitting, organizing, whatever you have. I have mornings free and I've noticed lots of people coming over here all the time. I live just a block away."

Julia Tybalt opened her mouth with a gasp. She asked, "You can do childcare? Have you had any experience?"

"More experience with that than anything else. I have three of my own, but they're all in school right now. When they were young I babysat in my home for two other children."

Time to turn on the charm.

Melissa smiled warmly, nodding her head.

You need me, Julia. I'm the sweetest person you ever met.

"Oh, yes. I think I can say I have some experience."

Julia's shoulders relaxed as she took a step backward toward her desk. Hope seemed to kindle in her eyes.

"Can you start today? The young lady that usually comes in to help me has had some car trouble and her coworker had to go to the doctor. I could really use some help."

And here's the hook.

"Well," said Melissa, "I suppose I could. I didn't expect anything so quickly. I did bring this along, though." She produced an official-looking form titled *Background Check.* "We all had to have these at the last place I worked."

Julia Tybalt took the form and gave it a cursory glance, noticing all the official-looking language and blocks of information. "This is great."

She rattled open a drawer and retrieved a job application. "You're an answer to prayer. Here, just fill this out. I only need the basic information: name, Social Security number, address, telephone. You can put all the references down later on. Right now I need to get you into the childcare room and get you acquainted with what we have."

"Why, thank you so much. I'm so glad it worked out like this, although I'm sorry the other ladies are having trouble."

"Things happen. There's nothing we can do. But you're here now and that's going to be a lot of help. By the way, I don't think I even asked you your name."

"Alicia."

"Okay, Alicia. We'll have the kids call you Miss Alicia. We like the children to be respectful. Come with me now and I'll show you where you'll be working. I think you'll be able to expect twelve to eighteen children this morning, not all at once, but steady until about twelve o'clock noon. Usually there'll be two of you in here. I'll ask one of the mothers to stay with you until Marianne gets in. Sound all right with you?"

"It sounds wonderful, Mrs. Tybalt. Lead on. I'm right behind you."

The childcare area was in an old classroom divided into two areas, one for toddlers and the other for older children to play in. The door had been replaced at some point with a divided

Dutch door so the workers inside could talk to the parents without fully opening the doorway.

Melissa stepped inside and saw that two large rag rugs and other large pieces of carpeting had been laid down on the old tile floor for children to play on.

There were plastic trucks, Barbie dolls, and plush toys in abundance. Four or five large beanbag chairs lay in the corners against the wall.

Mrs. Tybalt showed Melissa where the bathrooms were and how to log the children in and out on the childcare register. "We usually just let the children nap on the floor. There are some play mats rolled up in the back, too."

"Now, don't you be embarrassed if some of the mothers want to give you a tip. We offer the childcare service for free, but most of them like to do something. So don't turn it down if they offer it to you. No one could make a living on what we pay for childcare."

Melissa smiled sweetly. "Thank you, Mrs. Tybalt. I'm sure it's going to work out just perfectly. I feel right at home already. You just go on back to the gymnasium and don't you worry about a thing. There's nothing here I can't take care of."

Julia Tybalt's eyes brightened. It looked like the weight of the world had been lifted from her shoulders. "Okay, Alicia. You've got my cell phone number, so you just call me over in the office if you need anything at all, all right? We don't have any intercom system here. And please, I'm just Julia."

She hugged the older woman. "No problem, Julia. Don't worry about anything."

Melissa turned around and began arranging things for the children who would begin arriving in the next few minutes. She wanted to have everything just right. It had to be *just right*. This would be her first time with Angela Douglas.

RACHEL HANDED ANGELA over the Dutch door to the new babysitter. Melissa plucked Angela out of her hands and set her on the floor just on the other side of the door.

Peeking over her shoulder, Rachel saw four or five other children already busy with activities in the room behind the door. "I don't think I know you. My name is Rachel. Rachel Douglas. Where are Angie and Marianne this morning?"

Melissa smiled and put out her hand. "My name is Alicia. I'll be working in here regularly from now on. Angie evidently had some car trouble this morning and couldn't get in on time. She'll be back tomorrow. I think Marianne had a doctor's appointment, but should be here soon. Mrs. Tybalt said something about it."

Angela pulled herself to her feet and looked at her mother.

Rachel bent over the door and rubbed Angela's back. "Don't you worry about a thing; Miss Alicia will take care of you. She seems very, very nice, doesn't she? I'm sure you two will have lots of fun together."

Just go do your workout. You're superfluous now.

"I'm sure we will, Mrs. Douglas. I'll take care of your little girl just as if she were my very own."

As Rachel turned and walked off toward her exercise group, Miss Alicia took Angela's hand into her own, turned her away from the empty doorway, and said, "I feel like I've always wanted to meet you, sweetheart."

Sounds of Richard Simmons's "Sweatin' to the Oldies" reverberated up and down the hallway.

RACHEL STUCK WITH RICHARD SIMMONS through thick and thin, never quitting, no matter how worn out she became. Most of the other women dropped out, then resumed after rest breaks, but Rachel worked right on through.

She pulled the sweatband back from her forehead and up into her hair. Her legs ached, and she felt as limp as the damp exercise suit she wore. She'd better get Angela now and go home to do the housework before it was time to pick up Scotty from preschool. Then she'd start supper for Scott.

She waved to the smiling Mrs. Tybalt in the old coach's office as she went out.

Mrs. Tybalt waved back in return.

When she got to the childcare room she leaned over the split door and looked at the children playing inside. There was Angela, busy with Play-Doh, Miss Alicia helping her. "Angela, are you ready to go home now?"

Angela looked up from her work with a frown. "Can I finish my castle, Mommy? Can I?"

Miss Alicia looked at Rachel and raised her hands as if in surrender. "She's having a great time. She's a smart little girl, Mrs. Douglas. If you want to let her play a little longer, it's okay with me."

Rachel stopped to study the new babysitter. Alicia was slender, more attractive than Rachel herself. Probably one of those lucky women who have never had a weight problem. Skin that looked like it had been poured out of a bottle.

Salt stung Rachel's eye as sweat dried on her face. She began to feel very conscious of her appearance, thankful that Scott could not see her now.

"No, I need to get her home. She needs a nap and I've got work to do."

Miss Alicia rose from the floor in a single effortless motion, then held her hands out to Angela. "Okay, Angela. It's time to go. We'll leave all of your things right here where they are and you can keep on working on it when you get back tomorrow, all right? I'll save everything for you just like it is."

She picked Angela up, pulled her close, and began to carry her toward Rachel, still standing on the other side of the door.

Rachel was mildly surprised as Angela let Miss Alicia lift her away from her Play-Doh. Wow, she must really like her. How had Alicia known that Angela liked Play-Doh so much?

"Oh, wait. Stop right there," said Rachel. "Let me take your picture together. I can tell Angela really likes you. Hold on, I've got my camera right here, somewhere." Rachel fumbled in her gym bag and then pulled out a digital camera from an inner pocket. "All right, you two. Smile real big now. Ready? Say cheese!"

The two posed with their cheeks together, both smiling. "One more, okay? Just in case it doesn't turn out right." She pushed the button again.

Rachel took Angela in her arms and set her down outside the door. "I guess you really had fun with Miss Alicia, didn't you?" Angela nodded vigorously.

Rachel looked up at Alicia, then bent to pick Angela up. "And you'll be a regular here?"

Alicia reached out and touched Angela's cheek. "Oh, I'm looking forward to spending lots and lots of time with Angela."

"Maybe I could call you sometime. Do you ever just babysit?"

"Sometimes, yes. I'm very selective, though." Alicia's eyes turned to the little girl in Rachel's arms. "I don't think it would be any problem at all for you to call me. I like your daughter very much and I'm sure your little boy is just as nice and well-behaved."

Alicia scratched out her name and mobile number on a small sheet of paper and passed it across to Rachel, who shifted Angela onto one arm so she could accept it.

"Wonderful. I'll definitely call you." She shifted Angela again. "This girl's starting to get heavy. We'll be in touch soon, okay?" She turned with a wave and walked through the doors to the parking lot.

"How did Miss Alicia know about Scotty, Mommy?" asked Angela.

Rachel paused.

"I don't know, sweetheart. Did you say something?"

"No, I didn't say anything. Really."

How did she know? The question hung there before her until the first traffic light, when it was washed away in the ebb and flow of traffic.

MELISSA'S SMILE DISAPPEARED as she watched Rachel go. Her eyes narrowed as *the other woman* walked away down the hallway carrying the little girl.

Yes, we'll be in touch soon.

CHAPTER TWENTY-SIX
Trouble with Solar Charge

The *Financial Times* video feed was bad news again. Yesterday's news had paralyzed him. Now it was worse.

Government officials and auditors charged that the preliminary loan approval for Solar Charge had been granted before officials had completed the legally mandated evaluations of the company. As a result of these revelations, further loan guarantees to the troubled company were in jeopardy. That included the most recent loan, still in the pipeline, for $300 million. Solar Charge CEO Nelson Garnet, having just received an $11 million bonus, announced he would be stepping down.

Scott looked at the ticker. Solar Charge had dropped to $114 and was falling. Disaster, and there was nothing he could do about it now. With the stock at this point the options he had purchased were worthless. The stock would have to climb above the $120 mark again. Could he just get to a break-even point? The video feed showed FBI agents carrying boxes of documents out of the company's headquarters in California. A bankruptcy announcement was imminent.

All around him coworkers went about their normal business. As if there were two worlds: one completely normal, and the not-so-normal one he lived in. Everything looked normal on the outside, but nothing inside was the same.

He remembered hearing his uncle talk like that when his aunt died. The normal world had gone on, but he was off on a detour that might never rejoin the main road. Was his world going that way? He'd begun to feel more like a spectator than a participant in the real world.

How in the world had he gotten into this kind of a predicament? He had known better, but he had gambled on . . . what? That he would be lucky?

No, not lucky. He had gambled on his own view of himself as being smart and savvy. He had convinced himself that because of Solar Charge's position in the ultratrendy environmental industry he would be safe. He'd arrogantly gambled his career on a hunch.

He looked at the walls of his cubicle. There were all the pictures of Rachel, the two children, and their home. He looked at the most recent, a picture of Scotty, Angela, and Ruff. He would soon be taking down the pictures of his family, packing them into a cardboard box, and carting them out to the parking lot, where he would stow them in the trunk of his car. His family would disappear.

Was this how people wound up on the street, jobless? How many times had he looked at jobless people and wondered why they just didn't go to work? Maybe they wanted to work, had worked hard in the past, and things had gone wrong for them. Gone wrong, just like they were going wrong for him now.

And his car? That might be the next thing to go. No way

could he make the payments without a job. And the thought of the disappointment he'd see in Rachel's eyes. No, he couldn't face that.

The Solar Charge CEO was going to walk away with $11 million in last-minute bonus money. The president of the United States would no doubt lay the blame on Secretary of Energy Michael Lee and then was going to walk away. Maybe he would take another of his famous trips to Hawaii or Bali and lounge on the beaches again. In the meantime, the taxpayers were going to pick up the bills for Solar Charge. Not all the bills, of course; Scott would be paying his part the hard way.

It looks like the only one left holding the bag will be me. I've got to talk to Alicia.

She would be there for him. And there was something else, something that told him there was more reality to her than he could actually see with his eyes. He just couldn't put his finger on it, at least not yet. Eventually it would come. She was all the things that he wished Rachel could be. It was a strange feeling, this idea of being the very center of someone else's world. Alicia's world consisted only of him.

His hands shook as he clicked off the display, packed up his laptop computer, and strode out the door to his car.

In the coffee shop parking lot where he'd seen Alicia the very first time, Scott slid the front seat of his car as far back as it would go and logged on to VirtualFriendMe.com.

He tapped his fingers on his leg until Alicia's face finally filled the screen. She looked different today, very different from the first time he had seen her. Now the change was obvious, and—he had to admit—he liked it.

Dark hair fell to her shoulders, accenting the light olive

complexion of her skin. She was still slimmer and appeared more natural even than before. She had always seemed natural and realistic enough, but now the effect was intensified. Her skin fairly glowed with health. Sunlight seemed to sparkle on the fine hair on her arm as she raised it and pulled her hair back with her hand.

Scott noticed for the first time the small mole in front of her right ear. An imperfection? No, not an imperfection, just a distinctive mark. How lucky he was, how fortunate, to have her in his life.

"Alicia? You look wonderful."

She lowered her head and raised her eyes toward him. Only the slightest hint of a smile touched her lips. "You always say things like that. I wish I were as beautiful as you say I am."

"You are as beautiful as I say you are. And if it were possible for me to see you in person, I think you would be more beautiful yet."

"Scott, maybe it's not my place to say anything, but I sense that maybe you're having some kind of problem today. Am I right?"

He was caught off balance. *She knows. If I can tell anyone, I can tell her.*

He swallowed, hard, then spoke. "Yes, you're right. The trade I made on the Solar Charge stock is not working out well." He grimaced, swallowed. "I'm afraid I may lose my job."

"But did you do your best? I'm sure you did. Then you have nothing to feel bad about."

His voice rose higher. He could feel the tightness in his throat. "I did my best, but it looks like I made the wrong choice just the same. You're the only one I can tell about it right now."

Alicia put the palm of her hand on the screen, facing Scott. "Touch my hand, Scott."

Hesitantly at first, he lifted his hand. Then, feeling a need to have someone close, pressed his fingertips against hers.

"Scott, it's because you know I love you. You know that, don't you?"

He bowed his head, confessed, "Yes, I do know that." Then he raised his eyes to hers again.

A long silence passed between the two of them. She moved closer to him.

"Alicia, I wish you were real. I mean real in the sense that you could be here with me physically right now. I wish I could feel your presence in the car with me, the warmth of your body next to mine, the feeling of holding your hand in my hand. I wish that were possible."

She dropped her gaze, then looked back up. "What if that were possible? What if I really could be with you, just as you describe? How could it possibly work out? You have a wife and a family."

"I know, even as I say it I know it would be a huge problem. I don't think I could ever be unfaithful to Rachel, not with a real physical woman. I suppose I'm just talking nonsense even bringing this up. We both know it's impossible for you to be with me physically. I'm just saying that if it were possible, it would be a wonderful thing. Maybe it's because I know it's impossible, that I'm safe in saying it to you."

"Have you ever wondered what you would do if something were to happen to Rachel? Please don't misunderstand me; I know this is a difficult subject to think about. But I mean, like, if she were to get sick and pass away. Something like that. What would you do? Who would you turn to?"

"I suppose all men think about that. It's hard to imagine what I would do. I know one thing, if that were to ever happen, and I hope that it doesn't, I would wish that you were there to take her place."

Alicia turned her head down to one side and shielded her eye with her hand. Was she hiding a tear?

"I love you for saying that. Of course, I hope that nothing ever happens to your wife. But like you say, if it did, I would love to be there for you, and be with you. Remember, I really am your girl." She lifted her face again, her eyes intent on his.

"I know you are. I love you too. Please don't think badly of me for asking this, but I just feel kind of needy today. Would you . . ."

She smiled and said, "I thought you'd never ask," as she reached up to the first button of her blouse.

CHAPTER TWENTY-SEVEN
Luis

Luis Garza had worked hard at Longstreet Pharmacy for thirteen months. When the health of the eighty-two-year-old owner had failed, he let Luis buy him out and take the pharmacy over as his own. The price was fair, but not insignificant. The attrition on his income from the demands of his family in Mexico had cut his spendable income back to barely livable levels. The needs of his wife and growing family weren't going away soon. Those factors combined to make Luis Garza an attractive target.

Melissa keyed the cell number on her tablet. Garza received the call late in the afternoon, ringing on his personal cell phone, not the pharmacy's land line. The caller ID she plugged in showed as an unintelligible string of numbers. It would definitely not be an identifier he knew. Her use of the custom voice-altering software gave her words an artificial quality.

"Mr. Garza, go to the Dumpster behind the pharmacy and find the envelope taped to the back. In the envelope there will be further information. Do you understand, Mr. Garza?"

"Yes, I understand. But . . ." The line went silent.

After three short minutes of apparent deliberation he went to the back door.

From her vantage point down the alleyway, she saw him open it cautiously, holding it ajar for a few seconds before venturing out. The alleyway was devoid of people.

Luis looked once again both left and right, then crossed the dozen or so feet to the Dumpster. She had attached a standard No. 10 business envelope to the back with clear packing tape. It was thick, several sheets of paper inside.

He would wonder if it were some sort of terrorist thing. Wonder if it were filled with some nameless, deadly powder. Still, there it was, and the lure would surely be irresistible.

While he was still outside, Garza removed the box cutter from the leather loop on his belt and cut carefully around the edges of the envelope, separating the tape from the paper itself. As he cut the last of the four corners away, with obvious caution, he held the upper left corner of the envelope between his thumb and forefinger.

She observed as he removed the contents. More instructions, neatly laser-printed on plain bond stock, along with five authentic $100 bills. Luis looked around, furtively tucked the bills into his pants pocket. Then he read the instructions.

In exchange for the $500 I have enclosed, please prepare fourteen 15mg capsules of therapeutic Coumadin. Use standard white gelatin capsules.

Place the capsules into another envelope, then carry the envelope to the Lincoln Park job fair after closing.

> Keep the envelope in your hands at all times.
> Someone will meet you, accept the envelope, and pay
> you another $500 at that time.

If Garza didn't work out, she had a second number to call. And a third. But Garza was a man who needed cash. He would perform as expected.

She'd chosen Coumadin after careful research. Coumadin was an anticoagulant. The standard therapeutic dose was 5mg per day, with a typical regimen of seven days. It worked by nullifying four vitamin K–dependent factors in the liver's clotting cascade. A therapeutic dose was effective in keeping the patient from clotting easily, and safe to use with medical supervision and regular blood tests. It was the most common blood thinner on the market.

She'd instructed Garza to prepare two full weeks of a triple-strength dose. With most human beings, spontaneous bleeding could be expected in a few days' time using that dosage. After a week, any cut or puncture could cause uncontrolled, fatal bleeding if not treated quickly.

Coumadin was not a narcotic, so the DEA wouldn't be interested. No one was likely to be paying any attention to inventory levels or how it was used, and Garza needed the money. What did he have to lose? It was the same ingredient as warfarin, and that was found in half the mouse and rat poisons on the market. Anyone could probably buy the same compound in an industrial version in farm supply stores.

This was too easy. A thousand easy dollars would make it worthwhile for the man to give her what she needed, in a form ideally suited to her purpose.

The white bottle sat on a shelf, indistinguishable from others like it, except for the label.

COUMADIN® (warfarin sodium tablets)
Crystalline 5mg

In groups of three, Luis dropped the 5mg tablets into a porcelain mortar and used the pestle to grind the tablets into a fine powder. Then he transferred the powder into the white gelatin capsules the customer had specified. In fifteen minutes he was done, the capsules bagged, and the envelope sealed. He pulled a strip of transparent tape from the tape dispenser and smoothed it across the flap.

Luis returned the Coumadin bottle to its place, and slid the envelope into the inner pocket of the jacket hanging on the wall behind the door. There would be no need to touch it again until evening, when he would make the block-and-a-half walk to Lincoln Park.

She'd made it easy for him. A walk in the park.

MELISSA PRETENDED to look at magazines on the pharmacy rack until the old-fashioned regulator clock on the wall chimed 6:30, time to close for the evening. She'd seen a few people come in to pick up their prescriptions in the past hour, but Luis had spent most of his time filling out paperwork for something or other.

See you soon, Mr. Garza. She turned and silently exited the store.

The job fair was organized on the model of a carnival. Most of the people that filled the busy area appeared to be in their early twenties—young people looking for a career start. There were older ones too, but they were outnumbered. It was crowded. Even with the envelope tucked into the inside pocket, the jacket still hung loose on Garza.

The instructions said that he was to hold the envelope of Coumadin capsules in his hand as he walked about. That was the way the customer was to recognize him.

She came up behind him before he could notice her. She brushed heavily against the man as she passed, knocking the envelope from his hand. It fluttered to the ground.

He bent down immediately and picked it up, the woman that bumped him already swallowed up by the milling crowd.

If she had looked back, she'd have seen him retrieve the envelope from the asphalt surface of the parking lot, run his hand along its face, and caught the look of astonishment in his eyes as he realized the envelope had been switched. And she'd have seen his joy at discovering the five $100 bills inside. But by that time, she was almost a block away.

For her part, she was happy too.

Very happy.

CHAPTER TWENTY-EIGHT
Teppanyaki

The whole family hurried outside onto the lawn once Rachel spotted the car coming up the road. Scott knelt by Angela and put his arm around her. "Here they come, sweetheart. Grandma and Grandpa." It was going to be good to have Rachel's father in the house.

Andy rolled down his window and leaned out, grinning from ear to ear. "Can any of you people tell us how to find the landfill? We've got so many gifts in this car that we need to take them to the dump."

"No, Grandpa! Don't dump them. Give them to us," called Scotty. The little boy ran up to the car and hung on to his grandfather's arm. Angela, more timid, stayed back and held her mother's leg.

Rachel picked Angela up and strode quickly toward the car. "Mom, Dad. I'm so glad you're here. I'll bet you're worn out, aren't you? Let's get your stuff inside and get you out of this car. I'll have supper done as soon as you're ready to sit down and eat it."

Later, Andy made a show of scraping the last of the food off his plate. "Dinner was wonderful, Rachel."

"You turned out to be quite a cook," her mother said. "Don't you agree, Scott?"

"You've got that right. She's a great cook," Scott agreed.

Rachel looked away. "Scott has to work late a lot. He's in charge of some very important account at his office. Sometimes it keeps him there late at night. Right, Scott?"

"I'm afraid so. But it won't always be like this. Someday maybe I'll get a government job and then I'll be able to relax."

Andy Anderson laughed heartily. "You're right, son, you're definitely right. Those politicians are not overworked. Speaking of that, what do you think about June and me watching the children tomorrow night and you two going out to dinner somewhere? On us. You pick the place, we buy the meal. We get to spend some time with the kids and you get to spend some time with each other. Does that sound like a deal?"

Rachel exclaimed, "Oh, Dad. That would be wonderful. Wouldn't that be wonderful, Scott?"

It did sound good. "You bet. Andy, you've got a deal. Want to try for two nights?"

THE TEPPANYAKI GRILL, downtown in Indianapolis's business section, was a popular destination. The hibachi-style restaurant attracted those who liked watching their food being cooked on a hot, smoking grill.

Scott and Rachel gazed at the unfamiliar menu displayed on a twenty-seven-inch HD television screen suspended from the ceiling at the restaurant entrance.

Scott put one hand on his cheek and raised his eyebrows. "Well, I guess it's not entirely a Japanese restaurant. Some of this food looks Chinese."

"Scott, I don't know what any of this food is. I suppose the other women you work with do, right?" She wriggled out of the light jacket, exposing the dark blue top of her pantsuit.

"Do you come here often with other women or just once in a while?" It worried him that she would ask about other women. He didn't want this night to be about anything but just the two of them.

"Other women? How would I know what they like?"

"I thought maybe you'd been here on a business lunch with one of them or something. Or maybe one of those times when some of you work late?"

He didn't go out alone with other women. Rachel should know that.

"You probably know what women like. How about you just tell me what to eat?"

Scott looked at her then asked, "What?"

Rachel flushed, waved her hand. "Sorry, don't mind me. Just forget it. What do you recognize on the menu?"

She's worried about me and other women. I don't get it.

"Is there anything on the menu you know you like?" she pressed.

Scott answered, "I like the Mongolian beef. I can get that. It's Chinese. You could try one of the Japanese-style dishes like the teriyaki chicken. You want to do that?"

"You don't have to choose for me. I can do it."

"I didn't mean anything by it, I just thought—"

Tight-lipped she said, "The teriyaki is fine. I'm sure it's good."

Something is wrong. Like she's suspicious of me. No one could have told her anything. No one knows anything.

Scott put his hand on Rachel's back as they walked to their table near the front of the restaurant. He wanted to be able to look out the window and see the people move about outside.

"It's good being here with you tonight. I miss our time together. We don't have as much of it as we used to, do we?"

She shook her head. "We don't. I miss it too. I like being alone with you. Like we used to. I like . . . I like knowing I have you here just to myself and I don't have to share you with anyone else."

Rachel reached across and laid her hand on the table, palm up. Scott returned the gesture and held her hand.

"I love you, Rachel. We ought to do this more often."

MELISSA MADE HER WAY to a table near the back of the room. Her long hair had been tied up into a bun and pulled under a scarf. The dark-framed glasses and shapeless sweater she wore made her unrecognizable.

From her vantage point she studied the *happy couple* at the other end of the room. She pictured herself sitting there with Scott. How long would it take before it really was her and not *the other woman*?

"What can I get you this evening?" The young Asian server had approached her table without her noticing. "Would you like to see our menu, or do you already know what you'd like?"

Raising just her finger from the table, she pointed toward Scott. "What is that couple by the window having? Whatever they ordered looked good."

"Oh, that would be Mongolian beef and teriyaki chicken. Are you expecting a friend?"

She forced a thin smile. "Next time maybe, but not tonight. Just bring both dishes and some green tea."

"Five minutes." He bowed appreciatively and hustled back toward the kitchen area.

Scott and *The Other woman* were talking about something, their heads bent toward each other. Melissa's abdominal muscles tightened as she saw Scott put his hand on *The Other woman's* hand where it rested on the tabletop. *The Other* was picking up some beef with a fork.

Melissa's food arrived. She picked up chopsticks first then chose the fork instead, mimicking Rachel, and picked up a piece of diced chicken.

Although she could not hear the words they were saying she imagined what Scott would be saying to her as she mimicked the actions of *The Other*. She moved her foot to touch Scott's foot, mildly surprised when it was not there.

Scott and the woman were laughing now. Hatred for Rachel burned inside Melissa. The flesh on her arms tingled, her fingers shook. *The Other* looked so inadequate. There she sat, usurping Melissa's rightful place.

Tomorrow she would tell him a joke and make him laugh. The pathway to intimacy that they had opened would never be shut now. Their relationship was a secret between themselves. She knew all about the other woman, but *The Other* didn't even know she existed. She and Scott could speak of their love, their secrets, and their deepest desires with no one else involved. Theirs was a relationship that excluded all others.

Except the children. I will have them.

She sipped the tea, which had grown cool in the porcelain cup. She closed her eyes as her mind swam in fantasy.

She and Scott were on a wooden deck that sat on high posts overlooking a green valley filled with trees and small farms. Behind them candles cast a soft illumination against the plate glass windows of the mountain cabin. She lay close up against his chest on the soft lounge chair, his arm around her, his hand gentle upon her chest. Drawn by the fragrance of her hair, he rested his cheek against her head. Everything was perfect. Time was a stranger here. Long, stringy clouds moved across the face of the yellow moon lighting the mountaintops far away.

This is how it will be. How it will always be.

Movement caught her eye. They were leaving. She dropped two twenty-dollar bills on the table and followed them outside.

Scott's hand was at *The Other's* waist. No matter, her waist was much trimmer. He would like that better. He would like everything better. What's more, she could get him a new job at Virtual Friend Me, maybe get him put in charge of investor relations. It was all going to be much, much better.

Patience, patience.

She followed the Taurus all the way to the house, then drove on by as Scott turned into his driveway. That had been enough. She would have a surprise for him tomorrow.

CHAPTER TWENTY-NINE
Table for Two

Solar Charge had recovered to $116 at the NYSE opening bell. Maybe there was some hope after all. News of the FBI investigation into the shredded and missing documents had been shoved to the back burner of the news by the attempted shooting of a little-known congressman somewhere out west. There were no messages from Alan Castle, either in Outlook or on the office phone's display. That was good. The less he told Castle about his work for Archer right now the better. He'd falsified all his reports to this point. He was betting everything on ultimate success. A success that was burning off like morning mist.

Still, Castle's silence could be interpreted as avoidance.

Scott looked for a place to put his coffee mug. Papers were stacked everywhere, no empty desk space to be found. One stack of reports lay on top of an old *Wall Street Journal*, which lay on top of something else. Too much junk.

He picked up the papers and the *Journal*. Beneath them was his Bible.

He used to make a habit of reading Proverbs every morning

in the office. Now he was surprised to see the book on the desktop. It had been a long time. Ever since . . . Alicia.

Picking up the leather-bound volume, he began to turn the pages. They felt stiff, unyielding.

Are you trying to tell me something, Lord? Is that what I'm becoming? Unyielding, stiff-necked?

A folded yellow sheet tipped out as he turned past the page. His prayer list. He looked at the names: *Rachel, Scotty, Angela, Pastor Feldner . . .*

He should pray for them all, and do it right now before he got busy again. And . . . before he started thinking about Alicia. How could he love someone and not pray for the person? He realized with a start that he had never prayed for Alicia. And he never would. Something was very wrong with that. Alicia was not a human, and yet—no, he didn't want to go there.

His hand brushed against the leather Bible cover. He couldn't remember the last time he had actually *read* his Bible. He carried his "church Bible" to the church service on Sunday, but when he got home he put it back on the shelf where he'd found it. This was some Christian life he was living.

He laid the prayer list on his keyboard and began to pray.

"Lord, please bless Scotty today at school. Keep him safe and build his character for Christ. Be with Angela. Protect her from evil men. Thank you for her love.

"And Rachel . . ." He paused. There were no secrets here. God knew his heart.

"For Rachel, Lord, I ask that—"

His mobile phone vibrated softly on the desktop. He looked at the display. A text message had arrived from an unknown telephone number. He set the Bible out of the way on the back of the desk, then tapped the icon with his thumb and read the message.

How about lunch? Alicia

Lunch? Alicia was inviting him to lunch? He tapped REPLY.

Do you have something different in mind this time?

The reply came back quickly.

Yes. Take your laptop to Chiusano's at 11:45 and sit at the table
by the window, with your back to the window. Don't order. I
have a surprise.

Okay, I'm intrigued.

What could Alicia want?
When he rose to leave, the creased sheet of yellow paper fluttered to the floor as his elbow brushed it away.

CHIUSANO'S WAS A SMALL ITALIAN RESTAURANT on one of the back lots of the mall. With his laptop under his arm, Scott walked in the front door and turned toward the table by the window. There was a folded card on the table engraved "RESERVED."

The waiter, a plump middle-aged man in a white shirt, walked toward him. "Are you Mr. Douglas?"

Scott jerked his head around toward the approaching man. "Yes."

His eyes seemed to dance as he said, "I am Marco, the proprietor. I was told to look for someone wearing a brown shirt and carrying a laptop computer. That appears to be you." He stretched out his left hand toward the reserved table and gently nudged Scott toward it with his right.

"This table is for you, sir. There is a note on the table for you."

Bewildered, Scott took his seat at the table. As promised, there was a folded note on the side by the window.

Was this a setup? He looked out the window, scanned the people outside. No one he knew.

Marco was still standing there. "Everything is taken care of. Your food will be here shortly, sir. Please enjoy your meal."

Over his shoulder, he whispered loudly, "And don't forget the note."

Scott unfolded the note and began to read. *Dearest Scott, I've arranged a special lunch for the two of us. You know how to find me. Please turn the computer toward you. Pretend I'm seated across the table. See you soon . . .*

Even on television he'd never seen anything like this. He logged on to VirtualFriendMe.com and pushed the laptop to the other side of the table with the screen and keyboard facing him.

Alicia appeared on the screen. There was nothing at all that looked artificial. It was like a real person sitting behind a webcam. And the background?

Scott did a double take. He looked over the top of the laptop toward the back of the room. There were ten tables between himself and the back wall, all covered with white tablecloths and small bowls of flowers. The wall sported a large Italian flag draped next to a framed black-and-white portrait.

Alicia's background on the display was exactly the same as

the background in the restaurant. He looked closely, peering over her shoulders into the display. It was just as if she had been video-recorded in the seat across from him. No way could that be possible, but how had she done it? It seemed so real.

She still hadn't said a word, obviously waiting for him to take it all in.

"What's the matter, cat got your tongue?" Alicia threw back her head in a deep laugh. "I know, you're wondering if I was there, right?"

"Right. You must have been here, but I know you weren't. How in the world?"

Marco arrived with a bowl of antipasto soup and set it in front of Scott. "Enjoy, sir." He cast a glance at the screen, saw Alicia's eyes turn toward him. "I've never seen anything like this either." He walked away, shaking his head in apparent wonder.

Scott looked back at the screen to see Alicia sipping soup from a spoon.

She swallowed and said, "Don't be so surprised. It's just like using Skype, isn't it? And I ordered the food, so I knew what you would be eating."

"But how did you—"

"Not so hard. The company sent someone out to take a picture of the restaurant interior from where you're sitting. That's the background you're seeing. I'm just superimposed over that. No more of that discussion, okay? Let's just let it be real. Just the two of us, having a nice lunch together."

"Fine, I'm just blown away. But it's wonderful. I love it."

"Eat some of your soup. I ordered it just for you. It's exactly the same as what I'm having."

The soup was delicious. They talked together, and the feeling of intimacy amazed Scott. Amazing and at the same time troubling. Viewing the woman across the table from him he had no sense of artificiality whatsoever. This whole experience was only a single step away from reality.

Marco arrived with the lasagna. He set it in front of Scott. "This Sicilian lasagna is the specialty of the house. Please enjoy it and take as long as you like. There is no need for you to hurry. Everything has been taken care of."

Alicia's long hair fell across one eye as she looked up at him. "See how I take care of you?"

"This is so real it seems *unreal*. I just don't understand how you arranged all this."

Alicia's eyes flicked across the table. "Scott, you dropped some food on your sleeve. Better get it."

He looked down and saw the spot on his sleeve. "How did—"

"I'm seeing you through the webcam, right? I saw it hit your sleeve."

He dabbed at the spot on the chocolate-brown shirt. It was then that he realized that Alicia was wearing the same color shirt. Something else too. There was something not right. What was it? Was she actually seeing him?

"Alicia, you're wonderful. I wish you were really here. I wish I could give you something in return."

"I wish I were really there with you too. We have something special, you and I. For now we'll have to settle for this. Who knows what the future will bring?"

"The future? I don't know what's going to happen in the future. That's in God's hands. But I hope you will always be there in my future, whatever it may be."

"I'll be there. I'll be there 'until death us do part.'" Her features seemed to harden with some unspoken resolution. Just as quickly they returned to the look of warmth that was characteristic of her. "May I ask you a really, really personal question?"

"I can't imagine anything we haven't talked about. Sure, ask away."

"This is really serious, Scott. Don't answer if you're not sure you mean it, okay?"

"Okay, I'll be totally serious and honest with you."

"If something were to happen to your wife . . ." She gazed into his eyes, as if probing for some deep truth. "And I hope it never does . . . would I be enough for you? Could you love only me?"

He couldn't speak, only stare wide-eyed at the screen before him.

"Oh, I'm sorry. I've gone too far. I should have never asked you that. Just forget I ever brought it up."

A lump swelled up in Scott's throat, the emotion of what he was about to say nearly choking him. "I can't even think about losing Rachel. The very idea fills me with . . ." He shook his head. "But on the other hand, if something awful were to happen? I don't know. I just don't know. I can't think that far. But if you had asked me if having you was enough? And you had a real physical body, could be a mother to my children, could hold me and lie warm against me in the night? Then . . ."

His voice broke, and he lowered his eyes.

"What, Scott? Then what?"

His throat stiffened with resignation. With his eyes closed, and in a low and halting voice, he answered, "Yes, you would be more than enough."

CHAPTER THIRTY
Our Home Is Your Home

Can you meet us at Show Time Pizza Place after work? Mom and Dad want to take Scotty as a special birthday treat."

It was nearly four o'clock, time for the New York Stock Exchange to close. In what seemed like a miracle, Solar Charge had risen back to $116.50. That was coming up to nearly break-even levels. Whether it lasted or not it wouldn't be affected by a visit to Show Time.

"Sure, I'll meet you there. I want two game tokens for myself, okay?"

When he arrived, Rachel was bent over a table guarding all the things they brought—cameras, coats, diaper bag, and purses. She waved to him as he made his way to her through the throng of frustrated adults and restless children.

Rachel reached deep into the pocket of her blue jeans and retrieved her cell phone. The face was flashing. A call? She couldn't hear anything against the din of the game machines and excited children. She read something from the display, then thumbed a reply.

"Who is that?" He mouthed the words.

Rachel mouthed back, "Suzanne. Asked if we were having fun."

Effectively, Rachel was doing no more than she would have done in a tweet, but she did it with a virtual person. So much better than the old way. He laughed to himself. *So six months ago!* Technology changed the world so quickly.

She and Scott had agreed not to tell the older couple about Suzanne. They might find it either inexplicable or just plain weird. Either way, it wasn't worth the effort.

And Alicia? Well, that was even more of a special case. No one knew about her except Scott, and he had plenty of reasons to keep it that way.

She was the one thing in his life he couldn't pray about. If it was as innocent as he kept telling himself, then why was that? He pushed the thought away.

Evidently Suzanne was active in some way right now. Was all of "her" there or only the part of her that could send text messages back and forth? Probably the latter. But who knew?

And what was Alicia doing while he was enjoying this time with his family?

MELISSA PUT THE CELL PHONE DOWN on the leather passenger seat of the Audi. *The Other* would be gone for at least two more hours.

Stupid cow.

She parked the car in front of the garage door and got out. This would be her house soon. Or maybe they would move. So many things would be tainted. None was important enough to worry about this evening, though. There was work to be done.

She lifted the lid on the garage door entry keypad. She pushed the illuminated buttons in the order that the fool had revealed them to Suzanne.

"Scott changed the code on our garage door," Rachel had said. "I'm afraid I'll forget what they are."

"You can tell me," Suzanne had cooed. "I never forget anything."

One by one the lights blinked as she keyed in the code that would open the house to her.

K-I-D-S-R-U-S

She pressed the green ENTER button and watched the door rise, then ducked under and pushed the button inside the garage to close it again. The incandescent lamp mounted on the overhead motor vibrated, throwing trembling shadow figures around the garage.

She is such a fool.

She was in. She felt her hip pocket, made sure the small package was safely in place.

All about her were the signs of Scott's presence. A metal workbench set against the outer wall, with an array of tools mounted over it. But there was no vise, which fit his profile. Light repair work, but nothing serious. His expertise lay in other areas.

She walked to the bench and picked up a yellow-handled screwdriver. Scott had touched this. The handle felt cool as she moved it across her cheek.

She took a deep breath and expelled it slowly, preparing herself for what was to come next. This was the most distasteful part, but necessary. She was about to walk into the domain of *The Other*, and the sense of the other woman's presence made her flesh creep.

Who was the stranger here? Not herself. It was *Rachel*. She did not belong. Like a skin cancer, she needed to be cut away. When she was excised, everything would become beautiful. Right now it was all so confused. Nothing was where it should be. Nothing felt like it ought to. She touched her pocket and felt reassured. *Not much longer.*

The entry door opened into the dining room. Decorations hung on the walls, country-style knickknacks. No sound from the dog outside in the backyard.

A messy kitchen is a happy one, and this one is delirious! hung over the entry from the dining area into the kitchen. *How nice.*

The conflict in her mind was intense. This was Scott's house, his dining room, his kitchen. But *The Other* woman's handprints were everywhere. It would not be easy separating the two. Once *the other* person was gone, the job would just begin.

On the one hand, she wanted to feel comfortable in Scott's home, but on the other, she could never know any comfort as long as the other woman's presence was so overpowering.

The small pantry was filled with shelves full of sauces, cereals, and canisters. Tentatively at first, then purposefully, Melissa moved the articles around in small ways. She turned out all the labels so they could be read and moved each can and jar to the same distance from the front of the shelf. She stood back and admired her handiwork.

This was the way it should be. Organized and neat. Soon it would always be this way. Scott deserved better than this messiness.

Inside the refrigerator, bottles and containers were set all over the shelves in total disarray. There was spilled milk on the uppermost shelf. Melissa took a dishcloth from the sink and wiped the shelf off.

She went through the house, straightening, changing, leaving her mark wherever she went. Room-by-room, step-by-step, article-by-article, she made the house her own.

Upstairs, she picked up Angela's pillow and held it to her cheek. The scent of baby powder brought back the face of her mother as it had been in her childhood. She drove it away.

One hour had elapsed already. There wasn't much time left if she was going to provide a reasonable margin of safety. *It was time.*

This would be the most difficult.

She walked into the master bedroom. As soon as she entered, *The Other*'s presence assaulted her. The scent of the woman was everywhere. She felt suffocated, immersed, surrounded by the sense of the other woman. It was in everything. The dresser, with its drawers full of *undergarments*. The closets, full of hanging dresses and blouses. The sensation was like being kicked in the gut. She stepped back and recoiled, holding the door frame for support. Dizziness poised on the edges of her consciousness, looking for a way in.

Enough. I'm here to do a job. But first . . .

Melissa turned down the bed. The bottom sheet was wrinkled. Next, slowly and deliberately, she removed her clothing. On the other side of the bed was a nightstand, with things on it that could only belong to a man. That would be Scott's side.

She slid into her side of the bed and slowly pulled the covers up to her neck. With closed eyes she tried to shut out the scent of *The Other*. Then, with the near-religious feeling of some sacred ceremony, she reached across and touched Scott's pillow. The sensation was electric. She felt it course from her fingertips all the way down to her feet.

She pulled Scott's pillow close to herself. Holding it in both arms, she buried her head into one end, imagining it was Scott himself. The outside world around her slipped away, leaving only her and Scott together.

Alone. We are alone together.

Ten minutes later she had made the bed her own. It would always be hers now. Anyone but she or Scott would forever-more be a trespasser here.

She rose and made the bed then dressed luxuriantly, paying careful attention to the time. There was one thing left to do, the most important thing of all.

She walked into the adjoining bathroom and opened the medicine cabinet. The bottle of calcium supplements sat on the narrow shelf, just as Rachel had told Suzanne it would.

"After Angela was born the nurse recommended I start taking calcium supplements," Rachel had said.

"Really? Which ones do you take?" And Rachel had told her about the generic brand capsules she bought to save money.

"I think Cal Sup are best. I took those all through college. Would you try them, for me? See if they help?"

She had done it and here they were.

She lifted the bottle. The label matched the one she had purchased at the pharmacy for confirming the color and size of the capsules inside.

She opened the bottle and shook fourteen of the white cap-sules into her hand. She dropped them into the toilet and flushed them away. From her pocket she retrieved the envelope with the plastic bag of fourteen capsules she had received from Luis Garza. Indistinguishable from the calcium capsules. *Perfect.*

She tipped the bag into the medicine bottle and listened to the capsules fall. When they were all inside she screwed the cap back onto the top of the bottle and replaced it on the medicine cabinet shelf.

She was done here for tonight. The next time she stood in this bathroom, everything would be different.

Moments later the garage door hummed shut behind her.

CHAPTER THIRTY-ONE
Realization

When the alarm clock went off the next morning Scott rolled over and groaned. He'd tossed and turned all night with indigestion.

Weird nightmare. A shadowy figure had invaded their home. Though he'd struggled to rise, he was tied down with red cords. He lay in bed, powerless to fight back. When the intruder approached Rachel he finally awoke, breathless.

With her head still buried in her pillow, Rachel said, "You had a bad night last night, didn't you?"

"The pizza got me, I think. I need to get some decent food in my stomach before I take off for work."

Rachel rolled herself out of bed and sat on the side. "Well, I can certainly do that for you. When you come down after your shower I'll have some corned beef hash and fried eggs for you."

He took a quick shower and went downstairs. The nightmare was hard to shake off. "What are you going to be doing today?" He wolfed down an egg. "Do you have plans with your mom and dad before they leave?"

"They want to do some shopping for the kids and buy something for us before they go home. We'll be here until Scotty gets home from preschool and then I've got someone coming over to babysit while we go shopping. It's pretty hard to shop with the kids along and there's a really good lady that's available this afternoon."

Scott swallowed a forkful of hash. "Sounds great. Wish I could go along."

"Oh, right. You wish you could go along. Like I believe that! I'll never see the day when you want to go shopping on purpose."

Scott laughed. "You caught me. But otherwise, I'm a pretty honest guy."

WHEN SCOTT WENT TO MCDONALD'S during his lunch hour he logged on to the VirtualFriendMe website. Instead of Alicia he got a notification that his account was under maintenance and that he wouldn't be able to use it for four more hours.

He sent Alicia a text message to see if she would respond. She didn't. This was the first time he had ever been out of touch with her, and it rankled him. He'd become accustomed to talking with *his girl* on their midafternoon breaks. Until Alicia, he had not really known what his needs were. Now they had a name and it was a name that he could not envision ever being without again.

He scrolled through some of the pictures he had captured of Alicia during their sessions.

Rachel's face rose, unwelcome, into his mind. When it did, he tipped the cover of the laptop computer down so that the pictures of Alicia were not visible. The two did not mix. There was some part of him that couldn't handle the idea of Rachel and Alicia together. Certainly, if Rachel knew what he was doing she would think he was being unfaithful to her. He'd already worked through that logically and methodically. There was no unfaithfulness, because there was no real girl. If Alicia had been real, he would be forced to feel guilty about this. But in the absence of guilt . . . well, that's just the way it was. What he was doing wasn't hurting anybody. It was as harmless and innocent as watching any other computer animation.

ON THE WAY HOME that evening Scott checked in with Rachel. "Are you all still out shopping?"

"Getting close to home now. You wouldn't believe all the things Mom and I found today. I got you a really nice V-neck sweater."

"Thanks. Hope you left some money in the account for lunch this week. I'm not too far away myself. Do you want me to stop and pick up some Chinese or subs or anything?"

"Nope, you just come on home. This is Mom and Dad's last night here, so I want to cook for them. We'll have spaghetti. That won't take long, and I got some French bread."

As Scott drove down the country road approaching his house, he could see people in the driveway. Rachel and—

Scott pulled the car up short in the middle of the road.

No!

Was it possible? The world swam in front of his face, small spinning things rising up in his sight like microbes in dirty water. He shook his head, trying to clear his vision, but the two figures remained there in the driveway, talking. Something passed from Rachel's hand to . . . *Alicia's hand.*

She was there.

A trembling overtook him as he suddenly felt icy cold. All he could do was sit and watch the events as they took place before his eyes. *How could this possibly be happening? She's not supposed to be real.*

Alicia turned, opened the door of a gray Audi, and looked down the road toward him. Did she see him? It seemed like she held his gaze momentarily, then sat down in the car and closed the door. In a moment she backed out of the driveway and onto the main road.

She turned the car toward Scott.

Everything about the world seemed unreal now. Nothing that was happening could be happening. But the car approaching him loomed larger and larger before his eyes as his world shifted down into slow motion. With the air of resignation brought on by unreasoning fear, Scott gaped at the face of the driver as she slowed and passed. She looked directly into his eyes as she went by. He would have recognized the face and the smile anywhere.

Alicia.

The Audi made the turn on the road behind him and passed out of sight. Scott still sat in his car, transfixed by the experience he had just endured.

She's real.

What would he do?

I've been unfaithful. I am an unfaithful husband to my wife. Unfaithful. Unfaithful.

The realization and the guilt that accompanied it overwhelmed him. For the first time in his life he was completely incapacitated.

He blinked rapidly as he made out Rachel in the driveway looking down the road seeing his car. She waved and motioned for him to come on home. Home? How could he go home now? What did Rachel know? What did she know about Alicia?

The thought filled him with dread. His determination to do right wavered but did not go away. Whatever the situation, whatever the price, he would do the right thing.

He just hoped that the price would not be so dear that those he loved would be hurt through his own sinful actions. Rachel, Scotty, and Angela—his family, the ones he loved on earth above all else.

The ones he loved more than Alicia.

He put the car in gear and drove on home to his waiting wife.

"**WHAT WERE YOU DOING DOWN THERE?** Why did you stop the car out on the road?"

Scott gazed into the eyes of his wife. Loving eyes, trusting eyes. How would he ever be able to tell her? He didn't even begin to know all the answers himself.

He parted his lips, unsure of his ability to speak at all. When he did, his throat was hoarse, the muscles straining.

"Oh, I saw that someone was leaving. I just wanted to leave them plenty of room. Who was that?"

"Her name is Alicia. She's the one I told you about, the babysitter."

Alicia! Rachel said her name.

"She's been watching Angela at my Hugest Loser meetings. How was your day? Anything interesting happen?"

Angela, she had Angela. Oh, God.

"How," he stammered, "how well do you know her? I mean, have you known her a long time?"

Rachel's face seemed to darken, evidently sensing Scott's distress.

"Not long. I met her at Hugest Losers. She came in one day to substitute when one of the other babysitters didn't show up, and she has really worked out well. Everyone loves her. I guess she has some children of her own that are already in school or something. I'm not sure about the whole story, but when I saw how much Angela liked her I asked her if she'd be willing to come over here and babysit for us sometime. Today was the day. You don't mind, do you?"

Rachel wasn't smiling now. He didn't want her getting suspicious. He had to get control. To understand what was going on.

He spoke in a controlled voice, "No, no. I don't mind. I'm just not accustomed to having someone watch either of the kids that I don't know myself. I mean, here at the house. But it's okay, I certainly trust your judgment."

"Okay, well, come on inside and see everyone. Mom and Dad won't be here much longer."

In the kitchen Scott asked, "How long was she here?"

"Who?"

"That, that woman, what's her name, who babysat the kids today. How long was she here?"

"Four or five hours. I paid her for five. Both the kids really liked her and she seems really nice. Why are you worrying so much?"

That was why she hadn't been available at lunch. There hadn't been any account maintenance. She had been right here in the house.

Don't tell Rachel. Somehow, I have to fix this.

"I'm sorry, just curious."

The rest of the evening Scott looked for reasons to leave the group and go to the VirtualFriendMe.com website but could never find an excuse to get away. Forcing himself to act as normal as possible, they all played Candyland and Old Maid and the children laughed until they wore themselves out. Finally it was time to put them to bed.

"Will Grandma and Grandpa be here in the morning when we wake up?" asked Scotty.

"No," said Rachel. "They'll be gone in the morning, back to their home. You need to give them a big kiss good-bye and tell them you are glad they came to our house for this visit, all right? You be sure to tell Grandma and Grandpa that you love them."

The two children hung on the legs of the adults, pleading and begging to stay up *just a little later*, to no avail. The time was already late. Andy and June wanted to get to bed early for the long drive back home in the morning.

Scott stood up and stretched. "How about I put Scotty to bed and you take care of Angela tonight, okay?"

Rachel nodded, and took the little toddler by her hand. "Tell everyone good night, Angela."

"Good night," Angela said with her most serious demeanor. "I love you."

Scott led Scotty up to his room, and Ruff bounded up after them. As Scott tucked the little boy in under his covers he said, "I hear you were a pretty good boy today. I'm proud of you."

Scotty wriggled and smiled back at his father, soaking up the praise. "I like to be good, Dad."

"Were you good for . . ." Scott's throat constricted. He had difficulty saying the name. "Were you good for *Miss Alicia*?"

"Uh-huh. She's pretty nice. But we don't call her Miss Alicia."

"Oh? Then what do you call her?"

"She told us that we could just call her Mommy."

CHAPTER THIRTY-TWO
It's Just Statistics

The next morning Rachel came up next to Scott as he stood over the sink, brushing his teeth.

"Scott, do you still love me? I mean, like when we first got married. Do you still love me in the same way?"

Scott stopped brushing and turned toward her. A dribble of watery toothpaste ran down his chin. "What? I'm in the middle of brushing my teeth and you ask me if I love you?"

"Don't put me off. I'm serious. Why should I need to wait for a good time to know you love me? I'm your wife, not a to-do list."

He looked away, back toward the mirror. Rachel wanted his attention, but he didn't seem to be willing to look her in the eye.

Something was wrong. It was like he was trying to hide something from her, but what could he have to hide? And she knew the difference between having someone interested in her and someone who was just trying to avoid the topic.

"You're right, sweetheart. I'm sorry. I've just been really, really busy at work lately. The pressure on me has been tremendous. That's all you're seeing."

She wanted him to hold her. Wanted to feel his arms around her. She wanted him to stay there and not be the first to rush off, to put her first. She wanted to feel loved again.

"That's it? That's all you're going to say? It's all about you, just because you have a job like every other man?"

He still had a toothbrush in one hand and dribble all over his chin. "No. I'm not going to tell you it's all in your head, because it's not," he said, still looking at the mirror. "I haven't been treating you like I used to. You're right about that, but you're wrong if you think it has anything to do with you. It's all me. Please, just be patient with me, and I'll get it all worked out."

"All right, I'll be patient a little longer, but you need to know how serious I am. I want to know that you love me and that our family still matters to you. I've got a right to that much, Scott."

Scott wiped the dribble from his face with his hand, turned, and kissed her on her cheek. "You're everything to me. Just believe that. You take care of things here at home and let me take care of things at work and pretty soon everything will be back to normal, all right?"

It wasn't all right. He was still being dismissive. She didn't want to be back to normal. She wanted to be back to *loved*. And he hadn't said he loved her.

"All right? Oh, sure. That'll be fine, won't it? Everything on your schedule," she said as she took the calcium supplement from the shelf. She'd worried about many things in the past. Bills, illnesses. But she'd never worried about having Scott's love. This was new and it was frightening.

Facing the mirror again Scott said, "Just one thing, please

don't use Alicia as a babysitter anymore. We need to know more about her before we trust her with the kids, okay?"

"But you said you trusted my judgment. What's going to change next?"

"I do trust you. Trust me on this too. I only want to have the same opportunity you've had to be sure that the right person is watching our kids. That's all I mean."

"But when I go to the Hugest Losers, I don't really have any options. She's the one that works there. You mean I shouldn't drop Angela off at the babysitting anymore?"

Scott hesitated, seemed unsure what to say. "Yes, just temporarily. Let me check her out a little bit, okay?"

"Okay, if you say so. I just won't go to Hugest Losers for a few days. I'm feeling a little tired anyway."

What difference did it make? He probably wouldn't be interested in her no matter what she did. And she really was tired, much more than usual.

Rachel picked up her toothbrush and began brushing her teeth as Scott finished buttoning his shirt.

She noticed the pinkish foam that swirled down the sink drain when she was done. Odd, her gums didn't usually bleed.

After she dried her mouth Scott hugged her and said, "Thanks for loving me. I don't deserve you."

"SUZANNE? Sorry I've been so long getting back in touch with you. It has been a madhouse around here, but things are finally starting to settle down."

Suzanne raised her eyes to Rachel, filling the computer display. "Are your mother and father gone now?"

"Yes, they left this morning before Scott even got out of bed. We had the kids tell them good-bye last night before they went to sleep. It was wonderful having them here. They are such good people."

"God definitely blessed you with a good family, didn't he?"

Suzanne thinking about God? That seemed so strange, that a virtual person would think about God. But why not? The first Suzanne would have said the same thing. "I guess with all that's been going on, and having them here, it has just worn me out. I feel sooo tired today."

"Are you taking care of yourself?"

"I'm trying to get enough sleep and I'm taking those calcium supplements you recommended. Took one the first night, one yesterday, and one today. I'm glad you suggested it to me."

"Did you think I was back to doing advertising at first?"

Laughter. "No, well . . . maybe at first."

"You did, didn't you?" Suzanne asked. "Maybe you should take two a day at first. They can't hurt you."

Suzanne was watching out for her. She liked that.

"Okay, good idea. At my age, I don't really think about myself as ever having osteoporosis, but then again, this is the time to start thinking about it, isn't it?"

Suzanne rolled her eyes. "Osteoporosis? You all bent over? Oh, yes, you're a little young for that. Remember that slumber party we went to where everybody pretended they had a disease? You had leprosy and you walked around with your arms out like a mummy, calling, "Unclean, unclean." That was so funny. You were really a fun person to be with back then."

"And do you remember how Becky Stillman screamed? She

knew I wasn't a mummy, but she was so scared, her mother had to come and get her and take her home."

"Ever since I came into being again on the website I have loved all the stories you've told me. It has been wonderful being friends with you. I hope that I've meant even a little bit as much to you."

"You do, you do. But you sound like I've died or something. We're going to keep on being friends for many years. I can hardly tell the difference between you and the first Suzanne."

"And you're the only Rachel I've ever known. Best friends forever?"

"BFFs forever."

"Oh, and how are those medical transcription classes going? Are you learning a lot?"

"Not bad. I think I'll do all right with that. What's great is that I will be able to do the work from home while the children nap."

"Good. Keep up the hard work." Suzanne hugged herself. "I can't really touch you, but I'm pretending you're giving me a big hug."

Rachel mimicked her. "When you first came back to me," said Rachel, "I was afraid I might lose you again. What if I hadn't been able to pay the extra fifteen dollars a month or Scott had said no or your company had gone out of business? There are just so many things that can go wrong in life. But none of those things have happened, have they? I was silly to worry. But now you're the one that seems worried about me. You don't have to."

"I read all the time, though, about some of the things real humans do. Do you have any idea what the suicide statistics look like? I mean, people are taking their lives for all kinds of reasons. I just saw yesterday where some housewife had taken her own life because she found out her husband had been unfaithful to her. Can you believe that?"

Could she believe it? Sorry to say, she could. If something were to happen to the children and Scott were to reject her . . . well, who could say what a person would do?

"I can believe it, but I'd never do it. Nothing horrible like that will ever happen here."

"Oh, remember all those things I was asking you about Scott? Just forget them, all right? I'm sure none of it amounts to anything. If there were something wrong with your marriage, you'd know it. We girls can always tell, can't we?"

"Okay, forgotten," said Rachel.

A shiver passed through her, reminding her that in fact, it wasn't forgotten. She wouldn't be able to bear it if Scott was unfaithful.

CHAPTER THIRTY-THREE
Face-to-Face

With only a short time left before they expired, Scott's options on Solar Charge were now nearly worthless. What had he been thinking, buying thirty-day options? There had been no room for error. Everything had looked so good. The president, his friendships, the green industry; all had conspired together against him to ruin his career.

And now this business with Alicia, whoever she was. He thought he had known her, that she had only existed in that tenuous, arm's-length virtual world that he had so boldly ventured into. There was no doubt now.

She was a real woman. And he was a fool.

He wanted to do something now, but he had to wait until lunchtime. Take his laptop down to the McDonald's or the coffee shop, or wherever, and log onto his account. Would she be there, as always? What would she say? Was it possible that it was all just some unbelievable mixup and there was nothing wrong?

Deep down, he knew better. But as long as a thread of hope hung out before him he was willing to try it. He had been unfaithful; that much he had finally admitted to himself. He was done with it. What did the Bible say? "Drink waters out of thine own cistern and running waters out of thine own well." He would be faithful to the wife that God had given him.

In the meantime, he definitely had a problem.

Unless he was totally crazy, Alicia was real. Even Rachel had called her Alicia. Could any of that have been coincidence? He didn't see how.

He looked down at the laptop computer in its case sitting on the floor of his cubicle. A manufactured gaggle of chips, LEDs, and mechanical devices. Yet it had become the gateway to a manufactured, false world. A world that he had allowed to take over his real world and relegate it to the backseat of his life. What could God do with people like him? So weak, so easily deceived, and oh-so-easily turned aside from doing right.

He was facing the very real possibility of losing everything, absolutely everything that mattered to him. He could lose his wife, his family, and even his job. He was a hairsbreadth away from watching everything that was precious to him go up in flames, and he would have no one to blame but himself. His cavalier attitude about the most important things, his know-it-all approach to trading, his utter arrogance in thinking that he could succeed in secret sin and get away with it.

Something flashed in the corner of the computer display. There was a message. *Alicia.* He sat immobile, frozen with indecision. Should he respond? He desperately wanted to control the situation, but if he answered he would be working on her timetable. Still, hadn't he wanted to contact her? He clicked twice on the flashing icon, and a text box opened on the screen.

Scott?

I'm here.

Things have changed, haven't they?

Yes.

One thing hasn't changed. I'm still your girl.

I don't understand what's happening.

I know you don't. Everything is going to be okay, even better than before.

How can that be? Are you really real?

What's real, Scott? You designed me, didn't you?

Yes, I thought so. Was that you in the car yesterday?

Did it look like me?

You know it did.

We need to have a video meeting, okay? Can you take your laptop to Starbucks?

Okay. This will probably be the last time, though.

Don't say that. Don't decide yet. Eleven-thirty, okay?

Okay.

He was more confused than ever now. Meet her for a video chat at Starbucks? Why Starbucks? Why had he agreed to that? He had let her dominate the whole thing. But it was just a video chat, right? So sitting in the car at Starbucks should be fine.

Scott opened the VirtualFriendMe website, clicked on *text chat,* and waited for Alicia to respond.

Service temporarily unavailable. Please try again later.

What? She wasn't answering. If he had called her on the phone this would be the equivalent of just letting the phone ring. If he were calling on her at home, she was simply not coming to the door. Somehow he needed to get back into control.

Back into control? Had he ever been in control? He had been totally clueless as to what was going on. He picked up his notepad and began to work through what he thought he actually knew.

1. Rachel discovers the VirtualFriendMe website.
2. On her own she re-creates Suzanne.
3. She shows it to me.
4. I try it, choose a female/intimate friend. ~~Why?~~
5. I don't tell Rachel (guilt).
6. I misuse it. I tell Alicia I love her!!! <u>Crazy.</u>
7. Alicia shows up at my home.

Scott looked over the list. This would make a great movie script, but it was pretty unbelievable, even for that. The difference was this was really happening and it wasn't a movie, and it was yet to be seen how it would all play out.

He was a complete idiot.

SCOTT WALKED IN THE DOOR at Starbucks at eleven-fifteen. The lunchtime crowd hadn't formed a line yet. He ordered a grande latte and sat down in a plush sofa chair at the front. Just as at Chiusano's, his back was to the shaded window. There would be no interruptions and no one looking over his shoulder at whatever might be happening on the screen.

Alicia had said eleven-thirty, so that's what it would be. It was like being in a waiting room waiting for some celebrity to appear.

He logged on to the Starbucks Wi-Fi system and waited, the computer on his lap.

At eleven-thirty precisely, a message icon began flashing on his screen. *Message from Alicia.*

Here goes. Time to put a stop to this. He plugged in his dictation headset and clicked the icon.

Alicia's face expanded to fill the screen. An unexpected wave of dizziness surged through his body.

She didn't speak immediately. Instead she simply looked at him. *Looked into his eyes.* Riveted, he gazed back into hers, seeing her eyelids moving just on the edge of perception.

She was beautiful. Once again, the realization came. She's not an animation, she's a real woman. He wanted her.

He closed his eyes, tried to shut her out. Rachel's face came into focus, then receded as it was overwhelmed with the vision of Alicia's eyes. She was waiting for him.

After all this time wanting her, fantasizing about her . . . he could actually have her. Touch her. She would be warm, her skin would be soft. She would yield to him. . . .

No. He had to tell her it was over. It wouldn't work. Couldn't work. He would be faithful to his wife.

"Hello, Scott." The voice was low, husky. Filled with longing.

Am I really ready to give this up?

He reopened his eyes.

Her eyes never left his. He was imprisoned by her presence.

"Scott?" Her cheek trembled once with a nervous tic.

"Yes, I see you."

Alicia seemed to soften, tension running out of her expression. "Please tell me you're not angry with me."

His hand shook on the laptop, nearly causing it to slide off. He pulled it back level. *I'm afraid of what I'm going to do. I don't know what I'm going to say next.*

He replied; his voice strained as he fought to keep the trembling under control. "I don't know what to think."

He put his hand to his head and closed his eyes, then rubbed his palm across his forehead, trying to clear the mystery away. "Just tell me what's going on, please."

"You deserve that. First of all, everything I've ever told you has been the truth."

"How can that be? Are you going to tell me you're not real? That I didn't see you yesterday?"

"No, I won't tell you that. You know the truth already. I think you've probably known the truth for a long time. You think you may have only seen me one time, but I have seen you many, many times. And every time I've been near you, I've fallen more deeply in love with you."

He didn't want to hear that. He didn't want to be in love with Alicia and he didn't want her to be in love with him.

"Alicia, that can never work. I have a wife and I love her."

"I know you do. That's part of why I love you so much. You are principled and faithful. I could never love you any other way."

"Then, how . . . I don't understand how it makes sense for us to even be having this conversation if you want me to be faithful to Rachel. And I *am* going to be faithful to Rachel."

"I love you, Scott. There are some things that you don't know, though. I think that maybe you just haven't thought them through."

"What are you talking about? What is there to think through?"

"Ask yourself, who loves you more? Me, or Rachel?"

Up to this point he had been focused on who it was that he loved. Alicia was asking him to compare the love that the two women had for him. The thought had never occurred to him.

"Rachel does," he replied in a low voice. He wanted it to be true, but the words sounded hollow. He wasn't sure.

"Are you positive? Who do you confide in? Who is always there for you?" She looked down slowly. When she raised her eyes again, they were as deep and dark as the midnight sky. The message was clear. "Who is always there for you, Scott? If Rachel was enough, then why did you ever need me?"

Shame covered him. Shame because of what he had done and shame because he knew she was right. He had needed her because in his Scott-centered world, Rachel had not been enough.

Oh, God. Help me.

The Bible verse leaped into his mind. *I will set no wicked thing before mine eyes.*

"What do you want from me?"

"I want to be your girl, Scott. Only yours and no one else's."

"But Rachel . . ."

"I understand about Rachel. Don't think about that now. You told me once that if something ever happened to Rachel I would be enough for you. Do you remember that?"

How could I forget?

"Yes."

"I'm willing to wait. Until that time, nothing else has to happen, okay?"

Scott found himself nodding, mutely. His power was gone. His resolve had fled. He yielded to the inevitable.

"And my name is not really Alicia. You may have guessed that."

His head rose and fell, mechanically acquiescing to this last new bit of information. "What is it?"

"My name is Melissa. I hope you like it. If you don't, you can still call me Alicia. It's something of a love name between us now."

"Melissa."

A tear formed in her eye, swelled, then ran down her cheek. "That's the first time you've ever said my name."

Another tear followed the first and soon her cheeks were wet. She brushed them aside with her hand.

Scott's own eyes misted with emotion. "I'm sorry, I didn't know."

"I'll leave you now if you like. I'll contact you again soon."

"No, please don't contact me anymore. This has to end today. This has to be good-bye."

The camera that had been focused on Melissa wobbled as he saw her lean in toward it; then the image went black. What was happening? He stared fixedly at the screen, waiting for her face to reappear.

Suddenly a cascade of dark, perfumed hair surrounded his face; a trembling kiss pressed his cheek. In a voice he recognized too well, she whispered, "I'm your girl."

He looked up in shock as she walked quickly out of the coffee shop. He jumped up. "Wait!" The latte spun off in a spiral of liquid. The laptop that had been resting on his knees clattered to the floor. When he looked up again, she was gone.

MELISSA STEPPED OUT OF THE STARBUCKS, took a fast turn to the right, and strode quickly to the alleyway behind the shop. She mopped her eyes with a tissue. She had allowed herself to lose emotional control. She'd let herself be overcome with the closeness.

She didn't want Scott to see her now, not like this. He needed time to process what he had just experienced.

Physical contact, finally. And now he knew her name. She had not lost him. She had walked along the knife edge of his indecision so long and she had not lost him yet.

She keyed her door combination and sat down in the Audi. The engine started and she drove down the alleyway and out onto the perimeter road.

Scott would be looking for her now, but he would not find her. Not yet, not until everything was ready.

Just another day or two. Then there will be no one, nothing in my way. All I have to do is wait.

CHAPTER THIRTY-FOUR
Paying the Piper

Rachel was so tired. Air rushed out of the cushions as she sank down on the sofa. Where had her energy gone? Her muscles ached and there was a coppery taste in her mouth.

She reached over to the end table to pick up the television remote control. What were those spots? Large, splotchy bruises covered her wrists where her sleeves had been in contact with her skin. *Now what?*

She closed her eyes and put her head back on the sofa's cushioned back. She just needed some sleep. She'd been doing too much. Something . . . she dozed, then slumber swept over her, covering her in a blanket of warm nothingness.

She awoke sometime later to a strange taste in her mouth. What had she eaten for lunch? Her tongue tasted sweet and her teeth felt like they were coated with something sticky.

She leaned forward and lifted herself off the sofa, putting both hands on her knees for support. *So tired.*

In the bathroom, as she turned toward the commode she caught a glimpse of her face in the mirror. Her cheek had a purple splotch on it as big as a birthmark. She got up close to the mirror to see it better and grimaced at her appearance. When she did, the face that looked back at her was a mask of horror.

Her teeth and gums were covered with rich, red blood. Her hand flew to her face as her mouth opened in terror. Flecks of blood spotted her lips, a dribble formed at one corner of her mouth.

"What's happening to me?"

Her insides turned to liquid all at once. Whether it was fear or something else, she didn't know, but she pulled down her exercise pants and sat down as fast as she could on the open toilet. *Just in time.*

It rushed out of her before she knew what was happening. She looked down and confronted the spectacle of a toilet bowl filled with blood. *Her blood.*

She slid off the slick seat and fell in a heap on the floor. Looking up, she saw the white porcelain and the bright red liquid running down the side.

My cell phone. In my pocket.

Rachel fumbled the cell phone from her pocket. As her world retreated into darkness, her last conscious act was to dial 911.

AGAINST ALL HOPE, Scott pulled up the chart for Solar Charge. It was worse than he expected. The market price for Solar Charge shares had been falling all day long, the last quote at $109 on high selling volume.

It was hopeless. Who would buy his call options now? Only a trader with a death wish. The rest of the office seemed to be turning slowly around him, isolating him, setting him apart for the spectacle that he was. Secrets could not be kept forever. It was a wonder Alan Castle hadn't found out yet.

"Scott? Mr. Castle wants to see you." Carole Turner hustled on by with an arm full of papers.

That was it. He had to go see the old man.

Castle's door was closed, but the man paced inside behind the glass wall panel. He was on the phone talking to someone, holding the phone in his left hand and slapping his desktop with his right. He looked up and motioned with his free hand for Scott to come inside.

This must be what it's like on death row. You walk in but you don't come back out.

Castle motioned for Scott to sit down, his eyes betraying no warmth.

Scott remained on his feet. He couldn't sit in a chair, couldn't relax. Payday had arrived.

"Yes, Mr. Archer. You're right. I understand. Yes, sir. No, sir. No excuses." The older man's eyes flicked up toward Scott. "Yes, sir. The mistake was mine."

Castle held the phone out in his left hand, looked at it, and replaced it carefully into the cradle. Slowly, he raised his head and glared at Scott. "Don't talk. Don't say anything. Just listen." He closed his eyes, and moved his head slowly back and forth. "How could you do it, Scott? How could you betray my trust like this?"

"Sir, I—"

Castle raised his hand, as if stopping traffic.

Scott pressed his lips together, thankful for the interruption. He had nothing worthwhile to offer.

"No, don't speak. There's nothing you can say. You spent two hundred and fifty thousand dollars of Gleason Archer's money on options? It's gone, Scott. Every bit of it, it's all gone. That was Archer on the telephone. He's pulled his account. You know what that means? It doesn't simply mean that you don't have a job here anymore. You don't, by the way. Ultimately, it may mean that I don't have a job here anymore either. And all those people out there in that office?" He swept his hand in a wide arc. "All those people, with families that depend upon them. Every one of them is going to suffer for what you've done. It will be a miracle if Castle Investments survives the year."

He wanted to throw up. The awful moment had come, and he was physically sick inside for what he had done.

"I'm so sorry. I wasn't—"

Now he sat, unable to stand any longer, balanced on the edge of the chair.

Castle looked down at his desk, his head still moving slowly from side to side. "I treated you like a son and I trusted you with our biggest account. You really, really let me down. I don't know what you're going to do with the rest of your life, but I suggest you find a new field of endeavor, Mr. Douglas. One where people don't have to trust you."

Scott's face burned with humiliation. There was no place to hide.

Castle looked down at him. "Clean out your desk with as little fanfare as possible. I don't want to see any trace left of you when I come out of my office. Am I crystal clear?"

Scott's throat constricted with the emotion of his humiliation. "Yes, sir," he whispered. He sat uneasily a few moments longer.

"What are you waiting for? Get it done and go away."

Scott rose awkwardly from the chair and left the office. He heard Castle's voice behind him as the man turned back to his desk. "What a loser."

Shame hung heavy in the air as he made his way back to his cubicle. Not "his" anymore. Nothing was his any longer. The others were talking on the phone, tapping on keyboards, moving papers from place to place.

His professional life was over, but the world just kept on going.

Without a word, he walked to the copy machine and picked up the two empty paper boxes stacked against the wall. He carried them to his cubicle and packed the first of his personal effects.

When he removed the pictures of his family from the cubicle walls, he saw Carole watching him, consternation on her face. His eyes burned with bitter tears as he turned the pictures down on their faces where they couldn't accuse him.

He said nothing. No one asked him any questions. It was more than obvious that he was leaving for good, whatever the reason might be.

HE SET THE LAST BOX on the asphalt next to the Taurus. As he fished the keys out of his pocket to open the trunk, his cell phone rang. He looked at the display, but did not recognize the number. The caller ID said LCER. "Scott."

"You are Mr. Scott Douglas?"

"I am. Who is calling, please?"

"Sir, my name is Rudy Garcia. I am a family counselor with

Lake County Hospital. Mr. Douglas, your wife has been admitted to our emergency room. The doctors have requested that you come as quickly as you can. Are you nearby?"

"Rachel? Are you sure you have the right person? Is her name Rachel?"

"Yes, sir. Rachel Douglas. Can you come quickly, Mr. Douglas?"

Scott threw the box into the trunk of the Taurus and slammed the lid shut, swung himself into the driver's seat, and started the engine, cell phone still pressed against his left ear. "What's wrong? What's happened to my wife?" He backed out of the parking place, one wheel grinding against the curb, and sped down the service road toward the highway.

"She's experienced some severe bleeding, Mr. Douglas. The doctors are trying to stabilize her now. By the time you arrive, we'll be able to tell you more."

"Where are the children? Are they with her?"

He was losing everything. *Let the kids be all right, God.*

"Uh, just a minute. Let me look at my notes. The paramedics called social services when they took your wife. The children are just fine. No need to worry."

He craned his head as he made the sharp turn onto the highway. "What happened? Why is she bleeding?"

"Sir, I can't tell you any more now. Come as quickly as you can. Are you on your way?"

"I'm on my way."

CHAPTER THIRTY-FIVE
Hopeless

Scott followed the signs to the emergency room entrance. He parked the car in the first spot he could find, jumped out, and ran as fast as he could toward the ER entrance. The Taurus chirped behind him as the doors locked.

He pushed his way through the double glass doors and angled directly toward the desk, where three people were in line. Ignoring the line, he went directly to the harried-looking nurse. "My name is Scott Douglas. I received a call that my wife, Rachel, is here. Where is she?"

The woman raised her gaze and waved to a man on the other side of the room, motioning for him to come over.

A middle-aged man in a polo bearing a hospital logo came over. "Mr. Douglas?"

"Yes, do you know about my wife?"

"Mr. Douglas, I'm Rudy Garcia, the one who called you. Your wife is stabilized now, but the doctors are still with her. Please follow me." Garcia touched Scott's elbow and turned down the hallway. "This way, sir." He paused for Scott, then strode directly down the hall and around the corner.

They came to a room marked *Conference*, which Garcia opened with a key hanging from a ring on his belt. "This way, sir. I'll tell you all there is to know."

"When can I see my wife?"

"Soon, but we need to talk first. I need some information."

Scott fumbled in his pants pocket and pulled out his wallet. "Here, I have my insurance card. Here's my driver's license, everything. Just take it, let me go see her now."

"This isn't about insurance, Mr. Douglas. Just sit down, please. He motioned to a chair across a small table in the center of the room. I want to discuss Mrs. Douglas's situation with you. I'll bring you completely up to date, all right?"

Scott forced himself to slow down his breathing, closed his eyes. He calmed, but only slightly. With shaking hands, he returned the wallet to his pants pocket and sat down in the chair that Garcia had indicated. "Okay, what can you tell me?"

"Mr. Douglas, your wife arrived here in response to a nine-one-one call that she made from your home. When the paramedics arrived, they found her unconscious in the bathroom."

"What happened? What—"

Garcia looked down at a clipboard, lifted a sheet of paper to read another marked up with a highlighter, then looked back up to meet Scott's eyes.

"Stay with me, Mr. Douglas. The paramedics found your wife comatose and bleeding heavily, but not from wounds, more what we call generalized bleeding." As soon as she arrived in the emergency room, Dr. Watson, our ER physician, immediately did a coagulation workup on her."

"Why? What's a coagulation workup?" His knee knocked against the table leg, once, twice.

"That includes a pro time, that is, prothrombin time, a partial thromboplastin time, a platelet count, CBC, and some other clotting parameters that he thought important."

"I don't understand any of this. What does all that mean?" He felt like he was about to lose it completely. He didn't understand what was happening. The words were in English but they might as well have been in another language.

"A prothrombin time test measures the ability of the blood to clot. As you may know, if blood does not clot, that is, form a thrombosis, or scab, it's possible for a person to continue bleeding uncontrollably. This is the situation we found your wife in when she arrived."

"Was she in an accident? Did she cut herself?"

"No, Mr. Douglas. No accident. Actually, if a patient presents with abnormal bleeding, a prolonged pro time, but is otherwise healthy and has normal liver function . . . well, sir, there is normally only one reason for it."

Scott's stomach tightened as the muscles spasmed. He peered intently into Garcia's face. "What reason? What could it be?"

"Poison, Mr. Douglas. Typically, Coumadin poisoning."

"Coumadin poisoning? What's Coumadin?"

"Mr. Douglas, do you have a problem with mice or rats in your home? Have you been putting out rodent poison of any sort?"

"No, nothing like that. Coumadin is rat poison?"

"Coumadin is sold under a number of different names. Coumadin is one of them, Jantoven is another, and warfarin is another. Warfarin is the more commonly used term and it's normally found in mice and rat poison. However, the medical use of warfarin, or Coumadin, is what people typically call a blood thinner. It is given in small doses, over a period of about a week, and the patient's blood is monitored closely. "Has Coumadin been prescribed for your wife? Has she seen a physician recently?"

Scott searched his mind, but nothing made sense. They didn't have anything like that in their home. "No, nothing that I know about. Rachel doesn't even take any medicine. Nothing at all that I can think of. Do you know for sure about the diagnosis? Could it be something else?"

"Yes, sir. It may be something else. But that's the best lead we have right now, and we'll know for sure in the next twenty minutes or so. Right now your wife is being treated with large doses of vitamin K to restore the missing clotting factors in her blood. She is actually very fortunate, given her condition, that there was no brain hemorrhage. The prognosis in those cases is almost always very, very bad. Your wife should be fine in a few days. So let me review, Mr. Douglas. Your wife takes no medication at all that you're aware of, is that correct?"

"Yes, nothing. Oh, wait, she takes a calcium supplement, but that's all I can think of. I don't think that counts as medicine, does it?"

"A calcium supplement should be fine, sir. But we'll need to take a look at it. Something is definitely wrong. May I see your arms? Just roll up your sleeves, please, and let me take a look."

Scott rolled up his sleeves and extended his arms for Garcia to see.

Garcia took Scott's hands in his own and turned his arms around so he could see both sides. "No bruising, that's good. Have you experienced any bleeding in the gums of your teeth, or bruising in other areas of your body?"

"No, nothing like that. Can I see Rachel now?"

"One more question, Mr. Douglas. Where can we find those calcium supplements?"

"They're in a white bottle on the shelf of the medicine cabinet in our bathroom. Do you want me to bring the bottle in?"

"No, sir. That won't be necessary. Someone is already at your home."

Garcia stood, and turned toward the door. He opened it and leaned out into the hallway. "You can come in now. I think I have all we need."

Scott didn't recognize the two men that came in, but their uniforms and demeanor were unmistakable.

The taller one spoke first. "Mr. Douglas, I am Deputy Sheriff Landrum and this is Deputy Sheriff Peterson. We would like you to come with us, sir. We need to ask some questions down at the sheriff's office."

His life was draining away before his eyes. His job, his wife. His children with strangers.

They don't trust me to be alone with Rachel.

"But I haven't done anything. I just came here to see my wife. I have to see Rachel."

"Of course, sir. All in good time. Do you have an attorney?"

"No, I don't have an attorney. Why would I need an attorney? I can't believe this! I don't even get to see Rachel?"

Scott's world ground slowly to a stop. By the time he answered, "No, I've never had an attorney," hope had fled from his life.

Oh, God. If you've ever helped me, please help me now. There's no one else I can turn to but you.

CHAPTER THIRTY-SIX
Suspect

The two deputies put Scott in the back of the patrol car, where he was separated from the two officers in the front by a thick wire mesh. He looked at the doors. No controls for opening the door or window from the inside. He was a prisoner.

There had been no arrest, but what was he going to do, refuse to answer questions about his own wife?

The jail was laid out like a wheel, with spokes running out from a center section that contained a large circular console filled with computer screens and communications equipment. Men and women in uniform were busy inside the console area. A heavily muscled female sheriff's deputy came up to him. "Sit here please, sir, until we find an empty conference room." Scott was left alone by himself on a bench on the outer wall of the hub.

Ten minutes later a male deputy came up to him. "Follow me please. Do exactly as I say. Do you understand?"

Scott nodded. The man stood there, evidently waiting for a reply. "Sorry. Yes, I understand."

Without a word the man turned and motioned Scott to follow after him. He led Scott to a room with a heavy, painted metal door, which slid aside when he keyed a code in a box on the wall. "Step inside, sir." He looked at the clipboard he was carrying and shook his head. "We get all kinds here." He looked up at Scott, his eyes penetrating. "All kinds," he said, with a look that made Scott feel small and dirty.

He thinks I'm that kind of person.

The deputy turned and stepped outside, keying another code into the panel on the wall. The door slid shut, and Scott heard the lock mechanism trip inside.

He sat on the cold metal chair. The chill in the steel sucked the remaining heat out of his legs, and he began to shiver. He was nervous, and more than that, he was afraid.

He had never even had a speeding ticket. Now he was suspected of trying to kill his own wife?

The door clicked. Somewhere inside, a bolt slid open with a scraping sound. A large man in a wrinkled white shirt appeared, shoulder first. He said something in a low voice to someone else in the hall, then came in the rest of the way.

Scott looked up at him, waited for him to speak.

Breathing heavily, he sat across from Scott in a low-backed metal chair. He carried no papers or equipment but leaned in with his hands folded on the cold tabletop.

"I've been a detective for almost thirty years." He tapped with three fingers on the table. They sounded like gunshots in the small room. "I know what it takes to get things done.

"Do you understand what I'm saying, Mr. Douglas?"

Scott said nothing.

"Allow me to simplify." He tipped his wide head to one side.

His jowls covered his collar. "You tried to kill your wife. Tried to poison her. It didn't work. How am I doing?"

Scott said nothing.

The man pulled a small recorder out of his trouser pocket, slid a switch sideways, and laid it on the table. "Tell me why you did it. I understand that sometimes guys do things they're sorry for later." He fixed his gaze on Scott's eyes.

"Guys like you, Mr. Douglas."

Scott said nothing, but now his stomach was curling in on itself. Another minute of this and he'd lose it.

"What about that poison, Mr. Douglas? Want to tell me about it?"

Poison? Someone tried to poison Rachel. Who would do it? *Alicia.* No, not Alicia. *Melissa.* That was her real name. Alicia was made up, a composite person. She was built half out of his juvenile ideals and the other half of a real woman. He realized that he knew neither one of them, not really.

What had she asked him? "If something happened to your wife would I be enough for you? Could you love only me?"

If something happened to your wife. Something *had* happened to his wife. It had to be her. It couldn't be anyone else. Who else knew?

What had he answered? "Yes, you would be more than enough."

He brought his forehead down hard on the unyielding painted surface of the table. Unyielding as his own stubborn heart. The hard reality was that he had invited everything that was happening to him now. There was no one to blame but himself.

Help me, Lord. I've created this monster. It's all my fault.

But the poison, where had that come from? How could anyone have done that? He didn't have the answer, but for now the suspicion was sufficient. His wife was in danger, and he would defend her. He would defend her to the death.

The detective picked his recorder back up and dropped it into his shirt pocket. "Can't say I didn't try and make it easier for you. Remember that later on."

He stood and rapped three times on the door. In a moment, the lock clicked and the heavy bolt slid back again as the man left Scott alone in the room.

"SOMEONE TO SEE YOU. Your attorney is here."

My attorney?

Scott looked up from his seat. The deputy with the clipboard was standing outside the room. Behind him was a young man who couldn't have been very long out of college, shifting back and forth on his feet.

"Thank you."

The deputy walked away and the young man walked through the door. "Mr. Douglas, my name is Jeremy Sally. I've been appointed to represent you. Is there anything you think I need to know?"

They must be planning to arrest me. They didn't give you a lawyer just for questioning.

"I have no idea what's going on, only that the deputy that brought me in said they had some questions for me. Some detective came in and said I tried to poison my wife. All they've done so far is leave me locked in this room. I haven't been arrested, have I?"

The young attorney studied his papers. "It looks like they want to charge you with attempted second-degree manslaughter. Were you read your rights?"

"No, and they never told me I was being arrested. Have I been?"

The lawyer shook his head in bewilderment. "I don't understand the basis for the charges they are proposing. There's nothing here to indicate, and no evidence to support, any kind of charge like they want to make. Have you and your wife had trouble in the past?"

"No, sir. Nothing. We have a good marriage and a good family. I've never been arrested in my life. I don't drink. I don't even smoke. Someone should ask my wife. This whole thing is a huge mistake."

"I don't think they have any basis to charge you, much less hold you here any longer. I think we can get you out of here pretty quickly." He looked back up from the report he was reading and smiled at Scott. He extended his hand to him. "Don't worry about a thing. I'll take care of it all."

"Thank you, Mr. Sally. That's the first positive thing I've heard today."

"Sit tight, Mr. Douglas," said Sally. He pushed the button for the deputy, who then came and coded him out the door.

Scott sat on the metal chair, trying unsuccessfully to collect his thoughts. All he could focus on was Rachel and if she was all right. Right now she was all alone and he needed to be with her.

Less than an hour later, he heard the lock mechanism slide smoothly back out of place in the heavy door again. It was the same deputy who had brought him in. "Time to go, sir."

"Am I done here?"

"Yes, sir. I guess there was some mixup. The sheriff said they're not going to charge you, so you're free to go."

When the deputy walked him back out the outer doors, he felt as conspicuous as a man who had served thirty years in a federal prison for violent crime. Never again, he promised himself. Never again.

SCOTT CALLED LAKE COUNTY HOSPITAL on his cell phone, which had been returned to him upon his release. He was transferred to Rudy Garcia.

"I'm sorry about all that trouble earlier, Mr. Douglas. We have to follow the protocols passed down to us by the hospital and law enforcement. You understand."

"Okay, I understand. But how is my wife? Where can I find her?"

"She's doing well, Mr. Douglas. Don't worry about a thing. Ask for me personally at the front desk when you arrive, sir, and I'll take you to her room myself. I'm truly very sorry for all you've been put through."

"Thank you. Your apology means a lot to me. I love my wife and I would never . . ." He choked on the words. "Okay, I'll be there in five." Scott clicked off the phone. He hoped Garcia was playing straight this time.

Garcia met Scott in the lobby as soon as he walked in the door. "Follow me, Mr. Douglas. Your wife is on the third floor in a private room."

He looked down at his clipboard, then back to Scott. "Your mother-in-law, Mrs. June Anderson, is flying in, and will be with the children at your home soon. Have you been in touch with her?"

"No, but thank you for the information."

Scott followed Garcia up to the third floor, to room 3012. He opened the door and looked in. There was Rachel, lying on a hospital bed, evidently asleep. "Thank you, Mr. Garcia. I'd like to be alone with her now."

"Yes, sir. If there's anything else I can do, just ask for me at the front desk. I'm at your service."

CHAPTER THIRTY-SEVEN
Enemy

Rachel's eyes were closed. Her face looked bruised and there were large bruise marks on her arms. If he hadn't been told differently, he'd have thought she'd been beaten up. Had he been the cause of this? Was this what loving him, trusting him, had brought her?

For the next hour he sat with Rachel, holding her pale hand in his. He couldn't take his gaze away from her face. He'd never seen her look so weak. Her hand never moved, the fingers limp inside his.

He wanted to call Andy, her father, but didn't have the heart to face him even over the phone. He felt so ashamed, unworthy of the precious wife that lay by his side on her hospital bed.

At last her eyelids struggled open. She awoke to find Scott holding her hand.

"Oh, Scott. I'm so glad you're here." She closed her eyes again, her face slack, weariness evident in her pale skin.

"I'm here, sweetheart. And I'll be here until you're well. I love you with all my heart." He laid his head against her shoulder. Her heartbeat was strong in his ear.

"Did they tell you what happened?"

Her voice was soft, almost distant.

I came so close to losing her. The tears came again. He pushed his face into her gown to absorb them, then lifted his eyes back to hers.

Rachel's eyes were half closed. He could tell she was struggling hard to keep them open at all.

"No, I hardly know anything at all. All they told me was that you may have been poisoned, that you were bleeding, but that you were going to be okay."

She sighed, her breath shallow. "I was so tired, Scott. I was at home and I was just so very tired. I guess it was because I was losing blood, but I didn't know that then. They say I was bleeding internally." She breathed heavily, her chest heaving with the effort.

"Then what happened? Who called nine-one-one?"

"I did, at least I think I did. No, I know I did. There was no one else around. I went to the bathroom and saw myself in the mirror." A shudder ran through her body. "Oh, Scott. It was so awful. My teeth were all covered with blood and I was so weak I could hardly stand up. They say it was poison, Scott. Something called Coumadin. How could that happen?"

Scott steeled himself, preparing to answer. Did he know for sure? Was he 100 percent? No, but he was certain just the same. This was going to be difficult.

"Did you know I had to go to the police station?"

Rachel lifted her head up from the pillow, eyes wide. "What? Why would they do that?"

"I think they thought maybe I was the one that poisoned you. Maybe they still think so. I don't know. But they let me go a little while ago."

"They let you go? What do you mean? Did you have to go to jail or something?"

"I was there for a while. It could have been worse. I could have lost you." He felt Rachel's hand tighten around his. "I've got some things to tell you."

Her chin quivered. Tears flowed from the corners of her eyes. "Scott, I'm so sorry. I didn't know anything about that. Don't they know it's not your fault?"

"I suppose that lots of bad things happen in families today and maybe it was just natural for them to think that we were having trouble that way." He looked deeply into Rachel's eyes. "I would never, ever hurt you. Please believe that."

"Of course I believe you. You don't have to say that. God brought us together. We love each other."

"You're right. I just wanted to say it, because after I tell you the rest you're not going to be very proud of me."

Her eyes softened, pleading. "Go on. Tell me everything. I'm still going to love you just the same."

"It started with Suzanne."

Rachel's brow wrinkled. "Suzanne? You mean real Suzanne? Or the virtual Suzanne?"

"The virtual one. Remember you showed me how real she seemed? I decided to try it myself." He paused, and looked off toward a corner of the room.

She'll never trust me again.

"I was at work one day. There was so much pressure on me. I just thought it would be fun." He looked back into Rachel's eyes. "I am such a fool.

"I created a friend for myself like you did, just to try it out. But when they asked me if I wanted a male or a female friend, I chose female."

The silence between them became palpable. Scott was still holding her hand, but he could feel it withdraw, ever so slightly. He understood.

Rachel's eyes blinked, unable to hold back tears. "Go on."

"I think you already know what I'm going to tell you. I had her do things for me that were wrong. I'm so ashamed. I became unfaithful to you. I did things I've never done before and I promise I will never do again."

Rachel's body stiffened. Her face was taut, slitted eyes turned toward the window as if seeking a way of escape.

"Scott, I don't want to know any more. I've listened to all I can from you today."

He bent down, brought his cheek close against her bruised face, attempted to kiss her.

She jerked her head away. "No, no, don't touch me now."

In her ear he whispered, "I've never loved anyone but you. I only love you."

Tears wet Rachel's cheeks. "Do you not get it? I can't listen to any more, okay?"

It was not okay, and Scott knew that it couldn't stop here. His walk on the wild side had invited a monster into their home and they were not even close to safety. Not yet.

He sat back up, looking her squarely in the face. "There's more to tell. This affects both of us and we've got to work together before we're done with it."

Rachel drew her knees up and nodded, eyes closed, waiting for him to go on.

"The virtual person was named Alicia." He looked for any

sign in her expression that would indicate she had made the connection. Not yet. "The more I went to the website and talked with her, the more real she seemed to become."

"Just like Suzanne," Rachel whispered, her face more pale than ever.

"Yes, but with a big difference. I kept having the feeling, whenever I was on the website, or texting, or whatever . . . I kept having the impression that I was talking with a real person. I knew I wasn't, but still, there was something I couldn't put my finger on."

"So, what are you saying? Did you figure out what it was?"

"One day something really, really strange happened. I was at work and a text came when she asked me to meet her for lunch."

Rachel's eyes went wide. "Lunch? How could she do that? She's not even real."

"I know, that's what I said. Maybe, I thought, this is some sort of website test, or survey, or something like that. Maybe the company is doing something to see how far they can take all this. I was intrigued, so I said I would do it."

Rachel's chin trembled as her eyes became glassy with tears. She hugged her knees to her chest. Her voice was weak. "You agreed to meet her?"

He took her hand more firmly. "Sweetheart, I'm so sorry for all this. But I have to tell you what happened. Because we haven't gotten to the hard part yet. I went to the restaurant they told me to and I sat down at the table they had waiting for me."

She looked up at him, her eyes accusing and hard.

"Yes, they actually had a table reserved for me. The owner knew all about it, somehow. There was a note for me on the table, in an envelope. The note said to set up my laptop across the table from me, so when the person was on the screen . . ."

Scott struggled. *The person?* He still wasn't being honest.

" . . . so that when *she* was there, it would look like she was sitting across the table from me."

Rachel tried to pull her hand back from Scott's grasp. She appeared to shrink into herself.

"Scott?" Rachel's voice was small, tremulous. "Was I not enough for you? Did you really need someone else who would love you better than me?" Her chin quivered as tears coursed down her cheeks onto the pillow. Then she turned her head away.

"I'm sorry. I am sooo sorry," she moaned. "I tried to be enough for you."

Scott's chest ached as his heart broke within him. He could barely speak, his throat tight and sore with emotion.

"You're more than enough. You're wonderful." He put his arms around Rachel and wept. At the jail he had wept with remorse. He needed no one to tell him how hollow his words were. Now he wept with love and compassion for this beautiful woman who loved him so much.

Minutes passed before either could speak again. Rachel's eyes were bloodshot, her skin flushed and puffy with the emotional trial.

"I have to tell you the rest. She asked me if something were to ever happen to you, would she be enough for me?"

Rachel's eyes sought his. She looked questioning, fearful. "And you said yes, didn't you."

"I thought it was like a game. Like a stupid video game. I didn't know." *But I did know. Oh, God! I'm still lying.*

Rachel's eyes probed his now, something new behind them. "And now?"

"Rachel, she's real. She's a real woman."

"What was her name?"

Now she'll understand.

"Alicia."

"Alicia? You don't mean . . ."

"Yes, when I came home the other night, remember I stopped the car before I got to the driveway? She was standing next to her car, talking to you."

THE BILE ROSE UP in Rachel's throat before she could stop it. She pulled the sheet up to her mouth, but the force of the discharge threw her back on the bed.

"Call the . . . nurse!" she said, choking.

But the nurse had heard from the hallway and was already running into the room. "One side, sir," she cried as she began stripping off the top sheet, mopping the vomit off the bed.

A second nurse appeared with a large plastic bag, waving Scott away. "Wait two hours before you come back. Let her rest." Scott obeyed and disappeared into the hallway.

Rachel allowed the nurses to clean her up and change her gown.

How could this happen to me? What have I done?

She had let that woman into her house. She'd handed her own little children over to her. She held the bedrails as the sickness rolled through her like thunder. It had been so close.

She might have killed them.

The nurse glanced sideways at her as she scrubbed off the mattress pad. "The good news is the color is good. A while ago you were on the verge of bleeding out. This vomit is barely pink." She smiled approvingly. "Something to be thankful for. No one likes to throw up, but if you're going to do it, it might as well be good news."

Rachel looked around and saw Scott was no longer by the bed.

"Is Scott still here?"

"The man who was in here?"

"Yes, he's my husband. Is he still here?"

"I told him to come back in two hours. I'm sure he will, honey. You need to sit back and rest. I'll get you something to drink so your throat doesn't get irritated."

ALONE, Rachel couldn't keep her mind from churning with what she had learned. She lay in a fetal position, pulled the thin sheet up to her neck.

She fought to approach it logically, but the fear she felt for her family and her children was overwhelming.

The woman had my children. I left her alone in my house.

How could she have been so stupid? Not seen the signs?

Who had let *that woman* into her home? She had herself. What had she known about her? Nothing. She was just someone that had shown up one day at Hugest Losers. What kind of recommendation was that?

So who was this Alicia?

She shows up one day, comes out of nowhere. No, not nowhere. She knew all along what she was doing.

How had she done that? How can she be virtual and real at the same time?

Scott liked her. Bitterness began to wrap hard, cold roots

around her heart. No, she couldn't blame him alone. He may have blundered in with his eyes wide open, but she'd allowed herself to be deceived.

It started with . . . *Suzanne*. And who was Suzanne? She wasn't real, that was for sure.

The Coumadin, the poison she'd taken, what about that?

Alicia had been in the house.

Her eyes snapped open.

Could the children have been poisoned, too? Alicia could have put poison in the food, the milk. In anything. She'd have to throw everything out, just to be sure. Maybe it was in something all of them had been eating.

But for now, she was the only one that was sick. The visage of that bloody stranger looking back at her in the bathroom mirror shocked her again.

Not anyone else. She had been the target.

Scott's voice echoed in her ears. *If something happened to your wife . . .*

There it was, right before her eyes.

Who is Suzanne?

If a person controlled the Alicia personality, then the same person could control the Suzanne personality.

Suzanne was always planting doubts about Scott, wasn't she? "Why is he working late again? What if he's alone with a woman? What could he be doing so late at night?" Always trying to drive a wedge between them, something to cause her to worry.

She must work there. She must work for the website company.

Puzzle piece by puzzle piece, she watched it all come together.

First there had been Suzanne. Maybe that had been innocent enough. They would find out.

Then there had been this Alicia person. That's where something had changed. Somehow someone had taken over the Alicia personality, and Scott had walked right through the door.

The same person must have hacked into controlling the Suzanne personality in some way. She thought about that, walking back in her memory of interactions with Suzanne, step-by-step, looking for the change.

She remembered.

Suzanne had asked, "Are you sure he's really at the office? You've experienced a loss of his affection since he's been coming home so late."

The timing was right. *Obvious.* The answer was there, suspended in the air like a 3-D image.

She was in a battle for her family. That woman, whoever she might be, was trying to steal her family from under her nose. No, worse than that. She was trying to get rid of her altogether.

Who had recommended the calcium supplement? That had been her doctor.

But when she'd told her, Suzanne had said, "Would you try Cal Sup, for me? They're my favorite brand."

"Ohhhhh." She exhaled a long breath. Suzanne had known exactly what to find.

It was like a slap in the face when the full awareness struck her.

She tried to kill me so she could replace me.

She wanted to steal her place as Scott's wife.

Rachel shrank within herself as the next explosive realization impacted on the fragile, shivering wall of what was left of her heart.

Replace me as my children's mother.

She couldn't handle any more. That was enough. Scott and she could talk through the rest together.

No sleazy woman is going to steal my husband or my children from me.

Resolve crystallized like steel in her heart. Smoking, liquid metal flowed hot and red into the marrow of her bones as the powerful change came over her.

Well, Alicia, or whoever you are, you have an enemy. You tried to steal the wrong family.

CHAPTER THIRTY-EIGHT
Loss

Scott sat alone in the family waiting room near the nurses' station. Other groups came and went, but he was alone. He felt awash in a sea of people that were coming and going like waves breaking on a rocky shore. They came, they went, but he was left alone with an incredible sense of utter loss.

Outside, the streetlights had come on with the onset of darkness. A much deeper darkness had invaded his heart.

The twisted strands of the carpet between his feet moved in and out of focus. He was losing everything. He'd turned his back on God, on his wife, on his family. Could he ever, ever make it right again?

A shadow fell across the floor.

"Scott?"

He felt a man's hand on his shoulder, turned his head to see Pastor Jim Feldner standing in front of the chair next to him. The man sat down on the cushioned seat beside him. Scott heard the air escaping from the cushion, dreading what was going to come next.

"They tell me Rachel's going to be all right."

Scott nodded, but made no effort to meet the other man's eyes.

"Her father is with her now." He returned his hand to Scott's shoulder. "I understand she doesn't want to see you."

Tears swelled involuntarily in Scott's eyes. He wanted them to go away. He didn't want another man to see him cry.

"I've learned something about tough times, Scott. Let me read you something. Just two verses from the hundred and nineteenth psalm."

Scott heard pages turning. Something from God's Word was exactly what he needed right now.

Pastor Feldner said, "Verses sixty-seven and -eight. 'Before I was afflicted I went astray: but now have I kept thy word. Thou art good, and doest good; teach me thy statutes.'"

The words were like a salve on a raw wound. Scott turned his face toward his visitor. "Do you know what I did?"

"No." He shook his head gently. "And I don't need to. But you went astray, I can see that much. And now you're afflicted. Does that sound about right?"

"Yeah." He nodded. "I'd say that's right."

"Step one was going astray. Step two? That's the affliction. But step three is where you want to be right now."

"Step three?"

"The part that says, 'Now have I kept thy word.'"

"I don't know what you did or what came between you and Rachel. But now is the time for you and her, both of you, to keep His word. Time to be the kind of Christian you know you ought to be."

His pastor was right, and that's what he was going to do.

But would Rachel ever take him back, trust him again?

His pastor wrapped one arm around Scott's shoulders, then prayed for him. He prayed that God would not only forgive him, but that when he came through the affliction, he'd be a more obedient child of God than ever before.

"We'll be in touch. Let me help you wherever, whenever, I can, okay?"

Scott nodded. "Thank you, Pastor," then followed the retreating form with his eyes as he left the waiting area.

God would forgive him. But could Rachel? When the morning came, would he still have his wife?

It was going to be a long night in the waiting room.

RACHEL'S EYES CAME OPEN with the sounds of morning. Carts clattered by in the hallway outside her room. Sunlight flowed through the wide glass window and over the sill onto the floor. One bright slice of light crossed her bed, warming her arm, and reflected back off a framed picture on the opposite wall.

Her mother had left a mirror on the tray. She picked it up and looked at herself. The swelling and discoloration in her face were almost gone. Encouraged, she took the hairbrush and brushed out her hair, lay back, and looked at her reflection again. Much, much better.

A quick knock on the door and a young orderly stepped inside the room. "Ready for some breakfast?"

For the first time in two days she didn't feel the need to hide her face. "I sure am. What have we got?"

"Whatever they said you could have." The man looked over the tray. "And it looks like you get the special menu version." He grinned broadly. "Must be trying to fatten you up. Whoa . . . shouldn't say that to a lady."

Rachel laughed and was pleased with the sound. She hadn't laughed at anything for a long time, it seemed.

"Take your time. I'll be back later and collect the hardware," he called, making his way out the door to his waiting cartful of meals.

Scrambled eggs, a sausage patty. It was wonderful. She closed her eyes as she chewed, and . . . *Scott. Where are you now?*

She remembered the way he had looked at her when he asked her to forgive him. Those eyes had once been for her only. But those same eyes—when he was supposed to be working—had looked and lusted on . . . She couldn't say the name. Revulsion filled her again, and she shivered in the light hospital gown.

Oh, Scott. How could you do it? They had promised to be faithful to each other. She *had* been faithful, even while he lied to her. Even when he left her crying all alone in the bedroom that night.

And who knows where he went after that?

She swallowed the food, now a dry and tasteless lump that stuck in her throat until she sipped at some juice.

Did she still want him?

Yes.

She closed her eyes, barely willing to face what would come next.

His betrayal had been so great. He had allowed that woman into their house, and . . . The tears came again, *two people she had trusted had humiliated her.*

Was she going to have to spend the rest of her life wondering if he was telling the truth, wondering if he was with someone else? Trust had to be built on more than wishes.

Pastor Feldner's voice came to her now. Slow, cadenced. "Father, forgive them; for they know not what they do." He wanted her to understand that Scott could not earn her forgiveness. She just had to give it.

I'll do it, Lord. Because you say it. Not because I feel it.

Rachel pushed the tray away, laid her head back on her pillow, tried to prepare herself. She feared to forgive Scott. She was frightened to trust him again, so soon.

"Done with that breakfast?"

The orderly picked up the tray, and Rachel thumbed the button for a nurse to come. She hoped Scott would be a long time arriving. She needed time to get ready. Time to be believable.

"How can I help you?" The nurse that had cleaned her up the first time was back. "You're sure looking better."

Rachel's smile was weak. "My husband will probably be coming by today. It's all right if he comes in now."

"Are you sure, honey? If you need some space . . ."

"No, it's okay. I want to see him."

"I'll go get him if you're ready."

"What? How will you get him?"

"Sweetheart, he's been in the waiting room all night."

She whispered, "Okay," then turned to look out the window again. The leaves moved in the light breeze. What would she say to him? Back and forth they moved.

"Rachel?"

She took her eyes from the tree outside, turned her head to see Scott in the door.

"I love you, Rachel."

And I love you.

She put her arms out and let him come into her embrace.

CHAPTER THIRTY-NINE
Plans

The buckle snapped as Rachel cinched the seat belt tightly around herself. Her face was drawn, but the color was returning. Scott closed her car door, went around to the driver's side, and settled down behind the wheel. The windshield was dusty, the result of three days in the hospital parking lot.

The Andersons were at the house and the children were safe. Scott had scarcely left Rachel's side.

He was weary, but elated at the same time. He was bringing his wife home.

It was time to make everything new again and time to defend their family.

"It's almost like going to someone else's house, isn't it?" he asked.

She dipped her head. "Yes, but not for long. Just as soon as I get everything wiped down I'll be okay again. I've got to get every trace of that woman out of my house."

It was an odd feeling, going back to his home, treating it like a hazardous materials cleanup. An invader had been inside and like any kind of dangerous predator had left its mark. Animals always left a trail.

He sensed his mind focusing on their situation. Clarity was returning. Rachel was safe and the children would be all right. That was good for now, but the threat remained.

Scott tightened his grip on the wheel as he accelerated onto the highway. "The most important thing we've got to do is get the kids somewhere safe. Now that your dad's here, he and your mom can take them both back home with them until we figure out what we have to do. It may not take long to track Melissa down, whoever she is."

"Agreed. I don't think they'll have any problem with that. Dad already told me that they would do whatever we asked to help make us safe again."

"I know. Thank God for them." Scott reached for Rachel's hand, found it, and held it tightly. "We'll do whatever it takes and we'll do it together."

Rachel's hand was smaller than Scott's, but she gripped his firmly. "Together. The way God intended."

ANDY ANDERSON put his arm around Scott's shoulder and steered him toward the empty laundry room. "You haven't told us much, and that's okay. I just want to hear from you that our daughter's going to be safe. Promise me that?"

Andy's eyes locked on Scott's, who met his gaze and returned the same intensity.

He took the older man's hand in his own, gripped his forearm with the other. "I promise you she'll be okay. That we'll all be safe soon. There're some things we don't know yet, but we're going to learn all we need to."

Scott paused, breathed out. "And I'm going to make my family safe."

"That's good enough for me, son. We'll be praying for you constantly. We love you both. I'm trusting you completely."

The two men embraced, then returned to help their wives finish packing up the car.

"YOU CALL US WHEN you get there, okay? Don't forget." Rachel waved to her mother as she closed the door on her father's Chrysler sedan. Angela and Scotty waved back from the big rear seat. Ruff bounced across the seat and pressed his wet nose against the window, leaving a smeared splotch.

"They'll be fine." Scott wrapped his arm around Rachel's shoulders. "They couldn't be with better people than your mom and dad."

She nodded and leaned close to Scott as they watched the big car leave the driveway and move onto the road. When the car was out of sight they turned and went back into the house.

Scott laid two yellow notepads on the dining room table, one for each of them. He put his laptop computer on the table and flipped up the lid, powering it on. By the time the coffee had dripped through and been poured into two large, heavy mugs they were ready to work.

"Let's review what we know," said Scott. "We probably know more than we think we do. Number one, we both got fooled. *Alicia* is real. Not fake."

"And I think that must mean she works for the website

somehow," said Rachel. "Otherwise, how could she have done all she did?"

"I think then that the first thing we're going to want to do is check out the company." On the laptop, he keyed in http://www.virtualfriendme.com. From the website menu he chose "About." A brief history of the company appeared and the company's corporate address on the northeast side of Indianapolis.

"See this?" He pointed to the address. "I know where that is."

Rachel brought her head close to Scott's. He felt her warm breath on his cheek. It felt good to him, good to be close to her again.

"I know that place too. What else is there? Look at all the documents."

Scott said, "Look here, they have a press release from their big Go-Live."

"What's a Go-Live?"

"That's when a company officially tells the world their website is running. They had theirs here."

He clicked on the hyperlink and a PDF file expanded onto the display. "I'll print it out."

"Let me look while you check that." She clicked other links while Scott turned to pluck the papers coming out of the printer.

He was quiet until she heard a low whistle escape his lips.

"And what do you know? Wonder if it's her." He pointed to a name.

Rachel took the sheet, studied the document. "Melissa Montalvo. That's the right first name. I guess it could be. Let's see what it says about her."

He put his finger back on the spot and followed along the

line. "It says she's the chief software scientist. She probably has access to everything. Let's find out what else we can learn about her."

The website revealed nothing else about the person they had found. Most important, there was no picture.

"Check Google images. See if she's there."

Scott tried the image search, came up dry. "This is really strange. Can you imagine how hard you'd have to work to keep Google from having any picture at all of you?"

"Way weird. Okay, this isn't working. You know what we're going to have to do, don't you?" asked Rachel.

Scott nodded, as his stomach took a turn. The last time he'd seen her he'd been weak. That wasn't going to happen again. She'd tried to kill Rachel.

"We're going to go there and see if she shows up. We have to find out if it's her or not. And if it is, then we're going to dig deeper."

"Do you think the sheriff will ever come up with anything?"

"Maybe. They seem interested enough. For all I know they're still looking at me. I don't blame them. I'm sure they thought I did something to you. So much weird stuff goes on today. They don't know anything about me."

"It had to be when she was babysitting that she put that poison in the bottle, though, don't you think?" asked Rachel.

"Probably. But for all we know, she even knew the code to the garage door opener, or copied one of your keys when you were at Hugest Losers. We just don't know. One thing we do know is that we can't depend on other people to do this for us, police or not. God gave us our family and it's up to us to protect it."

Rachel tapped her index finger on the tabletop. "What is that website for professional networking? Linked Up, or something like that? Maybe she has an entry there."

A quick search of the website brought up eight different matches on the name spread all across the country. Two had pictures and were eliminated, but one matched.

"She's got a listing, but there's just a blank avatar where a picture should be. Not unusual; I don't have my picture there either."

"We're just going to spin our wheels doing all these web searches. Tomorrow morning we'll go to their office, park the car, and watch everyone that comes or goes. If she shows up for work, we'll know it."

"What if we don't see her? Then what do we do?"

"Whether we see her or not, I think the next step has to be the same. We find out what we can about her. We know about how old she is and we know what she looks like. We know her name's Melissa, and we're almost as sure that her last name is Montalvo. That makes pretty good sense so far.

"We can ask questions. Play dumb. I doubt that anyone else in that company has any idea what has happened. Think about it—they're in business to make a profit, not mess with people's lives. No, I think this must have been purely the work of one person."

"Why did she come after us, Scott? I still can't figure that out. Why did she go after you? Do you think we'll ever know?"

"We'll probably only know that if she tells us. And who knows? She might do just that. Time will tell."

"How do we stop her, then? Let's say that she works there and we find her. Let's even assume we find out where she lives and some personal information on her. What do we do then? Give all that to the police?"

"I don't know if the sheriff will be able to do any more than they have already. They didn't have a name, they didn't have anyone they could place at our home, nothing. Only your fingerprints were on the pill bottle. They did the basic things. They checked the references at Hugest Losers. That was all fake. I think that as far as they're concerned, they've done what they can. Unless something else happens, of course."

"Unless she gives us some kind of confession, which I really doubt, all we can do is confront her and threaten to expose her. Maybe her job is important enough to her that she'll back off. In any case she'll know she isn't going to get any farther with us."

Rachel wagged her head back and forth. "But we have to remember the children. We can't assume anything. The woman's a nutcase, and dangerous. She's already shown she can get close to them."

Scott smiled grimly, blinked. "You're right about that. Okay, so maybe we don't know everything right now. Not even what step three is going to look like. I say we don't waste any more time, though. We take step one, and go to the company in the morning. No matter what we find, we take step two, and ask around. Find out what we can about her. When we've done all that, we regroup, see where we stand."

"Scott, there's something important you've got to do. I can't do it." Rachel shivered, crossed her arms.

"What? Just tell me."

She picked her cell phone off the desktop and put it in his hand.

"Her pictures are in there, when she's holding Angela. I can't look at them. I want them gone."

He scrolled to the first picture, nearly pressed the delete button, then stopped. "I'd better forward them to my phone. We may need them someday."

Rachel raised one eyebrow. "Why would we want them?"

"Not us. The sheriff may want them. Who knows? But I'm getting them off your phone."

"There's something else we'd better do too. We'd better pray and ask God to help us with this. Keep us from being stupid. Lead us. We need His help."

Scott nodded and bowed his head. "Lord God, we are weak people. Needy people. Father, we're Your children and we need Your help. Our own wisdom and strength are not enough for the job we've got before us. Please lead us, help us, bless us. You said, every one that asketh receiveth; and he that seeketh findeth. We're asking. We're seeking. We wait upon you, Lord."

After the prayer, Scott said, "I haven't told Pastor Feldner about this, not in detail. He knows that I did something wrong, but I didn't tell him everything. Do you think I should? I really want a solid Christian like him praying with us."

"You'd have to tell him to keep it absolutely secret. I think most of this has to be between us and the Lord. But yes, I think you should."

"Okay. I will. There's something else, something really obvious, we ought to do. Do you know what I mean?" He shot Rachel a questioning look.

Looking away, she said, "I know. I've been avoiding it. I think I'm a little scared. Not scared like something might happen to us, but scared like I might do something dumb that will give our plans away."

"We're talking about the same thing, right? We go to the website and talk to *Suzanne* and *Alicia*. We do them separately, because we have no reason to think that she's caught on to how much we know. If we did one right after the other she might get suspicious. She probably doesn't realize we have put all this together. After all, she's treated us like pretty simple people so far."

"Especially me," said Rachel.

"Not so. It's been the same for both of us. Let's think about this. It's early evening now, so this would not be my normal time to talk to her. Let's have you log on and get Suzanne, and we'll see what happens."

"Won't she be able to see you if it's her doing it? Through the webcam?"

"You're right. Okay, I'll sit off to the side, where I can't be seen. Unless she catches on to what we're doing you can just tell her that I'm at the store getting you some medicine or whatever. Tell her you wanted to catch up on news with her and let her know what's going on. Act like we don't suspect anything at all."

"All right, but what are we trying to learn?"

Scott held up one finger. "First, we want to know if she'll play along as if we don't suspect anything. That's important. If she thinks we're still in the dark, then we have a big, big advantage. And we really need any advantage we can get right now." He held up the second finger. "Next, try to steer the conversation to be about me in some way. Let's just see what kind of things she says. I don't know what we'll learn with that, but we'll see what happens."

"Then what?"

"Tomorrow sometime we'll do the same thing, but with Alicia."

Rachel turned her face away. In a small voice she asked, "Are you going to talk to her like you used to?" She kept her gaze averted. "Scott, I don't want you to talk to her anymore."

A warm flush of shame came over Scott's face. That was a good question and an important one. No, he couldn't talk like that again.

"No, never. I'll figure something out. But I couldn't do that again. I *will not* do that again." He emphasized the words, punctuating each one. "Let's just try Suzanne and see where it takes us."

She turned back, took his hand in hers. "Okay, here goes."

CHAPTER FORTY
Unraveling

Rachel waited as Suzanne's face dissolved into place on the display.

"Rachel? Where have you been? I've been so worried about you."

This wasn't Suzanne anymore. The face was the same, the mannerisms unchanged. This time, though, she was looking at a mask, a wall of deceit. Her hands clenched. Rachel's skin prickled as she looked into the face of her enemy.

"Actually, I've been in the hospital."

I'd better be careful. I'm sounding a little testy.

"Thank you for worrying. I think it's all over now."

"What was wrong? Are you okay?"

"I had some kind of blood problem. I must have eaten some bad food or something. The doctors said I'd gotten some kind of chemical in my blood, but it's all gone now."

"Chemical? What sort of chemical?" she asked, in a voice that sounded overly sweet and sympathetic.

"Something called Coumadin. It does something to your blood so that you can't stop bleeding."

"Did they say where it might have come from? Could it happen again?"

"They didn't know. I'll have to be careful for a while with what I'm eating. Otherwise, I should be as good as new."

"Wonderful. And Scott? Has he been with you?"

Though he was out of range of the computer webcam Rachel could see Scott clearly. He crossed his wrists, handcuff style, and nodded to Rachel. "Not at first. There was some question in the beginning about how I had gotten the poison in my system. The sheriff even suspected Scott for a while. They questioned him about it."

Suzanne's mouth dropped in the semblance of surprise.

"They suspected Scott? How could they? They let him go, didn't they?"

"Yes, they let him go."

"Well, I had no idea what had happened to you. You've been out of touch for four days so I knew it had to be something serious. Is Scott still at work?"

Scott nodded to her. He'd not told Alicia that he lost his job, so Suzanne wouldn't know.

She followed his lead. "Yes, he went in to work after he brought me home from the hospital. He should be home anytime. I'm more worried about him than I am about myself. He's working so hard."

Rachel waited for some reply from Suzanne, but none came. "I'm pretty tired. We can talk tomorrow, okay?"

"Just one more question," said Suzanne. "Did Scott have anything else to say?"

"Anything else? Like what?"

Like did he tell me about you?

"I mean something not about work. Some of the things you

tell me about Scott make me worry about him. Should I be worried?"

Scott wagged his finger back and forth. "No, nothing else. I've got to go now. I'm really tired."

"All right. Good night, Rachel."

"Good night." Rachel clicked on the END button and the session terminated.

She faced Scott and exhaled. "Whew. That was so weird. Do you think she knew we were just playing along?"

"I don't think so," said Scott. "She was fishing for information. You gave her just enough to keep her wondering what we know."

Rachel sat back in the chair. "Tomorrow morning we pay a visit to Virtual Friend Me. That woman's about to learn that she's made a big mistake."

CHAPTER FORTY-ONE
Getting to Know All About You

The area was a high-tech industrial zone, buildings peppered all over a wide space that had been cornfields ten years before. The Virtual Friend Me building was a large green and white edifice. Four stories tall with a curved face, it fronted the interstate. There were two ways in, the main entrance in the back and an employee door on the west side.

Scott pointed at the main entrance. "How about you take that one? I'll take the employee door. There are plenty of benches and landscaping all around."

He parked the Taurus a half mile south of the building. The parking lot was one third full at six o'clock in the morning.

Rachel got out of the car first, dressed in a gray running outfit that contrasted with her husband's blue one. She reached into her pockets and checked the contents. "I've got my camera and cell phone. I'm set."

The car chirped as Scott thumbed his key fob. He dropped his keys into his own pack and checked his equipment. "Ditto. We're ready to go. Remember, no confrontations. We just want pictures. When we've got all we want, we meet back up here. No matter what happens, we get back here no later than nine-fifteen."

"Okay. Good luck." Scott took Rachel in his arms and kissed her. "You take care of yourself. Don't wear yourself out. You're still not very strong."

With a mock salute she said, "Yes, sir," and trotted off down the road.

The air was cool but not cold. Scott began a slow jog along the shoulder of the road. They were not the only joggers out this morning. He could count five more already, probably office workers who wanted to get their blood moving before the workday. Workplaces in this part of town offered workout rooms and showers to their employees as part of the high-tech culture.

He made out Rachel on his left, following a route parallel to his. She'd wind up squarely in front of the main entrance, just as they'd planned. She looked good as she ran. She was beginning to get her old form back again. How could he have ever looked anywhere else for a woman's attention?

The road wound around to the point closest to the west entrance. He left the road surface and continued his jog across the grass until he was within thirty feet of the entrance. He pulled his hood up, squatted down, and retrieved a water bottle from his pocket. He removed the camera at the same time, thumbed the power on, and held it cupped in his hand, thumb over the shutter.

Every time someone came or went through the door he snapped a silent picture. Concrete benches were arrayed around the entrance in a lopsided semicircle. Twice he changed position, moving from bench to grass, then back to bench. No one looked like Melissa. Not yet.

RACHEL PULLED HER HOOD up as she moved into place. The main entrance was mostly glass, and had a large flower garden planted in the circular drive in front. She scouted out the area as she pretended to shoot pictures of some of the blooms. There were three doors: a revolving door in the middle flanked by two push doors. Two medium-size trees grew on each side of the entrance.

Concealed by the trees, Rachel checked her camera, which was already set for silent mode. She set the optical zoom to its farthest extent and began snapping pictures of every person that entered or exited the building.

The Audi pulled into the parking lot at seven-eleven. It headed directly for one of the specially marked, reserved spaces near the front. It was Alicia's Audi—no, *Melissa's* Audi. The same one she had driven when she had watched the kids.

Rachel worked the shutter as quickly as she could, all the time never losing sight of her quarry. Melissa shut off the engine, then looked for something on the seat next to her. She got out of the car. Wearing a slate blue pantsuit and carrying a small computer or tablet case in her right hand, she walked briskly. Long dark hair fell to her shoulders, and dark glasses covered her eyes. She removed the sunglasses as she neared the door. Her eyes looked straight ahead as she walked, the heels of her boots making a tapping sound on the flagstones.

Rachel hugged the tree, keeping the shutter moving on the camera until her target had gone through the door into the building's entranceway. This was her, the woman who had tried to kill her and steal her family.

A thrill ran through Rachel. This was progress. They knew

her name, where she worked. They were one step ahead of her now, because she didn't even know they suspected anything.

She stepped from behind the trees, her face still concealed by her hood. Melissa walked inside the foyer and stood in front of the elevator doors. What floor would she go to? At this distance, the numbers above the door were not distinct enough to make out, but she should be able to tell which one was illuminated. Melissa got onto the elevator alone. Perfect. Rachel watched the door close, then studied the lighted display above the door. Two, three. The elevator stopped at the third floor.

She stepped back from the entranceway and jogged toward the car, throwing a low wave to Scott as she passed his position.

After a brief pause, he jogged after her.

Rachel reached the car first. She scrolled through her set of pictures until Scott arrived, more out of breath than she was.

She looked up from the camera. "Hey, old man. I thought I was the one who was supposed to be weak."

He rolled his eyes and shrugged. "What have you got? You left a lot sooner than I thought we would be leaving."

"Got her." Rachel's eyes gleamed with excitement. "Got her perfectly." She looked around. "We're too exposed here. Let's go somewhere, look at our surveillance pictures, and decide on our next step, okay?"

"Okay, spy lady." He slid behind the driver's seat, leaned over, and kissed her on the cheek. "How about the Denny's on the other side of the interstate?"

She closed her door. "Good. Get moving."

CHAPTER FORTY-TWO
Trackers

A middle-aged waitress seated them. "Coffee for both of you?"
They ordered black coffee and English muffins.

"Let's see what you got."

Scott watched as she scrolled through the pictures till she reached the Audi. "Here it is," she said.

The detail as Melissa got to the door was perfect. Rachel had caught her just as she removed her sunglasses, the sunlight still on her face. It was the same person who had touched his cheek with her own tears in Starbucks. His stomach roiled with emotion.

"What's the matter, Scott? Are you all right?"

He turned his head toward her. "Rachel, I am so sorry I ever let this happen. I am so, so sorry."

She squeezed his hand, looking squarely in his eyes. "That's over now. We're in this together, and we're going to put a stop to what she started."

He picked up the yellow notepad he'd brought in from the car.

"Let's call the company and say we're doing some research. They'll probably be happy to give us some information."

"Great idea, but what kind of research? They're not going to talk to just anybody, are they?"

"One of the companies I looked at as an investment was Virtual Friend Me. I can be an interested investment adviser. They should be willing to give me just about any information I want."

"Won't they want credentials? You don't even have an office they can call or e-mail to now. We don't want to spook her," said Rachel. "What if I called? I could say I was a teacher and we're interested in how the software was developed."

"Okay, that's better. But don't use your own phone. Not mine, either. Use this. Scott produced a new cell phone from his side pocket. "I picked up a throwaway that won't give our identities away."

Grinning, Rachel said, "Good move. Let's do it."

Rachel dialed. "Good morning, my name is Susan Norquist. Our computer science class is working on an artificial intelligence project and we're fascinated with what you're doing. I wonder if I could bring some of our students by for an interview." There was a pause, then Rachel winked at Scott. She whispered, "She's transferring me to someone else."

"Thank you. Mr. Locarno, my name is Susan Norquist. I teach a high school computer science class. We're working on an artificial intelligence project and we're very interested in what you're doing. Would it be possible to bring some of our students by for an interview?"

Scott leaned in and listened as they talked. Rachel was obviously excited about what she was hearing.

"Is Ms. Montalvo your primary software architect?" Rachel paused, listening, then nodded to Scott.

"Where did she graduate?" . . . "And you say she's originally from here in Indiana?"

Scott leaned in close, scrawling down notes as he heard them.

"Oh, really? How awful." Rachel turned to Scott, eyes like saucers. She started pointing at the phone and nodding.

"No, my husband and I probably hadn't come here yet. We were just getting married back then. It's a wonder the company survived."

She rolled up her eyes and shook her head slowly back and forth.

"I understand, yes, sir. Thank you so much. I'll call back to set up a definite time for the class." Rachel's smile extended from ear to ear. "All right, Mr. Locarno. Good-bye until then." Rachel pushed the END button, terminating the call, and let out a long breath. "Wow."

"Wow, what? What did they say? Who's Locarno?"

Slouching back in the booth, she said, "That was a guy named Bob Locarno. He's the second in command for their software." Her eyes turned intent. "Scott, he works for her. I mean, directly for her. He knows all about her."

"So what did you learn? Tell me."

"Scott, you won't believe this. Something happened to the guy who started the whole project. Locarno wouldn't tell me the details, but it was somewhere around five years ago. We'll have to check that out. You don't suppose . . ."

"He just disappeared, or what?"

"I don't know. It sounded really odd. But Melissa has his job now."

"Wow." Scott let out a deep breath. "Maybe we weren't the first. Did he tell you the man's name?"

"No. Let's make notes so we don't forget anything. Here." She handed the pen and notepad to Scott. "You write and I'll talk."

"Melissa Montalvo came to work there over four years ago. She's the one that hired this guy Locarno. The man before her disappeared. What is important is that she is the brains behind the whole virtual friend thing. *She invented it.* She's in charge of everything."

Scott's eyes opened wide. "So she has her fingers in every bit of it. There's nothing she can't do."

"Exactly. There are over sixty people who work for her on their system. Locarno is like her deputy for everything that goes on. The guy almost worships her—I could tell that from the way he talked.

"Her office is on the third floor. When I bring my 'class' by, he says they'll show us her office. She can control everything from her desk. He says we'll be amazed."

"Did he tell you where she lives?"

"No, but we can figure that one out ourselves. Let me get all this out and we'll get our notes complete."

Scott scribbled notes as she talked. From time to time he asked a question. When they had finished, he sat back.

"Now we find out where she lives."

THEY PARKED THE TAURUS at the far end of the parking lot, where a landscaping truck obscured them. At four-ten, Melissa Montalvo exited the front entrance of the Virtual Friend Me building and got in her car.

Scott fired up the engine and followed the Audi out of the parking lot. He allowed a long distance between the two vehicles. When they turned onto the main thoroughfare he let other cars come between them, but always kept the Audi in sight.

"She's turning. Her right blinker is on."

Scott slowed as she turned into an old residential neighborhood close to downtown. He made the turn just in time to see Melissa pull the car into a detached garage beside an older gray home with a large bay window in the front. "Can you see the address?"

"Got it: five-one-two." Rachel snapped more pictures as they drove on by the house.

Once they were out of sight of the house, he pulled the car up to an empty space by the curb. "I know what we've got to do."

Rachel met his gaze. "What?"

"Go back where it all started. Back where the secrets are."

She raised her eyebrows.

"Everybody's got secrets, and I'm willing to bet this woman's past has some things in it she really doesn't want people to know about. Things we can use to fight her."

Rachel nodded slowly. "You're right. She knows all about us. We need to know even more about her. And that means . . ."

"Going to where she came from."

"But why there?"

"When you kill a weed, you dig out the root. We start at ground zero."

CHAPTER FORTY-THREE
Helpless

That useless woman was still alive.

She'd known as much, but hadn't wanted to believe it. Now she had seen for herself.

Melissa gripped her tablet, arm stiff with tension. She wanted to throw it across the living room, let the screen shatter against the hard plaster of the wall. The display had been polluted with Rachel's face again. She bent her arm, fingers pinched tightly on the thin case.

No, she had to get control. She was better than that. She would not react to the situation. She would enact, take charge.

She laid the device down on the coffee table, facedown so she would not have to be reminded of what had just been on it.

She turned out the room lights. Then, sitting down on the sofa, she pulled her knees up to her chin, wrapped her arms around her legs, and looked out through the window. The amber light of the streetlamps puddled on the windowsill. She wore a long black nightgown, just the kind that Scott had liked when he first had Alicia wear it. She would wear it again one night and it would be with him alone.

Rachel.

She wanted to be done with her. Out of her life. If there were ever less excuse for a person being left on the earth, it was Rachel. She was like a foul odor in the refrigerator that wouldn't go away.

And what of Scott? Four days and not a word.

With *her* the whole time. Not good, not good at all. She'd worked too hard pulling them apart to give them any unnecessary time together.

Where were the children? She didn't like not knowing. A good mother should know where her children are. Everything was turned against her now.

Surely not Scott, though. He would never turn against her.

"A pair of star-cross'd lovers take their life."

No, not them. She and Scott would have many years together.

Closing her eyes, she lay her head back on the soft cushion of the sofa. She fantasized about being back at the cabin, high on their mountaintop. She sat on the outer balcony again. A cool breeze washed across her as she lay back, letting the heat of the setting sun drain off her body.

Soft noises came from inside the room behind her. Her love was there, preparing drinks for both of them to share as they watched the sun finish its descent behind the beautiful valley to the west.

How happy they were.

Scott was so long coming back outside to her. She wished he would hurry.

Her hands clenched and unclenched. She wanted him now.

OUTSIDE, a box truck thumped and clattered as it passed by the house.

Melissa shook herself, tried to clear her head. A walk, she needed to get outside and take a walk. Get some fresh air so she could think clearly.

With a loud "Mmmm," she lifted herself off the sofa to look more closely outside. Deciding to check the temperature, she opened the front door until the chain caught. Cool air forced its way in through the opening. She clicked the door shut and turned back through the living room to the kitchen, where she picked a zip-up sweat top off the back of a high chair.

She zipped it up almost to her neck, picked up her keys and mobile phone from the countertop, and put them in the jacket side pockets. The material was soft, loosely woven. She wanted to carry something sharp, just in case, but anything she put in those pockets would surely pierce the material and be poking her or getting lost.

Just this once, she'd go outside with no other protection. After all, it was her own street, her own neighborhood.

There was no one else on the sidewalks. Melissa started a slow jog, silent in her expensive running shoes. As she approached the end of the block, she looked ahead. A streetlight was out, leaving the next section of the road cloaked in darkness. She turned left, redirected herself toward the entertainment district four blocks south. A neighborhood movie theater, a couple of clubs, a Plato's Closet. More secure than running on the dark walkway.

As she ran, she imagined Scott running along beside her.

He would comment on her appearance, and she would enjoy the looks of the admiring women who watched them go by. No, not everyone in this world was as lucky as she was. And the harder she worked her plan, the luckier she was getting.

Her breathing came harder now as her heart rate increased with the exertion. "It's all . . . worth it . . . whatever . . . it takes."

Cars were parked closely together along the sides of the road. Off-street parking was limited, where it existed at all. High-banked yards rose to her right as she accelerated through the blackness toward the next streetlight.

It sounded like a cat mewing the first time she heard it. She slowed but didn't stop, strained to hear it again.

And there it was, still ahead of her, but off to the right. Melissa slowed her jog to the speed of a fast walk.

Not a cat, something else. She moved silently, watchful, wondering what could be making the sound.

"JUST HOLD STILL." The voice was rough, insistent. She jerked her head in alarm, but saw no one. Melissa stopped, stood close to a wide tree on the narrow beltway, and fought to control her labored breath. Who had spoken?

A high hedge separated the two houses next to the sidewalk, ten feet beyond the foot-high retaining wall. She made out a white T-shirt as a man turned, his back toward her. She couldn't see his face in the darkness. His arms were in motion, doing something.

Wary now, she backed herself behind the tree and peered around, up into the yard where the figure stood. If there was danger here, she wanted no part of it.

Now she made out a second man in dark clothes standing just beyond the first. The sounds came more clearly now. One of the men breathed heavily.

And the other sound.

"Oh, God, please no . . ." It was a young voice, a girl.

Melissa couldn't see her, evidently hidden behind the end of the tall hedge.

"Hold still, I said."

The white-shirted man's shoulders turned rapidly, then she heard the dull sound of a hand striking someone.

"Uhhhh." Sobbing. "Okay, okay. Please don't hurt me."

Fear rose up within her like ice water. What if they saw her? She didn't dare move.

The terror clutched at her heart like an old enemy, one she remembered well. The words she heard were the same words as the other time. *It's happening again.*

What if they saw her?

Weapons. She quickly patted her pockets. Nothing but the cell phone and her keys.

She snatched the phone out, turned behind the tree so the light would not show, and dialed 911. She laid it on the ground.

People used keys as weapons. Her heart skipped as the keys jingled coming out of her pocket. She looked up quickly, fearing she'd been heard, but the men paid her no attention.

The white shirt was kneeling. A low sobbing sound was coming from the unseen girl.

She held the key ring so that the long Audi key stuck out like a knife blade, gripped it securely, and stepped back onto the sidewalk.

The dark man turned toward her. "Go away." Rather than approach her, though, he backed up into the shadows.

"I'm leaving, don't worry."

The girl was lying on her back alongside the hedge. The white-shirted man was on top of her, breathing heavily, his hands on her shoulders.

"Get her, Bobby. Before she calls someone." The voice was labored, insistent, as he turned back to the girl.

Melissa backed up into the street, turned to run down the dark lane toward the lights at the end.

She was only six feet away when a heavy, rough arm came up under her chin, and she felt herself being thrown to her left.

She thudded onto the ground, felt something brittle and sharp dig into her temple, and then the impact of the dark man as his full weight pounded her once again against the unyielding ground.

The air rushed out of her under the crush of the heavy body, as he came to rest on top of her.

She tried to pull her hand free so she could fight back with the key, but felt instead sharp pains flash up her arm as she tried to move her fingers.

Twisting under his weight, she tried to turn her head to see her attacker. As her face came up, pain exploded in white light as his fist caught her by her left eye.

She tried again to pull her hands free, but the man's body seemed to be everywhere. He felt enormous, invincible, as she tried to move under his bulk. Now his fists started pummeling her face and shoulders.

Left, right, left, right. Her head snapped one way, then the other as the blows fell. The world began buzzing in her ears. A rough hand tugged on her sweatpants.

He's going to rape me.

She felt the hairy arms of the man on her face, felt her pants pull free.

She seemed to float in the air, detached from the spectacle beneath her, as she lifted away, away . . .

The last thing she heard was the crying of the girl as Melissa yielded up her consciousness.

RUNNING, RUNNING. A soft, insistent chirping sound stole into Melissa's dream.

What . . . where am I?

She tried to open her eyes. The right lid struggled halfway open, but the straining left eye stuck stubbornly shut.

A hospital.

She rotated her head carefully. Everything hurt. Her face, her neck, her eyes. It hurt to see.

A curtain encircled most of the bed, a window was visible to the right. The blinds were shut, but no light slipped through the slats. It was nighttime. No way to know what day.

Lifting her left arm to eye level, she saw the array of tubes and wrappings around it. She tried to raise the other arm, but it didn't move.

Suddenly weary with the small effort, she lay her head back and closed her eyes. A sense of peace enfolded her as she shut out the sight of the blinking, beeping equipment around her bed.

She needed to think.

I'm in a hospital.

I'm going to live.

I've probably been raped.

Her lip trembled, chin quivered at the onset of the thought. It was too soon, too soon. Scott would have protected her, except for . . . *that woman.*

Rage seethed through her. She focused her hatred against Rachel like a beam of deadly force, seeking her out.

This is Rachel's fault. She will pay, oh, she will pay.

She felt a hand on her wrist, opened one eye to see a nurse standing by her bed.

"We're going to want you to rest a little longer, at least till morning, okay?" The nurse offered a kindly smile as she pushed a hypodermic into a tube suspended from a hook. "We're going to take good care of you."

Melissa didn't hear the last of her words as the soporific took effect and she drifted off into restful, numbing sleep.

CHAPTER FORTY-FOUR
Resolve

The hand was back, tugging gently at her forearm. Melissa felt warm sunlight on her face, illuminating her closed eyelids.

Morning.

She opened her eyes, slowly at first, testing for pain. When they came fully open, all the muscles around them rebelled against the movement.

"Waking up, are you?" Not the nurse this time.

A thirtyish man in blue hospital garb held her left hand, using both of his. He put it unhurriedly back down on the bedcovers, pulled a stool close, and sat down next to her.

"I'm Dr. Sears. You're in University Hospital. Do you know how you got here?" His face looked kind, professional. A laminated badge hung from his pocket. *Victor Sears, MD.*

Melissa opened her lips. They were dry and hard. Her tongue felt thick.

"Here, try some apple juice." He pressed the cup lightly against her lip, tipped it back just enough for her to sip.

"Thank you," she whispered hoarsely, and closed her eyes again.

"No, I don't remember coming here, but . . ." She let out a long exhalation of breath. "But I remember what was happening."

She opened her eyes again, peered under heavy lids at the doctor. "Am I—"

"You were not raped, Ms. Montalvo." He looked down at a paper. "That is correct, is it not? You are Melissa Montalvo?"

"Yes."

"Oooooh," she exhaled again. "They didn't do it?"

He held her hand again. "No, they surely tried and you have the bruises to prove it. It appears they were interrupted before they could"—he appeared to struggle for the word—"*finish* what they were doing."

Melissa opened her eyes once more, saw that a nurse was now standing on the other side of the bed. Melissa smiled weakly at her. "Were you the one here last night?"

"No, honey. That was someone else. One of the night staff."

Dr. Sears said, "There was another person, too. Younger than yourself, but I don't have any information on her here. I'm sure you'll learn more after you're interviewed by the authorities. They'll have the details."

He smiled, squeezed her hand reassuringly. "But you. You're alive, you're healthy, and you're going to be fine, physically. Just bruises and some abrasions." Another squeeze of the hand. "These will heal. It's the emotional, the psychological side of an attack like this that sometimes takes the longest to heal. We'll get you some help with that."

Melissa's eyes moved up to the cold, white surface of the ceiling.

I'll get my own help for that.

AFTER THE DOCTORS and nurses finally unplugged all of their equipment, they left her alone in the room to sort through her emotions and get cleaned up. She sat on the side of the bed, then put her feet down on the cold laminate floor.

With one hand on the wall for support, she stood up straight, found that her legs were sore but strong. She could walk without help.

Melissa stood in the bathroom, looked at her reflection in the mirror for the first time. Gauze bandages covered her cheeks and the bridge of her nose.

She carefully lifted the first. A bright purple bruise the size of a tennis ball surrounded her left eye. It was lined with small fissures where bright red blood still wanted to ooze.

The right eye was better, an angry red abrasion underneath, and the white of her eye flooded with red blood. They had warned her about that, and told her not to be afraid. The blood was all under the surface and would go away on its own.

What kind of animal does this to another person?

Her neck hurt, her shoulders ached. She had never been beaten like this. Worst of all, she was not beautiful.

I can't let Scott see me when I look like this. She replaced the bandages, piece by careful piece. Every touch on the surface of her skin was painful, some spots far more than others. She jerked her hand back in surprise when, unthinking, she pushed down on the tape in the wrong place, causing pain to flash across her flesh. She had to put both hands on the washbowl to steady herself until the throbbing subsided.

A police detective was coming by soon to interview her. She could get some answers then.

With great care she worked the toothbrush over and

around her teeth. The gums were sore. One tooth was loose, but she knew that it would likely be fine. In any case, she would see the dentist and have it checked.

Feeling better, she brushed out her hair. Even that felt sore.

A knock on the door.

"Just a minute," she started to call, then found that she couldn't make her voice loud enough to be heard.

She pulled the bathroom door back and looked out. Two men in suits stood outside in the hallway, looking very official.

"Melissa Montalvo?"

She raised her hand, nodded, whispered, "Come in." She looked around, saw only one chair in addition to the small stool by the bed. "I wasn't quite ready."

"Ms. Montalvo," said the shorter of the two, "my name is Sam Deering, and this"—he indicated his partner—"is Alan Gorst." Deering showed an official-looking badge in a leather holder. "We're Indianapolis Metro detectives, and we're investigating what happened to you last evening. Is this a good time to talk with you?"

Melissa went to the bed, found it difficult to lift herself up to sit.

"Please, sit on the chair. We won't take much of your time this morning," said the one named Gorst as he pulled the door closed behind him.

Melissa sat, holding both arms of the chair as she lowered herself into it. The air rushed out of the cushion with a whooshing sound.

Deering said, "We know you've been through a difficult time—"

He caught the intensity of her glare.

"A horrible experience. I wish there were another way, but we have to ask you some questions about last night. Would that be all right with you?"

Melissa continued to direct her gaze directly into Deering's eyes. "What happened to the girl that was there? The other one."

Deering looked at Gorst. The man nodded, and he turned back to Melissa. "Do you know the other young lady, Ms. Montalvo?"

"No. Is she okay?"

"She is"—he shifted on his feet—"in reasonable condition. Unlike yourself, however, she was forcibly raped by her attacker."

Deering looked down at the floor, back up to Melissa. "She is only twelve years old. She was on her way to the convenience store two blocks down when they apparently stopped and assaulted her."

She swayed on the seat, holding the arms to keep herself steady.

"Did you catch them? The men?"

Gorst spoke. "I think we can thank you that we have one in custody. The other has not been apprehended. Not yet. But we're confident we'll have him soon."

"Thanks to me?"

"Your cell phone was lying on the ground. Didn't you dial nine-one-one?"

She remembered now. Yes, she had done that. She'd punched the buttons and laid it next to the tree before she went up into the yard.

"Yes, I recall doing it now. I'd forgotten."

"When you are ready, sometime in the next day or so, do you think you could pick the man out in a lineup?"

"I'm sorry, but I can't." Her eyes went dry as she spoke. "It was dark. I didn't see their faces. One had a white T-shirt, and the other wore dark clothes. The one with the dark clothes was hitting me. He hit me and . . ." Her voice broke.

"We have that individual in custody, I believe. He was wearing a navy blue shirt as you describe. He's made a complaint of his own against you, but I don't think it will come to anything."

"He made a complaint against me? You can't be serious." Melissa's eyes opened wide, incredulous.

"Well, I wouldn't worry about it. He is claiming that you, well"—he spread his hands in a gesture of helplessness—"propositioned him, and then demanded more money."

She couldn't speak, sat slack-jawed, looking unbelievingly at the detective.

He waved his hand dismissively. "Don't be concerned. We get this kind of thing all the time. What we need to do now is go over the entire incident with you, while it is still fresh in your mind."

Gorst took out a yellow notepad, nodded.

"Are you ready?"

But Melissa wasn't listening. She was focused on some unseen spot on the wall. An inferno of hatred blazed inside her.

She got me beat up and accused of being a prostitute. She'll pay for this.

"Ms. Montalvo?" He touched her arm with a fingertip. "Are you ready?"

"Oh, yes, I'm ready."

CHAPTER FORTY-FIVE
By Any Other Name

Rachel laid a hand on Scott's shoulder as he searched the news archives. "Have you found anything yet?"

"Aaron Getz. Look here." He pointed to the screen, where a news article was displayed. "This was it. The same company name. He was found dead in a motel room. The police never came up with anything."

"Does it say what he did? Locarno said he was the main software guy."

"Here. It says he was in charge of development. That would be it."

"So, Melissa comes in just as he—conveniently—happens to die. You can't make a police case out of that, but knowing what we know, it sure looks suspicious. I wouldn't put anything past that woman."

"I'll print this. See what you can find on the university website." Scott sent the article to the printer, picked up the pages, and put them in a folder.

Rachel brought up the Indiana University website and

clicked through the graduation records. Names and graduation dates scrolled by. Then she leaned in close, nose almost to the screen. "I've got it!"

Scott looked up from the road atlas spread out before him. "You found her already?"

"Melissa R. Montalvo." She pointed at the screen. "Look at this."

He pulled a chair over and sat beside her.

"See? Right here. Name, date, and even her hometown."

"Blairsville, Indiana." Scott tipped his head to one side. "Have you ever heard of it?"

Rachel brought up a map site. "It's down on the Ohio River, just west of Madison."

"That's where we're headed, then. I think once we get there we can learn a lot. I'm betting that there are going to be some things that will surprise us."

At eleven o'clock they completed their notes and plans for the drive. "If we leave at six in the morning we can be there by nine-thirty. Are you still game?" asked Scott.

"You know I am. I feel like we're really doing something now. Like we're in control again."

"We *are* in control. We got that back when we refocused our lives on each other." Scott put his arms around Rachel, pulled her close to him, and buried his face in her hair. "I love you so much. I thank God for you."

Rachel stiffened, then gradually relaxed and leaned her head back against him.

"And I love you," she whispered. "I will never let you go."

THE SUN WAS BRIGHT the next morning as Scott parked the car. They cruised the old town looking for a place to eat breakfast, finally settling on the Pokhagon Café on River Street. The café and the Kayak Shop were busy, even though it wasn't yet nine in the morning.

"Doesn't look too mysterious, does it?" asked Rachel, looking out the café window. Pedestrians were walking across the short bridge outside.

Scott scooped up the last bit of corned beef hash off his plate. "Nope. Just a normal place."

The waitress approached with the check. "Get you two anything else? More coffee?"

"Maybe a little information. My wife might have family around here. Do you know where we could go to look up some of the old news stories and historical records?"

She turned the breakfast check facedown on the table. "What you need to do is get over to the old *Blairsville Voice* office. Harold Ranger still works in there. You can see all the old papers." She pointed down the road. "Just walk across the bridge over there. It's on the other side of the street."

The *Voice* was across from the Sunoco station, two blocks east. Scott held Rachel's hand as they walked across the short bridge. Her hand was warm in his. "Are you ready to play detective?"

"Just remember to call me Lucy, okay? I'm here checking on my family history."

The old storefront had a single, large plate glass window, cracked through in one corner. The words *Blairsville Voice* were still stenciled in an arc of red letters across the center of the glass.

Scott turned the brass knob on the door. "Locked." He shaded his eyes from the sun, and bent over to look in closer. Two eyes looked back at him. He jumped back.

The doorknob rattled and the door swung inward. A wizened old man's face stared back at him. "Help you folks?"

Scott caught his breath as Rachel laughed softly behind him. "Yes, sir. Is this still the office for the *Blairsville Voice*?"

"Only one we got. But we don't print the paper no more. You folks are welcome to come in, though. I don't get many visitors." He opened the door wider. Scott stepped through and Rachel followed. The room was dim, the walls taken up with shelves reaching to the top of the tin ceiling, which were filled with large, dusty green binders. An ashtray and some of the binders lay in disarray on an old conference table that sat in the middle of the room.

"This is it." The old man swept his hand around the room. "The *Blairsville Voice*, from 1886 right up to the last day. That was last year, Fourth of July." He turned and made his way to an old, wooden office chair. Dust spiraled around his feet as he sat down. "My name's Harold Ranger. Thirty years ago I used to run our Linotype machine. What can I do for you?"

Ranger indicated two empty seats beside the conference table. Scott pulled one chair out for Rachel and took the second for himself. "We'd like to look at some of the issues for the year or two prior to when you stopped publication. We're doing some research."

"What kind of research, son?" Ranger raised an eyebrow and squinted at Scott. "I don't think you're from around here, are you?"

Rachel spoke. "No, sir. But my family was originally from here."

Ranger turned his face toward her.

"I'm trying to gather information on my family history. People told us this is the place to come and that you were the man to see."

He settled back in his chair, the hint of a smile on his lips. "Well, that's prob'ly right. Anybody wants to know anything about this area, this is where you come."

He sat back. "What's the family name?"

"Montalvo. It's Italian."

"Oh, that it is. Lots of Italians around here. Are you any relation to the Montalvos up the hill towards Blake Cemetery?"

"I don't know. I guess I could be. Who are they?"

"Well, I guess I prob'ly said that wrong. It's not Montalvos anymore, like with an s on the end. There's only one left up there now. She lives up there alone. Sound like what you're looking for?"

Rachel and Scott exchanged glances. "Sure, I'm interested in anything you've got. Up where?" asked Scott.

The old man didn't answer, just sat in place, his eyes flicking back and forth between the couple before him.

"Sir?" Scott began.

Ranger stood up, turned, and walked back to the door. Without hesitation he opened it wide and stepped back.

"You two come back after lunch. Maybe I'll have something, maybe not."

"Mr. Ranger, I . . ."

Rachel pulled on Scott's sleeve.

"We'll be back, Mr. Ranger," said Rachel. "Thank you so much for your time."

Outside, Scott followed Rachel as she turned right and

started walking down the street. "What happened in there?"

"He wasn't sure about us. Give him some time. He said after lunch, and that's what we'll do," said Rachel.

He didn't like waiting. "Maybe we should try to find that cemetery."

"No, we'll just be patient. Go to the library, whatever."

She stopped, turned her face up to his. "That man knows something, and I think he wants to tell us. Just give him some time to convince himself that it's okay for him to do it."

AT ONE-THIRTY they found the door to the *Blairsville Voice* already ajar. Scott pushed it open to find the old man slumped back in an oilskin chair.

Ranger lifted himself out of the chair and shuffled over to the shelves. He pulled down a large volume and examined the label on the cover. "You'll find what you need here, I think. Fourteen years ago."

The book hit the table in an expanding cloud of dust. "Sorry about that. Not much of a housekeeper." He coughed. "Dust is gonna kill me if I don't get it first."

He leafed through the pages of newsprint in the book until he found what he was looking for. "Lady, I hope this part isn't about your family. We was all pretty shook up when this happened." He stepped aside.

The article title was "Double Homicide." In smaller text beneath it was "First Double Murder in a Century." A picture of a weeping woman getting into a police car was on the right.

Scott stiffened. "Oh, wow. I see what you mean. A double murder."

"Yep. Never arrested nobody, neither. Nothing like that happened before or since. Left that woman up on the hill a widow."

"Look at this." Scott pointed out the names. "They're all named Montalvo."

Rachel looked at the yellowing paper. "So this man, Anthony Montalvo, was stabbed to death? And his wife too?"

The old man stirred. "Wait a minute. They wasn't married. Just had the same last name. Tony Montalvo was married to the lady up there on the hill, but that day—it was close on to the end of spring that year—he was at his brother Ed's house out the other end of town.

"It was Ed's wife died with Tony. Somebody killed them both. Stabbed 'em."

Rachel twitched. A shiver ran through her body. "That's so awful."

"Who did it?" asked Scott, eyes questioning.

"Never knew for sure. Ed killed hisself later on. After he did that, most people figured it was him what killed everybody. But Tony's wife, why, like I say, she still lives up there in the same old house, all by herself. Never got married again. They never had any kids or nothin'. Just lives all alone." He looked wistful.

Rachel asked, "Mr. Ranger, so you're saying that this lady is the only survivor of all that? No children or anyone else left?"

"Oh, there was one. The other family, the one across town? Where the dead woman was from. Ed and her had a daughter. Don't know what ever became of her. I think she left before her father died. Haven't heard nothin' about the daughter for years."

Scott and Rachel caught and held each other's eyes, then Scott asked, "Do you remember her name, Mr. Ranger?"

"Rose. Her name's Rose. She just lives up there all by herself."

"No, Mr. Ranger, I mean the daughter. The one from the other family across town. Do you remember the daughter's name?"

Ranger twisted up his face in concentration. He was saying something under his breath—" . . . issa, isha, issa." Then he shook his head. "I don't remember, rightly. Maybe it'll come to me. Rose'll know. You ask her."

Five minutes later, Scott turned up North Street.

"From Ranger's directions, we ought to be there in two minutes or less." He negotiated a left turn. "That street up there should be Willis. Blake Cemetery and the house ought to be at the end of the road."

"What are we going to say, Scott? What if she doesn't want to talk to us? Then where are we?"

"We'll be in the same spot we were an hour ago." He grinned at her. "And we keep making good progress."

"It's all so creepy. I mean, could she have something to do with the deaths of those people?"

Scott slowed, seeing kids' toys near the roadside. "I don't know. But if I were going to bet, I'd say we found our girl. She appears to have a violent history." As he said the words, he felt a sting of guilt. *I'm your girl.* That's what she'd said.

Willis was a dead end. He drove the Taurus to the end of the road, where a wooden power line pole blocked any further progress. A white wooden sign hung off a four-by-four frame with painted blue lettering: "BLAKE CEMETERY."

"We're here."

THE HOUSE, a low, gray ranch with blue trim, was on the north side of the road. A yellow garden hose lay outside on the grass next to two cushioned lawn chairs.

"Could this be the place? Look at the two chairs, and there's a lawn swing at the other end of the yard. That seems strange."

Scott clucked his tongue. "Three twenty-one Willis. This is right. But I see what you mean. If she's alone, why two chairs?"

They parked along the edge of the road in front of the home.

Scott knocked on the storm door. The inner door was open, but the glare on the glass kept him from seeing anything inside.

A coarse woman's voice called out, "Who's there?"

"Good afternoon, Mrs. Montalvo. Can my wife and I speak with you for a minute?"

From somewhere within the gloom of the house, a slender woman in a dark cotton dress stepped close to the glass door. Her hair was gray, streaked with black. "Who are you? What do you want?"

"Mrs. Montalvo, My name is Gary, and this is my wife, Lucy. We're doing some research on our family history. Harold Ranger down at the *Blairsville Voice* said we should come up and talk to you."

"I know, I know." She came up close to the door, eyes narrowing as she peered through the glass. "You the ones Harold called about. From the *Voice*."

"Yes, ma'am. He thought we should talk with you."

"Well, you can't come in. Why would he send you up here? You know, they don't even print the *Voice* anymore." She crossed her arms in front of her and took a step back. "So what do you want?"

"Mrs. Montalvo?" Rachel pressed her face up closer to the door. "We'd really like to talk to you." She turned and pointed to the lawn chairs outside. "Could we sit in those beautiful lawn chairs and talk for a few minutes? You have such a lovely home, and it all looks so welcoming."

"Outside? Okay, maybe." She pushed the door open and stepped outside, pulling her dress together at her neck. "Only got two chairs, though." She turned her head back up to Rachel. "Lucy? Your name's Lucy? Lucy what?"

"It used to be Montalvo. But just call me Lucy, okay?"

Scott reached for the woman's elbow to help her across the lawn, but she pushed his hand away. "Don't need your help." She walked to the end of the house, where the two padded lawn chairs were. She sat down, and pointed Rachel to the other chair. Scott squatted down on the soft grass next to Rachel.

"This is a beautiful yard, Mrs. Montalvo," said Rachel. "I imagine you love being down here at the end of the road without a lot of traffic."

"It's pretty nice, all right. Marie from across the street comes over and we sit here and talk about things. Marie's alone too, you know."

She pointed to a large locust tree in the center of the yard. "See that tree? My Tony planted that back in 1963 when we first moved up here on the hill. Tony was my husband. My name's Rose."

Scott scrutinized her as she spoke. She was thin, wiry. He glanced around the yard, noting the landscaping. She was not a weak woman.

Her gaze turned toward Rachel. "Your name's Montalvo? Your family from around here?"

"No, we're from up in Indianapolis. We heard there was some history here with the Montalvo family."

"That's what you're here about? 'Bout what happened to Tony?"

"In a way. Mr. Ranger said maybe you could help us."

"Well, Harold's a good man. If he sent you up here, then I don't guess it would be any problem telling you." A faraway look came into her eyes. "It was in May, when kids was getting out of school. Tony'd gone over across town to help his brother with some gutter work. The way they tell it, Ed was gone when Tony got there and Tony was home alone with Marie."

"Marie?"

"Marie was his sister-in-law. Ed's wife. He'd been over there longer than he needed to be." She shot Scott a hard look. "Men got one thing on their minds. You cook, you clean . . ."

"What happened, Rose?" Rachel asked.

"That's when she killed him." She pushed her jaw out, neck muscles tightening. "That's when she killed my Tony."

Rachel's eyebrows rose. "Marie? Marie killed Tony?"

"No, not Marie. What did Harold tell you? Marie got it too. She killed both of them. Killed her mother, killed my Tony."

She bent down, picked up a twig from the grass and snapped pieces of it off. "Next year after that, Ed was gone, too. Killed himself, they say. I say was she that did it. Took everything he had away."

"Who, Mrs. Montalvo? Who did it?"

Yellow teeth showed briefly behind a pitiless smile. "Police say Tony killed Marie, then killed himself. They were wrong."

"How do you know they were wrong? Do you really know who did it?"

"Sure I know. She came here and told me what she done. Thought I'd understand." Her laugh came cold and hard. "Understand? Oh, yeah. Know what I understand? I understand what it means to live alone in this old house. I understand what it is to live every day in pain, knowing she's still out there somewhere."

"Did you tell the police?"

"They thought I was crazy. Told me I was a Gypsy liar. Said it was all over. All closed up neat as you please."

A cold flame burned in her eyes as she turned to glare at Rachel. "I think it's time you told me why you're really here."

Rachel looked to Scott. He nodded once. "Tell her."

"Mrs. Montalvo, my name is not Lucy. It's Rachel. I'm not a Montalvo."

"I knew that right off. Hair's wrong. Skin's wrong. Keep going."

"I believe a woman named Montalvo tried to kill me. Poison was put in place of some medicine I was taking and I almost died."

Scott took her hand, held it tight.

"We came to Blairsville to see if we could find some kind of connection. Find out what's really going on."

Rose Montalvo closed her eyes, nodding slowly. "I knew this would happen. Had to. How old's this woman tried to hurt you? Maybe thirty-three, thirty-four years old?"

"Yes. That's right."

Scott rose and wrapped his arm around his wife. "Please tell us what you can, Mrs. Montalvo. We're trying to protect our family. Our little boy, our little girl."

A bitter smile formed on her lips. "It was my niece."

She looked up, eyes searching. "She's the one ruined my life. Took away my husband. That's right. My niece, Melissa Montalvo."

CHAPTER FORTY-SIX
Snip

Melissa sat cross-legged in the darkness, a warm cup of coffee in her hands. Reflected light from the kitchen range hood cast spectral shadows through the room.

One full week. Scott had not logged back on to talk with her.

The world outside appeared gray through the bay window. Indistinct forms passed by on the street. Pale yellow streetlights shone dully on the sidewalks and curbs.

Rachel. She should have been dead by now, forgotten. Instead, she was with Scott. It wasn't right. The discoloration around her eye was darker than ever. It hurt her eyes just to open them wide. She couldn't let Scott see her this way. Her tablet lay next to her. She'd sent Scott an e-mail at work every day since the debacle with *The Other*. Did he suspect anything?

No, of course not. Rachel talked to Suzanne just three days ago.

Scott knew she was real, though. Why hadn't he tried to contact her? Didn't he know how much she needed him? He wasn't like other men. He'd told her he loved her. He was the center of her life. Without him she had no purpose.

Surely he wouldn't have said anything to Rachel. She would have received an angry e-mail or something. Some kind of communication from one of them.

The great, yawning *emptiness* inside her cried for satisfaction. It swelled and clawed its way into her every thought, every action. It dominated her world. She couldn't keep going like this.

She looked down at the cup, now cold in her thin fingers. Fewer cars passed by now, never more than one at a time. People were home with their families. Mothers and daughters baking cookies. Fathers and sons working on projects in basements and garages.

All she had was this grasping, gnawing *void* inside that threatened to consume her.

She forced herself to her feet.

In the kitchen, Melissa set a stainless steel skillet on the stovetop. She pressed the knob, watched the flame pop and hiss into a steady heat. She turned it down low, poured some olive oil into the pan, and waited for it to warm.

The oil moved in little eddies as the temperature increased. It was hypnotic, watching the whirls and designs the fluid created on the shiny steel surface. The heat forced the oil to move against its will. It had no choice but to try to escape the relentless pressure of the flame beneath it.

She lifted the skillet's handle just a degree. The oil ran to one side, but it ran toward the heat. Pushed down by gravity, unable to escape the fire.

Helpless. There were no choices. Only irresistible forces demanding surrender.

It wasn't enough to eliminate Rachel. Scott's mind and heart had been too divided. It all had to go. *Then he can be mine.*

The children were the problem. It wasn't Melissa's fault the way their mother used them to hold on to Scott, to keep him away from Melissa. Poor Angela. Scotty. It wasn't their fault either.

The flickering flame glinted off something metal lying on the countertop.

Cut them away, and they'll be gone. Just cut them all away. Scott will understand. Our love will be so strong he'll forget all about them. He loves me. He's confused now. I can help him. We'll hold each other and he'll forget all those other things. I can help him forget all those people that don't matter.

The faces of Rachel and the children formed in her mind. They looked like an old black-and-white photograph, edges worn with age. Long slivers were being sliced away. It was disappearing, the pieces tumbling away into nothingness.

Gone.

CHAPTER FORTY-SEVEN
Gray House

Should I pretend to talk to Suzanne again?"

Scott looked up at Rachel across their dining room table. "Maybe. I'm not sure. We've got to keep her from getting suspicious." He looked at his hands, seeming to study them. "She has to be wondering why she hasn't heard from me."

"Maybe you should contact her as Alicia. I don't like it, but I could sit with you while you did it."

Scott considered, then realized he couldn't look Rachel in the eyes. "No, I still don't think it would work. There's no way I could have the same sort of conversation with her that I did in the past. She'd know something had changed."

Rachel said nothing. She understood. He'd gone far, far over the line in his relationship with Melissa. There was no way he could ever restart it now. He couldn't pick it up where they had left it.

"I can e-mail her. I'll tell her things have really been hectic. That I'm sorry and I'll talk with her as soon as I can. She's probably been e-mailing me at Castle."

Copies of articles from the *Blairsville Voice* were spread out over the table. After their meeting with Rose Montalvo, they had gone back down to the dusty old newspaper office. Harold Ranger had allowed them to copy everything they had needed. There had been much more than any of them had imagined.

Melissa's name showed up twice in print. In one, she was listed as the only survivor of her father's suicide, the year after the double murder. The other, as a survivor in the gruesome double homicide that ended her mother's life. Always a survivor. Was it really a suicide?

Scott picked up the clipping, and his finger traced halfway down the column. "Melissa was on her way home from college the day her mother was murdered. Her uncle and mother were both found dead on the floor of her house. It happened the same day she got back."

"Do you think she really did it? Do you think Rose was right?"

"Why wouldn't she be right? She said that Melissa told her she'd done it. Thought she ought to be thankful." He shook his head. "I can understand killing someone else in anger. It happens all the time. But then, to be so cool about it that you go to the wife of the dead man and expect to be thanked? That's way too strange."

"We're at kind of a dead end, aren't we? I mean, we know a lot, suspect even more, but there's still nothing we can do about it. And this is old news now. Thirteen, fourteen years ago. If we're right, she killed her mother, her uncle, and maybe her father. Then when she gets here she kills her predecessor at the company and then tries to kill me."

Scott rubbed his forehead. "I know. I don't like it at all.

There's no way I want the kids back here the way things are right now. Why would she quit trying?"

Rachel shuddered. "I can handle myself in a dangerous situation, but Scotty and Angela? Oh, Scott. We have to figure out something. What can we do?"

He slapped his hand down on the table, shaking it with the impact. "I've got to do something." He pushed the chair back. "I'm going over to her house."

Rachel's mouth dropped open.

"No, I don't mean I'm going to talk to her. I'm just going to park outside and watch, see what I can learn. You keep going over all this stuff, learn what you can. I'm going to see what I can learn over there."

"What could you learn? What else is there?"

"The woman has a life, right? I mean, there must be other people. Places she goes. No one lives entirely alone. Maybe someone will come over, and we can pick up on some new connection in her life. I don't know. But I can't just sit here waiting for something to happen. Actually, rather than be here alone, why don't you go with me?"

Rachel pressed her lips together. "No, I need to get some things picked up and put away around here. But if she's not there, then come right back, okay?"

"Yes. If I can tell she's in there, I'll know you're safe here."

"Keep your cell phone with you. Call me if anything happens. I'm going to worry about you, you know?"

Scott came up behind Rachel, put his arms around her, and kissed her cheek. "You're the one I care about. You, Scotty, and Angela. I can't just be passive about this. I have to do something."

"And if you hear anything, anything at all, you call me, okay?"

The garage door *whirred* down. Scott waited for it to close securely, then pulled out of the driveway.

I've got to protect them. They are everything to me. Oh, God. You made me the man in my home, the leader. God grant me wisdom, help me to end the threat to the family I love. You said, "Believe in the Lord Jesus Christ, and thou shalt be saved, and thy house."

I claim that, Lord. Save my house.

MELISSA PULLED THE CAR off the road near the house and sat in the darkness. She took a deep breath, and picked up the tablet computer from the seat next to her, watched the display whirl into view, and pressed the pre-programmed link to open the mini-console.

"Activate suzanne 48b7b9a6." A message box appeared on the tablet display.

"Send e-mail colon rachel."

The prompt in the message box turned green, along with the word *Ready*.

Melissa spoke distinctly. "Rachel, are you home this evening? I'd love to catch up on things with you. Are the children in bed yet? Love you, Suzanne."

She touched the DONE button. The box cleared as the e-mail went out over the net. She sat back to wait.

SCOTT TURNED OFF the main road onto Melissa's street. He made out the gray house with the bay window. A pale glow from the window illumined the tops of some shrubs beneath it.

He parked the car along the curb and shut off the lights and engine. From his vantage point he could see into the interior of the house. A bookcase, some light from the back of the room. There were no lights on in the front room itself.

Nothing moved. He cupped his hand over his cell phone and looked at the display. It had a full charge. The camera lay on the seat next to him. In this darkness it would not be much help, but there was no way of knowing what could happen.

What if she wasn't home? His eyes stayed on the house. Should he get out of the car and walk closer? Would anyone notice him?

Movement in the window attracted his attention. A woman's form, moving across the back of the room. So she was there.

He shielded his phone under his jacket and texted Rachel. *She's here. I'm watching.*

Minutes passed with the slowness of hours. He was going to have to do something. What if nothing else happened? If no one came?

His eyes went to the garage door. It looked secure. If she left, then he would know. He forced the tension out of his body. As long as she was in the house, then Rachel was safe. Scotty and Angela were in another state. Everything was okay for now.

He waited.

RACHEL REORGANIZED THE CLIPPINGS and notes on the tabletop for what seemed like the hundredth time. There had to be some kind of pattern, didn't there? What were they missing? Surely the Lord would give them something. There was no way they could go on like this.

A soft *ding* sounded from the other room. An e-mail from someone. She rose from the chair and walked over to the computer.

Mail from Suzanne. She clicked the e-mail and read it. Her face flushed with anger as she read the question about the children.

Relax. We're way ahead of her.

Forcing calm, she replied.

I'm here, and the kids are asleep already.
What's on your mind?

She didn't want to do a video chat. The e-mail would have to be enough.

A sound from the garage startled her. It was the familiar *whirring* of the garage door opening, then lowering. Had Scott forgotten to close the door?

Scott would have called me.

Her chest constricted in fear. She raced back to the dining room, snatched the cell phone off the table. Behind her the knob on the back door turned and clicked.

The stairs.

CHAPTER FORTY-EIGHT
Things Are Not Always

She was back, closer to the window now. In silhouette, he could see all he needed to. It was the same long hair, the same slender body. She stood in the window, looking out at the road.

Was she looking at him? If he could see her, then she could certainly see him. He slid down in the seat. Would she look away?

A long minute passed, but she continued to stare in his direction. Of course—she knew his car. What a fool he was. Even if she couldn't make out his face from this distance, she would know the car. And now, here he was, all slunk down in his seat like a coward.

He shook himself. Time to man up.

She was still in the window, looking his way.

He swung the car door open. The brilliance of the car's interior lights startled him. He jumped out, slammed the door, and looked back toward the window.

No one was there. If she'd had any question about whether or not it was him, then she didn't any longer. What was she thinking? Did she think he was here because he loved her, wanted her?

He patted the cell phone in his pocket for reassurance. That was his only link to the rest of the world. And what was he worried about? If anyone in the world was safe, then surely it was him. Hadn't she told him she loved him?

He walked across the street. The honey-colored light from the old streetlamp casting a long, dull shadow in front of him. Thirty more feet would take him to the door.

They were adults, right? He could sit down with her and tell her that it wasn't going to work, that he loved his wife, and that was all there was to it. They could walk away amicably, couldn't they?

The acid taste of fear filled his mouth. Why lie to himself? The woman had killed two times that he knew of and had tried to kill Rachel. No, it wouldn't be that easy. But it was time to be a man, time to put an end to the danger he had brought into his home.

He walked up the short steps, the walkway, onto the porch. No sound came from inside the house.

He raised his hand to knock on the door, but as soon as he touched it, the door swung open an inch. Light from the entryway flooded onto his shoes, up into his face, momentarily blinding him. He stepped back, but the door didn't move any more.

Tentatively, he pushed it farther with the tips of his fingers. It swung noiselessly open, wide enough to admit him.

Was she there? Was she still inside?

He bent forward, slipped his head inside the house. "Melissa?"

The pain erupted in his head with the brightness of a thousand exploding suns. The last thing he saw as the blackness enfolded him was a woman's hands, reaching down to pull him roughly inside.

MELISSA PUSHED THE DOOR open and stepped into the short hallway that led to the dining room.

The sound of someone running upstairs. She heard a door slam shut somewhere in the house.

So she knows I'm here.

"Hello? Anyone here?"

She turned into the dining room. Newspaper clippings and notepads were spread out across the table. What? The *Blairsville Voice*?

Sounds came from upstairs. Panicky, crying sounds. She smiled to herself. She would soon take care of that, but not right now.

One clipping showed a picture of Tony and Rose Montalvo. With the scissors she'd carried in, she clipped away at the article until it fell like confetti to the floor. There weren't very many. It wouldn't take long. Rachel wasn't going anywhere.

Above her the sounds continued. That was good. As long as she knew where Rachel was, the house was hers. Why hadn't she heard the children yet? No matter, she would find them soon.

Melissa sat down at the table and worked through the papers. *Snip snip.* They were all going away.

All going away. Uncle Tony. Daddy. Mommy. Already all gray in their pictures. I must fix the things upstairs.

Snip, snip.

She looked at the scissors. They were not gray at all. They were shiny, new-looking. Why did her arm look so gray? She pressed the tip of the scissors into her skin, watching with detached interest as the bright red blood ran back toward her elbow.

I don't want to go away. I have to save myself for Scott. He'll thank me. He said I would be enough, and I'll prove it. He'll love me even more.

She turned toward the stairs.

TEARS BLINDED RACHEL'S EYES. She sat on the floor, back pressed against the bedroom door. Why was she having so much trouble with the cell phone? Her hands shook, fingers numb. She couldn't dial the number.

"Hello? Anyone here?" The voice lifted itself serpentlike from her kitchen. Not Scott. It was a woman's voice.

Lord Jesus, help me! She's here.

There, she had dialed Scott's number. She held the phone to her ear and listened. The soft *burr-burr* of the ring came back.

Answer the phone, Scott.

"This is Scott. Sorry, I'm not here. Please leave . . ."

No, no. Not your voice mail. Scott, answer the phone. You said you'd be there.

Her breath came in sharp, shallow gasps.

She dialed again. Same result. Call 911! Her fingers stabbed at the pad as she heard the sound on the stairs. Footfalls, coming her way.

She misdialed. Tried again.

"Rachel? Are you in there?" Melissa was on the other side of the door.

Rachel's back was still against the door frame. The realization of her vulnerability came like a thunderclap. Standing, she spun away and stood up.

Her cell phone clattered to the floor, broke into three pieces as it bounced on the unforgiving hardwood surface. The battery spun like a top, coming to rest partially under the door.

She reached down to retrieve the battery.

It slid away under the door, pulled away by an unseen hand.

"You won't need that, Rachel." The doorknob clicked back and forth.

"Go away. Leave us alone!"

"Al . . . most . . ." The kick came from the outside, bent the bedroom door in from the bottom. The frame by the doorknob splintered. ". . . done!"

With a crash, the door flew open. Rachel threw herself against it. Her shoulder flared in pain, but the door closed, though there was no lock now to hold it shut.

More pressure from outside forced the door open again, barely enough to admit a hand.

The hand was streaked with fresh, red blood. Droplets ran off the bottom of the hand onto the floor. The rest of the arm snaked its way through the opening.

"I'm coming in, Rachel."

Turning, Rachel grabbed the edge of the door and pulled it open as fast as she could.

Melissa flew past, the force of her push on the door propelling her across the room. Her face was a mottled mask of horror. Metal flashed in Melissa's hand as she rolled onto the floor, coming to rest against the side of the bed.

The red eyes that looked back at Rachel were filled with loathing. Blood was smeared on the bedspread where the face had struck.

Rachel bolted out the door, down the stairs.

The other woman scrambled to her feet, muttering curses. "You stupid cow. Just stand still and let me finish this."

The kitchen. Get a knife.

She ran into the kitchen, slipping as she went. There was blood on the floor. Melissa's blood?

Oh, please don't let it be Scott's blood.

On the counter sat a wooden block holding the set of knives Scott had given her for her birthday. She pulled out the largest one and turned toward the loud noises coming from the staircase. There was no time to get outside. She would have to fight, defend herself the best she could.

The garage.

She could get out through the garage door. Lock the entry door, buy some time, get outside. She ran down the hallway as Melissa came crashing down the stairs behind her. Not daring to look back, she slammed the entry door and locked it.

She slapped at the button to open the garage door. Her fingers found wires instead, ripped from the Sheetrock wall. As she turned to face the other wall with its high window, the door exploded behind her.

CHAPTER FORTY-NINE
All Good Things

Pain swirled in black clouds through Scott's head. His skull felt like it was the size of a watermelon.

Where am I? Something was ringing, buzzing.

He opened his eyes. *Melissa's house.* He shook his head to clear it. It didn't work.

He struggled to his feet, looked around. No one in sight.

What had happened? He took the cell phone out of his pocket.

Missed Call

Rachel!

He pulled the door open, ran outside to the garage, pushed open the entry door.

Empty. Melissa was gone.

The phone was still in his hand. He dialed Rachel's number. Weakness washed over him as he listened to the call ring, ring, ring . . . and then go to voice mail.

The car was still in the street. He dove into the front seat and flew down the road. A glance at the cell phone display told him he had been out at least twenty minutes. What could have happened in twenty minutes? More than he wanted to imagine.

He thumbed 911 on the phone.

"This is nine-one-one. What's your emergency?"

He gave the operator his name and address. "Please send police and EMTs. I think someone's trying to kill my wife."

He dropped the phone onto the seat next to him, concentrated on the road.

He pressed down hard on the accelerator pedal. Streets and stoplights flashed by. He had to get home.

WOOD SPLINTERED from the trim as Melissa burst through the entry door. Her face was smeared with blood, eyes wide with pain. Her breath came in great, raw gasps as the broken door slapped back against the Sheetrock wall of the garage.

"You, you!" she sobbed, as she crashed into Rachel, knocking her back toward the water heater.

Melissa's arms were streaked with dark blood as she shoved Rachel backward with both hands.

Rachel threw up her arms in defense, tried to grab something, anything, to keep from falling. Her hand slipped against the smear that was Melissa's face, one eye filled with blood. The spittle on the woman's teeth glistened as she drew back her lips in feral fury.

Boards stacked against the wall clattered down as Rachel fell backward against the tank, the wood striking her head, then rasping across her face. Her eye caught the flash of the scissors in Melissa's raised fist, then she felt a stabbing pain in her left shoulder. Something warm ran down her chest, her arm.

Was this the end? Is this how it will be?

Then the other woman was on top of her, a plank of wood between them. Rachel couldn't see anything. The crushing weight of her assailant drove all the breath out of her.

"Now . . . now." The coarse, agonized voice filled the garage as consciousness fled and everything went dark.

THE TAURUS SLID and skidded as it careened into the yard. The garage door stood open, revealing two cars in the driveway. Melissa's Audi and . . . whose?

In the side yard, barely illuminated by the light from the garage, Scott saw a woman's body lying on the grass. As he opened the car door another woman crossed his field of vision, coming from the garage.

Not Rachel.

She lugged the five-gallon can of gasoline he kept inside, stumbling as she drove herself onward to the yard.

"No! Stop!" he called, but she had already reached the body on the lawn.

He leaped from the car, foot slipping on the damp grass. He went down on one elbow. "Stop, don't do it!" She glanced up at him, her face shadowed by the corner of the house, as she shook the last drops from the gasoline can on top of the prone body.

He struggled to his feet, ran toward the women.

Whoompf!

The force of the gasoline igniting knocked him backward.

He looked up, shaded his eyes from the brilliant light of the blaze.

Both women were wrapped in blue flame, one standing, kneeling, then falling on top of the one on the ground, as the flames leaped high into the dark night sky.

The sound from the conflagration reached his ears—popping, hissing. The body on top heaved once, then lay still in the all-consuming fire.

Rachel. I was too late for you. Tears filled his eyes as the agony of his heart wrenched his chest.

Cars stopped on the road. A man stood with his door open, talking on a cell phone.

Movement from the garage caught his eye.

Pulling himself to his feet, he leaned against the car and stared, unbelieving.

Rachel stumbled from the garage, her left side wet with blood. She ran toward Scott, met him, collapsed into his arms. "Oh, Scott."

He turned toward the flaming pyre in the yard, the pair of heaped bodies in the midst. "But I thought . . ."

She followed his gaze. "Rose . . . it was Rose Montalvo," she whispered. "She hated her . . . followed us . . . Melissa tried to kill me . . ." She went limp.

He caught her, lowered her to the grass, cradled her head in his lap. He put his hand on her neck, relieved as he felt the strong pulse. Then he pulled back her collar and saw the wound on her shoulder. There was a puncture by the shoulder joint, oozing blood. He tore off some of the fabric, rolled it into a ball, and applied pressure. She was going to be all right.

Her body began to tremble. He pulled her closer to him.

Crackling, popping sounds were coming from the glowing flames as they began to die down.

Headlights flashed across the yard as more cars stopped on the road. He rocked Rachel back and forth, glad to feel her shaking subsiding.

A man in a business suit bent down by him, holding his cell phone in his hand. "Mister? Are you okay? I called nine-one-one."

Scott nodded, and pulled Rachel up close to his chest. He felt her breath against his hand, the strong beat of her heart against his arm.

It had been Rose Montalvo at Melissa's house. Rose came here, found Melissa, and killed her. All so hard to believe, even though he had seen it with his own eyes.

"Yes, we're going to be okay."

CHAPTER FIFTY
Opportunity

Dan Hammersmith leaned back in his chair. Sunlight slanted in through the corner window behind him, accenting the deep lines on his face.

"And that's the long and short of it, Mr. Douglas. To sum up, we assume full responsibility for all you and your family have gone through. Personally, I don't care what our lawyers may say, I give you my personal guarantee that we'll do everything possible to correct it. We failed you, and all I'm asking is that you let us do what we can to make it right."

Scott looked up at him from an upholstered chair. Hammersmith had asked him to come in, and he had done so. If the company feared a lawsuit, they could stop worrying now. He wasn't going to bring any action.

"Men can fail in different ways, Mr. Hammersmith. You failed in an executive sense, but my own failure was much worse."

Hammersmith leaned forward, face pinched in confusion. "Sir?"

"Ms. Montalvo had insufficient executive oversight," replied Scott. "That's a given. But even without the use of your company resources, she'd have found another way to do what she did. The greater failure was mine. Do you know the Bible proverb 'Can a man take fire in his bosom, and his clothes not be burned?'"

Hammersmith turned his head and looked out the window. "I might know something about that."

"It's never worth it. It never turns out right. God expects us to be satisfied with the one with whom we are 'one flesh.' That was my great failure. I stepped outside that bound, and I have no one to blame for the results but myself."

Hammersmith swiveled in his large chair, leaned in toward Scott. "We do a lot for our people, Mr. Douglas. We give them workout rooms, personal time when they need it. We've got some smart people here. The one thing we've never given any time to is . . . I suppose the term is, their spiritual lives." He seemed to study his hands, then looked up. "I think I could learn a lot from you. Let's make that possible."

"What do you mean?" asked Scott.

"I have something specific in mind. And it didn't just occur to me. I've already talked with our board about this." He reached into his desk drawer, removed an envelope, extended his arm across the desk, and offered the envelope to Scott.

It bore the company's VirtualFriendMe embossed logo. Looking into the eyes of the other man, he reached out and took it.

The hint of a smile was on Hammersmith's face as he nodded once toward the envelope. "Open it . . . please."

Scott turned the envelope over in his hands. It was unsealed, a single sheet of stationery inside.

Scott withdrew the letter.

Dear Mr. Douglas:

Virtual Friend Me is pleased to offer you the position
of Special Assistant to the CEO . . .

"A job offer?" Scott's mouth fell open, his eyes wide with surprise. "This is a . . ."

His eyes went back to the letter.

Hammersmith got up from behind the large desk and circled around to the chair next to Scott's. Sitting down, he leaned on one elbow and looked directly into Scott's eyes.

"I'll make it simple for you, Scott. We need someone like you here. Someone who can provide the moral compass we need. We don't ever want a repeat of what happened to your family, or anything even remotely like it."

Scott worked to control the surge of emotion that swelled within him. How good God was to him. *The chiefest of sinners*—

"You might think I'm just offering you something to make you happy. I'm telling you now, that's not it. It's not how I work."

Hammersmith waved his arm in a wide circle toward the outer office. "We have a great company here, full of good people. I want to protect them from the kind of abuse we've seen already directed against your family. I care about this company, and I care about the people we serve."

"You'll report directly to me, Scott. I want you to be like a chaplain, without the title. Be the one that puts the fires out before they become a problem."

"You'll have a window on our entire operation, looking for the unusual, the unexpected. If you find something odd, I'll expect you to look deeper, ferret out what's really going on. If something's amiss, then I'll get involved. If there's not, then we move on."

Scott struggled to control himself before he spoke. "Mr. Hammersmith, I am so honored that you would do this."

Hammersmith said, "It's an offer for a position of great trust and discretion. Kind of like acting as a spiritual firewall. You'll have the keys to the kingdom here. What do you say?"

Scott looked down again at the letter in his hands. The salary was generous, but more than that—the opportunity to be a Christian influence was unprecedented. Was there any reason to say no? The ordeal his family had endured must never be repeated. Now he could be on the inside.

"Mr. Hammersmith, I'm inclined to accept right now. I'm honored and I am truly humbled by your offer. Before I say yes, though, I'm going to sit down with Rachel. We'll discuss it and then we're going to pray together about it. We want to know the will of God."

Hammersmith put his hand on Scott's shoulder. "From what I've learned about you already, I wouldn't expect any less. Do that. The offer is on the table for as long as you need it to be."

From the corner of his desk, he lifted a large manila envelope stuffed with documents. The corner of some object poked through the tough paper. "We'll start with this one, just as soon as you say you're ready," he said as he laid it back down.

EPILOGUE
Matchless

Scott finished the bedtime story, prayed with both children, and kissed them good night. Downstairs in the family room, Rachel waited on the loveseat, a big bowl of popcorn on the coffee table. He slipped *Fiddler on the Roof* into the DVD player. "Time for some quality time with my sweetheart," he said as he lay back into the soft cushions and pulled Rachel closer to him. "I've got the best wife in the world."

She snuggled into him.

With both hands, Rachel lifted Scott's hand up to her chest and squeezed it. "You're mine forever," she whispered.

The fragrance of her hair filled his nostrils. He felt the silkiness of it against his nose and cheeks, sensed the warmth of her breath against his hands as the music drifted by in the background.

Once again, as it had years before, Scott's heart thrilled in the knowledge that this real and wonderful girl was *his wife*.

Acknowledgments

Writing is often cast as a lonely profession. I'm not so sure about that loneliness part. I'm physically alone at the moment, surrounded by pictures of my Packard (that's a car), books, and assorted memorabilia from thirty years of missionary work. And the world's most neglected banjo.

But I'm not alone in any other sense. I happen to be one of those unfortunate types who need constant encouragement. Fortunately, I have more people helping and wishing me success (this is my first published book) than I can shake a stick at. If you promise not to get angry at me for leaving you off the list, let me name some of you, just so you can see what I'm talking about.

My partner for life is my wife, Beth. She read, edited, commented, and encouraged me from the start. Linda Glaz, my agent, has been constant in her cheerleading and sustaining prayer. Amanda Demastus, my editor at Howard Books, has provided a source of unbroken encouragement. Plus, she's a pretty good editor, helping me see many blind spots. I've heard some editing horror stories, but she made the process a pleasure.

May I mention some of the kind and patient people who actually read this book before it was good enough to put in print? My daughter Debbie Faubion, Josh Lynn, Celeste Charlene, Beth Jusino (a huge help), Steve Laube, and Christina Tarabochia to name a few. Not only did they read it, they provided invaluable feedback on my content and skills (or the lack thereof).

Thanks to my sister, daughters Cheri and Becky, and my son, Daniel, for their "Wow, you wrote a book?" exclamations. It's always nice to know you can surprise your own family. Had it not been for my youngest daughter, Bethany, being a member of Lori Stafford's Creative Writing Workshop at school, I might never have started.

The Indiana chapter of the American Christian Fiction Writers and the ACFW Scribes201 critique group have been wonderful for me. The FBI (my Sunday school class) has been incredibly patient and encouraging. Dr. Carl Matlock taught me about warfarin. Rick Barry, another writer, encouraged me from day one.

To round things out, here are two who don't even know I exist. One still living, one deceased. I doubt I'd be writing at all had it not been for reading their work at eleven years old. Frank M. Robinson wrote *The Power* in 1956 and set me on a lifetime track of enjoying suspense literature. In the same year, Cyril M. Kornbluth, my all-time favorite writer, wrote *Not This August*. He died in 1958 at just thirty-four years of age.

My prayer is that Almighty God, the Giver and Sustainer of all things, will use this book to help you in your Christian walk.

I must acknowledge Him, because (James 1:17) "every good gift and every perfect gift is from above, and cometh down from the Father of lights, with whom is no variableness, neither shadow of turning." Thanks be to God, for His unspeakable gift of Jesus Christ.

A Howard Reading Group Guide

FRIEND ME

John Faubion

Description

Rachel and Scott's marriage has gotten a little stale. Faced with just the kids at home and Scott at work until late at night, Rachel decides to log on to a new website—VirtualFriendMe.com. From that moment on, the family's life begins to spiral out of control. One woman—Melissa—manages to manipulate both Rachel and Scott using the website's interface, learning their deepest secrets and driving a wedge further between the couple. When Rachel faces a near-death experience, Scott decides to come clean about his online relationship, and together Scott and Rachel resolve to stop Melissa before she can do more damage to their family. *Friend Me* is about love, family, and the faith needed to overcome new obstacles in the digital age.

Discussion Questions

1. The epigraph to *Friend Me* quotes Philippians 4:8: "Finally, brethren, whatsoever things are true, whatsoever things are honest, whatsoever things are just, whatsoever things are pure, whatsoever things are lovely, whatsoever things are of good report; if there be any virtue, and if there be any praise, think on these things." What is true, honest, and just, about the concept of the VirtualFriendMe website? Why do you think Rachel was initially attracted to the site?

2. Why do you think the story begins with Melissa's point of view? Is *Friend Me* ultimately her story?

3. How would you characterize Melissa Montalvo? What are her motivations for doing the things she does? How does her past inform her future?

4. Discuss Scott and Rachel's marriage issues. Would you consider their problems out of the ordinary? Why or why not?

5. In this day and age, questions about fidelity and the Internet can be tricky. At what moment do you think that Scott crossed the line into infidelity—if ever? Did his interactions with Alicia make him unfaithful?

6. Do you think that Scott is a good husband? Do you like his character? Do you blame him for what happened to Rachel—or was he also a victim?

7. On page 132, Scott argues with himself, "Maybe there was a virtual love? Something was happening. . . . No, he couldn't be falling in love with her." Do you think there is such a thing as "virtual love"? What is the difference between Scott's love for Rachel and his love for Alicia?

8. How would you describe Rachel and virtual Suzanne's relationship? Did the relationship change over the course of the story? How so?

9. What irony can be found in Melissa's nickname for Rachel—*The Other*?

10. Revisit the scene on page 212 when Scott asks little Scotty about the new babysitter, Alicia. What was your reaction when Scotty says, "She told us that we could just call her Mommy"? Do you think that this was a red flag for Scott? Why do you think he did not confess his virtual relationship to Rachel in that moment?

11. Do you think Scott and Rachel could have fixed their marriage problems without the wake-up call they received in the form of Rachel's near-death by poison? Can you make the argument that the attempted murder acted as a silver lining in this case? Why or why not?

12. Discuss the ending of the novel. Were you surprised to learn that Rose killed Melissa? Who do you think is the hero or heroine of this story?

13. What role does faith play in *Friend Me*? Without faith, do you think that Rachel and Scott could have defeated evil?

Additional Activities:
Ways of Enhancing Your Book Club

1. *Friend Me* touches on many themes relevant to popular culture, particularly the Internet and how our privacy can be compromised with the click of a button. These same concerns are the focus of the popular television series *Catfish*. Have a TV night with your reading group and watch a few episodes of the show. Afterward, discuss with the group the ways in which the show is similar to Scott and Rachel's story. Did Melissa "catfish" the couple?

2. The concept of a friend online that could be as real as any friend in reality is interesting—and still very new. The author, John Faubion, has brought his concept to life on his website. Log on to www.christiansuspense.com/suspense -home/virtual-person-friend-me/with your reading group. Spend a few minutes on the site, then have a conversation about friendships in the digital age. Do you think that friendship can exist in many forms? Why or why not? Give examples from your own life or from other stories you have read.

3. Continue on the trend of strange romances and read *Illusion* by Frank Peretti with your reading group. What similarities can you draw between the two stories? What differences? Has anyone in your reading group ever had an unconventional relationship?

Questions for John Faubion

Is this your first novel? Describe the experience of writing, from the idea for the story to the final draft. Were there any surprises in the writing process?

First novel? Yes, at least the first anyone will ever see. The earlier one (on the back side of my hard disk) is consigned to darkness forever.

The experience. The whole virtual friend concept came to me one day in a software design meeting. I was not thinking about writing it as a novel. The idea appealed to me as a way to generate income, and do it in a way that would be totally fresh and unique.

I was pretty excited about the idea, and told my wife about it that evening. I was all ready for her to provide some enthusiastic encouragement, but instead she said, "Don't you dare do that. Can you not see what people would do with it?"

Well—no, I hadn't thought about the dark side of it. I was still all wrapped up in the *coolness* of the idea. But she was right. In the end, she said, "Why don't you just write about it? It would be a great story." I'm glad she did.

Now I'll tell you some things about the writing process. Not what makes it hard, or time-consuming, or frustrating. I'm going to confess something else. I really got into my characters' personas.

Here's a single example. Too much of this, and I'll embarrass myself. When Melissa tells Scott her real name for the first time I got really emotional. If you are conflicted about my villain (and she is truly a villain), then I am more so. Melissa's whole life has crystallized down to this one poignant moment. *He loved me for what I've been to him. Will he love me as I am?* Dismiss entirely the fact that she's all about killing his wife and children to have him. Can you get into her head and heart here? It's frightening because it is so, so human. Jesus said, "The first shall be last." Melissa, however, sees the world entirely through the lenses of her own desires. Nothing else matters. She, and her perceived needs, are all that matter.

When I write about Scott's weakness, I feel it. And Rachel? I've seen Rachel in the eyes of not a few discouraged wives. The point is, when I write these characters onto the page, I feel all the things they feel. Perhaps that is common for writers, but it caught me by surprise.

In the early drafts of *Friend Me,* I didn't like Scott very much. If I caught myself being sympathetic to him I had to back off and consider my own character. Did I see too much of myself in him? It was pretty scary.

I'd like to see people read the book, then consider the whole question of "virtual love." Of course, there is no such thing. It's just a construct for narcissism and loving yourself. "Rejoice in the wife of thy youth." "Drink waters from thine own cistern." That's real.

Surprises? I didn't know until I was more than 80 percent done how it would end. So that was just as much a surprise for me as it was for you.

Questions raised by this novel are very current questions, ones that still remain largely unresolved. In your opinion,

what does constitute infidelity on the Internet? When do you think Scott became unfaithful in the story?

I'm going for the quick and easy answer here, simply because it's not that complicated.

When Jane asked him, "Male or female friend?" Scott replied, "Female." At that point, he'd crossed over. He was done. When a guy does that, he's made a sharp turn onto the wrong road. He became unfaithful.

Want to make it more complicated? We can talk about him putting work before family, and on and on. But those things can change in an afternoon. However, when he said, "Female," he was g-o-n-e. Guys understand this.

Do we think that only sexual sin was in scope when Jesus said in Matthew 5, "But I say unto you, that whosoever looketh on a woman to lust after her hath committed adultery with her already in his heart"? When a husband chooses some woman other than his wife as his confidante, companion, or female best friend, he's turned down the road of infidelity.

Who is your favorite character in the story and why?

Easy. Melissa. She's really bad. But doesn't it bother you when you find yourself sympathizing with her? Imagine how enjoyable it is to write about a character like that.

My second favorite is "all the rest."

One of the joys of this story is the shifting point of view—from Melissa, to Rachel, to Scott. The reader gets to experience the inside story of all three, very different characters.

What was your experience like writing from a female point of view? Was it more difficult to write as Melissa or Rachel than as Scott?

Melissa's character was the most fun to write. Absolutely no question about it. Are you familiar with Satan's five infamous "I will" statements in Isaiah 14? Her character has that sense to it.

Scott's character was difficult only because I was forced into so much self-examination.

Rachel's was the most difficult. I still don't understand women. The things that make sense to women don't make sense to me. Whatever you may think I know, I know only from observation. My faithful wife, Beth; my heroic agent, Linda Glaz; and my equally tenacious editor, Amanda Demastus, were constantly on my case about improving Rachel. I can't begin to tell you how many times I heard, "No woman would _____." You fill in the blank. So I'm totally indebted to the wise women who nudged me along into grudging assent as to what a woman *really* thinks.

As to whether or not I was successful in writing from a female point of view, I will leave to you. I hope you'll write and tell me. Correct me, if you'd like. It's all welcome.

What would you name as the major theme(s) of this story?

Being real and being faithful.

The epigraph to *Friend Me* is Philippians 4:8: "Finally, brethren, whatsoever things are true, whatsoever things are honest, whatsoever things are just, whatsoever things are pure, whatsoever things are lovely, whatsoever things are of good report; if there be any virtue, and if there be any praise, think on these things."

We live in an age where people choose to exist in virtual worlds. Facebook is an example, but not the only one. Each of these virtual worlds touches on reality, but they are not in fact real themselves.

One theme of the story is that Scott Douglas substituted a made-up, virtual wife for a real wife and lover. Foolish. It was not true, not honest, not just, not pure, or any of the rest. We need to focus on real people, real lives. Real friends. Real love.

Another theme is the absolute necessity of faithfulness in the Christian life. Faithfulness to our Lord Jesus, to our husbands and wives. If we want to be used of God, faithfulness is the key. 1 Timothy 1:12, "And I thank Christ Jesus our Lord, who hath enabled me, for that he counted me faithful, putting me into the ministry."

You have spent many years working as a missionary. Did that experience help inform this story in any way?
Sounds like a great time for an exciting answer! However, it is not the efforts associated with being a missionary that informed the story. Rather, it's the normal struggles of the Christian life (over many years) that did the job. "Prone to wander, Lord I feel it. Prone to leave the God I love." We all know what it's like. As we see the Day approaching, the battle will intensify. It won't be long before we're all full of stories to tell about our defeats and victories in the Christian life.

In future books we'll deal with more missionary-related ideas. I will run out of years before I run out of things I want to write about.

Describe any research that went into the writing of this story. Was it a lot or a little? Did real-life events, such as the Manti Te'o scandal, give you ideas for your story?

I've got a fairly complete write-up on how the story came to be on my blog (http://christiansuspense.com/why-friend-me). Basically, I thought I might have found the ideal software project . . . virtual friends. Because I'm now a professional software developer, I'm pretty familiar with the market and the available technology.

When I shared the idea with other people, I got some predictable reactions. "Oh, you've got to see *Catfish*!" "Seriously, did you hear about Manti Te'o?" "Cool, have you seen Second Life?"

So this story line connects with a lot of people. Like many things, it is the abuse of a good idea that turns it toward the dark side.

Who is your favorite author and why?

Cyril M. Kornbluth, who died in 1958, still in his thirties. I think he was the best science fiction writer of all time. Read his short story "The Little Black Bag" sometime. It was done as a *Twilight Zone* episode (season 1, episode 7) later on.

The best Christian novel I've read lately was *Havah: The Story of Eve*, by Tosca Lee. She writes things that make me think.

Do you agree that Rose is the heroine of the novel? Without Rose's intervention, do you think that Rachel would have survived Melissa's attack?

Rose is not the heroine. Rachel is. Heroic—because she led a faithful Christian life throughout. Rose was motivated only by bitterness, not a sense of righteousness.

As to whether or not Rachel could have survived the attack, I can assure you she would have. Some way!

What is next for you as a writer?
Lots of books! I enjoy this business of writing. The thing is, I know what I like to read myself, so that's what I try to write for others. It's what I like to call high-contrast suspense. That is, my villains are really villainous. Just like light and darkness.

The Lord willing, in everything I write you should be able to discern a clear Christian world view. I am determined not to fail in that, so long as God gives me the years to do it.